Praise for Mark Has

"From the first sentence of *Baked*, wh
other writers eating their arms, Ma.
reader by the throat and half-drags, half-gooses them through a
laugh-out-loud, thrill-a-minute, tour de force of bad behavior,
weirdness, and contemporary illegal commerce. For years, the
author's work has been an open secret to connoisseurs of monstro
prose and outrageous, transcend-the-genre crime action. With
Baked, Mark Haskell Smith may have written his masterpiece. The
writing is addictively brilliant enough to render it a Schedule Three
narcotic. I defy anyone to put *Baked* down without wanting more.
It's so good you'll lose your short-term memory."   —Jerry Stahl

"Between these covers, my friends, Mark Haskell Smith has
harvested and served up the best kind of hybrid: at once a pulp
mystery, demented comedy, and meditation on little ideas like
greed, desire, and decency. *Baked* is original, subversive, a bit mind-
expanding, and fully irresistible—a laugh-a-minute romp through a
cultural moment just screwed up enough to be recognizably our
own. You won't have time to exhale. Nor will you want to."
                    —Charles Bock, author of *Beautiful Children*

"Connoisseurs of absurdist humor will find him working at the top
of his game here."   —*Booklist*

"Haskell Smith writes well, especially about sex and food . . . Think
Elmore Leonard meets Mario Batali."   —*Los Angeles Times*

"I look forward to anything Mark Haskell Smith writes."
                                                    —Jim Harrison

BAKED

Also by Mark Haskell Smith
Moist
Delicious
Salty

BAKED

Mark Haskell Smith

Black Cat
a paperback original imprint of Grove/Atlantic, Inc.
New York

Published simultaneously in Canada
Printed in the United States of America

FIRST EDITION

ISBN: 978-0-8021-7076-7

Black Cat
a paperback original imprint of Grove/Atlantic, Inc.
841 Broadway
New York, NY 10003

Distributed by Publishers Group West

www.groveatlantic.com

10 11 12 13   10 9 8 7 6 5 4 3 2 1

For Diana,
my fearless research assistant

BAKED

1

ONE BULLET can really fuck up your day.

He walked out of his house and into the white-light white heat of a bullet exploding out the end of a handgun. A bullet that flew out of a passing SUV and burned a perfect black hole in his jacket—the one he got at the thrift store on Sunset, the one that said "Tigers" in bright orange script—pushing bits of his T-shirt into his chest as it tore through his skin. One bullet, slicing through his body, puncturing his right lung, the soft metal expanding as it traveled through his chest, tearing and burning tissue, breaking two ribs on its way out. The bullet that almost killed him. One hundred and twenty grains of lead that fucked up his day.

The bullet didn't stop at his shattered ribs. It kept going, blasting out of his body, blowing a hole in the other side of his jacket, flying along Perlita Avenue until it embedded itself with a clank in the side of a clean white-and-orange van with the name GEORGE BRAZIL PLUMBING & HEATING painted on the side. The plumber thought someone had thrown a rock at him.

Miro blinked. He was looking at the world sideways, his face resting in the soft grass. He could feel something wet and warm, a sticky liquid flowing over him. The pain, the actual sensation of a burning hot piece of metal ripping through his flesh, was so extreme that he almost didn't feel anything. Maybe he was in shock.

He could hear people shouting, the distant sound of a siren, but he couldn't move. It took too much energy to move.

His neighbor's dog—a mangy old Pekinese whose body was riddled with hairless scabby patches from his constant chewing and clawing at his eczematic skin—walked up to him and started growling. Miro blinked. The dog crept closer and suddenly lunged forward and bit Miro on the arm. It was then that he had a thought, his first lucid moment since he saw the flash.

That fucking dog just bit me.

That's what he tried to tell the paramedics, the Los Angeles Fire Department emergency medical technicians who were flipping him over, urgently rapping in medical code, checking his ABCs—airways, breathing, circulation—sticking needles in his arm and tubes down his throat.

"A dog bite is the least of your worries, sir."

That's what the female paramedic said to him. She called him "sir." Like he was old.

Miro blinked. He saw his neighbors huddled on the other side of the street. He could hear the nosy Filipino granny who lived next door.

"He was up to something. I know that for sure."

That fucking dog bit me.

One of the paramedics injected something into a tube that was hooked to his arm.

"Try and relax."

Miro wasn't feeling particularly tense but he nodded; he'd take their advice, he would try and relax.

A large Asian man with a shaved head and a mustache loomed over him. A Los Angeles Police Department badge dangled from a chain around his neck. His shirt was brightly colored, patterned with little drawings of palm trees, tiki torches, and the iconic Duke Kahanamoku surfing at Waikiki. He stuck his face next to Miro's.

"Who shot you? Do you know?"

Miro smelled coffee. The smell triggered his second lucid thought of the afternoon.

Café pingo.

"We can catch the crumb who did this. But we need your help."

Miro blinked. A couple of young men wearing short-sleeved white shirts and ties stood off to the side. Their bicycles lay on the ground next to them. Mormons. One of them was praying out loud. Praying for him. The other, the one with a flattop crew cut, just stared wide-eyed.

As the paramedics hoisted the gurney into the back of the ambulance, Miro had his last lucid thought of the afternoon.

Elephant Crush.

Before the Bullet

2

IN AMSTERDAM, almost a month before the bullet, Miro looked up from his scrambled eggs and coffee and realized that he was totally baked.

He hadn't meant to get stoned at breakfast. But here it was, a Sativa buzz resonating through his cranium as he sat in the protective warmth of the coffeeshop surrounded by the smells of coffee and cake and skunk weed.

He was only slightly annoyed with himself. It was, after all, his first trip to Holland and he figured he'd need to give himself a couple of days to get into the rhythm of life in a foreign country. But it really wasn't much of a stretch to acclimate to the city; there was no language barrier really, and he found that sitting at a table in La Tertulia eating breakfast while smoking a joint and drinking an espresso was almost exactly like a slow Sunday morning in his kitchen at home. Even the music was the same.

Because he possessed offbeat good looks—the dark brown eyes and curly hair from his Jewish mother, the Roman nose and plump, almost girlish lips from his Greek father, coupled with a lean DJ physique—he attracted the attention of the cute Dutch waitress and was able to get the local perspective on which coffeeshops in the city offered the best cannabis. The waitress was tall, at least six foot one, with honey-colored hair and a warm, inviting smile that intimated, in his weed-tickled fantasies, an invitation to snuggle under a down comforter and explore her ridiculously long legs. Not that he would suggest something like that. For all his outward cool, Miro Basinas was actually quite shy.

He paid his bill, left a ridiculous tip, and shuffled out into the gray drizzle of the Amsterdam morning. Miro felt a blast of frigid air, which smelled of ocean and diesel exhaust, coming off the canal, causing him to shiver.

He stopped and looked at the strange Van Gogh–inspired mural on the side of the building as he flipped the collar of his leather jacket up around his neck and plugged in his earphones. He spun the wheel of his iPod, pushed the center, and felt the soft purr of a vibraslap in his ear as the sultry sugarcane voice of Freddie McGregor rose through a pulsing jungle of bass and drums. Miro smiled. He might be standing in the gloom and drizzle of a street in Amsterdam, but he had Jamaica in his pocket.

He hunched forward, leaning into the weather, his vintage Pumas slapping the wet sidewalk as he dodged bicycles and crossed the Prinsengracht canal towards his next destination.

...

Miro wasn't on vacation, he was in Amsterdam on business. He might not look it, his alt-rocker vibe disguising the fact that he was actually a successful underground botanist, one of the few propagators of ultra-high–grade and exotic marijuana in Los Angeles. He'd started off small, experimenting with plants, selling the successes to friends, and had even briefly considered a career in the import and distribution sector of the cannabis industry. But that occupation was fraught with dangers and consequences—like five to ten for possession with intent to distribute—so he'd stuck with the horticultural side of the business. Besides, that was the part he was good at, that was the part he loved.

He'd earned a BA from the University of California, Davis, studying plant biology and specializing in tropical agronomy—his senior paper on cassava crops and plantain farming in the Dominican Republic was even published in an obscure scientific publication—and it turned out to be a solid foundation for experimenting with cannabis. Using his understanding of the basics of genetic manipulation and his fieldwork in agronomy he was, through trial and error, able to grow some distinct, and distinctly potent, cannabis. Miro was inspired by his hero, Floyd Zaiger, the man who invented the *pluot*—a cross between a plum and an apricot.

...

Miro stopped at an intersection and consulted his rain-dampened map. He'd crossed over four canals, so he made a right turn and headed toward the coffeeshop at Singel 387.

Miro found the shop the waitress had recommended, pushed past a scrum of bicycles parked under the green awning, and went inside. He was thrown momentarily by the shelves at the back: they were canted at a severe angle, instantly reminding him that he was still buzzed from breakfast. He unbuttoned his jacket and approached the bar, where a lanky, longhaired dude was standing, rolling a cigarette, and looking pissed off about something.

Miro studied the menu. It was all select weed and high-grade hash from around the world. It was a kind of cannabis wonderland. Miro smiled at the dealer.

"What's the most popular weed you sell?"

The dealer looked at him for a moment, then pointed to the Silver Haze.

"How is it?"

The dealer finished rolling the cigarette, lit it, inhaled, and blew a plume of smoke toward Miro's face.

"Popular."

Miro coughed.

"What's your favorite?"

The dealer thought about it long enough to send a perfectly formed smoke ring into Miro's eyes before pointing to a clump of gray-green buds spotted with deep saffron blossoms.

"AK-47."

"What do you like about it?"

The dealer grinned and picked a piece of tobacco out of his teeth.

"It kills more Americans."

Miro didn't know what to say, so he smiled at the dealer and attempted a stoner nonchalance.

"Cool."

The dealer looked simultaneously skeptical and amused.

"Is it?"

Miro purchased a gram of AK-47, ordered a coffee, borrowed a pipe, and sat down to give it a try.

He exhaled a plume of AK-47 smoke up toward the

ceiling. Almost instantly he felt the THC begin its assault on his brain, rumbling through his cerebellum, wreaking havoc with his nervous system like some kind of cartoon motorcycle gang on a rampage.

Miro wondered how Floyd Zaiger had come up with the idea for the *pluot*. It was so weird, yet totally brilliant. Miro wondered if Floyd got high.

...

Floyd Zaiger had started out picking strawberries in the fields of central California in the 1950s before he began to research and experiment with cross-pollination of stone-fruit trees. He didn't splice genes or manipulate the DNA of the plants; Floyd wasn't high tech. He used natural selection, controlled pollination, and years of patience. He was a man with a theory and an obsession. Eventually he developed a tree that produced a cross between a plum and an apricot: a juicy and smooth-skinned fruit with a unique and vibrant flavor. The *pluot*. Along the way, Floyd invented lots of other fruits: the *aprium*, the *peacotum*, the *plumcot*, the *nectaplum*, and others.

Miro didn't have the luxury of hundreds of acres of pristine farmland in Modesto like Floyd Zaiger, so he turned three rooms of his small rented 1950s tract house into an indoor farm complete with grow lights, automatic drip irrigators, and charcoal-filtered aerators to keep the house from reeking. He kept his operation small enough that he didn't put a power spike on his electric bill—something the cops looked for—but big enough to experiment with various strains and

supply a network of select and legal medical marijuana outlets in Los Angeles.

Miro thought about smoking more AK-47 but then he
remembered he had things to do, he was in Amsterdam for a
reason. He was here for the Cannabis Cup.

3

O YE THEREFORE, and teach all nations.
It's hard to keep Matthew 28:17 in mind when you're humping your bike up a steep hill in the scorching midday sun, sucking in smog and trying not to get pancaked by the traffic. Yet it was his obligation to spread the teachings of the Church of Jesus Christ of Latter Day Saints to anyone who would listen. Elder Daniel Lamb was on his mission.

He had arrived in Los Angeles on a Greyhound bus and walked out into the heat and grime and Scientologists of Hollywood and stood blinking in the glare like the proverbial man who just fell off the turnip truck. He was blond and blue-eyed and would've been considered handsome if he hadn't come from a high school where every guy was blond and blue-eyed and on the football team. Standing there in his white short-sleeved shirt and tie, his gray slacks and black shoes, Daniel had waited for the local LDS coordinator to pick him up. Even the homeless man squatting over his freshly laid turds in the bushes, wiping his ass with an old Taco Bell wrapper, had thought Daniel looked like some kind of time traveling freak from the Soviet Union circa 1957.

Daniel heard the sound of a chain shuddering through the gears of a derailleur and looked behind him as he pedaled, checking to see if his mission partner was keeping up. Elder Collison always lagged behind. He wasn't much of a cyclist, that was for sure. Chubby, red-faced, and afflicted with a chronic wheeze, he looked like a pink, doughy Mormon dumpling straddling a bike. Collison was from somewhere near Kalispell, Montana, and claimed he was used to riding horses, not bikes, but he didn't look like a cowboy to Daniel; he looked more like a cow.

Their mission plan was simple, they were supposed to stick together, stay in each other's company all day, spread the word, do good deeds, and then share a room at night. It was a kind of spiritual buddy system. They would work together and keep each other from being tempted to do sinful things.

But Los Angeles is a long way from Boise, a small city where everything is nice and clean, everyone is white and well-behaved. Boise is a good place to grow up and be a thoughtful follower of the church. Los Angeles, however, is a whole other beast.

Together, Elders Lamb and Collison tooled around the sprawling neighborhoods of Silver Lake and Echo Park, stopping at various houses to offer a helping hand and to talk about the church. Not that the scrawny rock stars who eschewed food in favor of Wellbutrin and vodka needed their help or wanted to take Jesus Christ as their personal savior. To the locals, the missionaries were just a couple of annoying freaks. The indie-film editors and struggling screenwriters, they didn't care. The wannabe actors and actresses, the stylists and makeup artists, the graphic designers and schoolteachers, none of them gave the earnest young men the time of day. Occasionally they'd help an older person or a single mother carry groceries or move their trash cans out to the street. Sometimes a lonely gay man would invite them in and listen to their rap, always with that hopeful expression, like some porn movie scenario was about to unfold, like those things really happened. But mostly, day after day, they got doors slammed in their faces.

They got sneers.

They got ridiculed.

They pedaled on.

It wasn't easy to avoid temptation. Los Angeles is the living, breathing, personification of sex and no matter where Daniel looked he saw Satan luring him to sin. There were the women; in cars, on the streets and sidewalks, in shops, stores, and parks. Beautiful brown-skinned Latinas walking down the sidewalks wearing halter tops and short shorts; petite Asian girls with vintage dresses and thick-soled boots; long-legged honey-haired Amazons with gigantic breasts wearing tight T-shirts and tighter jeans; hipster women with severe glasses, asymmetrical haircuts, and slashes of neon-bright lipstick. All of them looking glamorous and forbidden and sexy-as-hell to a boy from Boise.

It wasn't like they talked to him, not with words anyway. It was their bodies, silently tempting him, urging him to touch them, to fornicate, begging him to ejaculate as he pedaled through the city in a pheromone fog.

And when the women weren't singing to him like so many bra-shunning sirens, there were billboards of beautiful actresses in provocative poses, bus shelters featuring posters of open-mouthed ruby-lipped harlots, broadsides on buses revealed models with erect nipples and perfectly rounded behinds, and on every corner, free adult newspapers shouted triple-X sex-sex-sex at him. Even the buildings, the bright reds and pinks, the cool greens and cobalt blues, the biomorphic steel of the architecture, were sexualized.

Flowers always seemed to be in bloom and the air was sweet with pollen. Even the cheap food they ate from taco trucks seemed to tease, riddled with chilies and flavors he'd never experienced, spices that seemed to wake up his body.

Daniel often rode his bike with a boner stiffening in his gray, missionary-approved, poly-cotton slacks, the rough fabric grating and stroking with every crank of the pedals.

But while the sexualized world of Los Angeles drove Daniel into a kind of teenage hormonal frenzy, Elder Collison found it to be proof that the end days were upon us. For him, Los Angeles was Sodom and Gomorrah times one hundred and cranked to eleven, like some kind of gay-pride parade love fest nightmare on steroids. It scared the crap out of him. Collison rode through the streets of Los Angeles on the verge of a panic attack, constantly looking over his shoulder, his sphincter clenched tight, fearing Satan would sneak up behind him and fuck him up the butt.

4

MIRO DIDN'T REMEMBER walking here—the city had become a rainy blur of small streets, bicycles, and bridges—and didn't know how he had found the place, but the coffeeshop on a street lined with bookstores and antique dealers was on his itinerary and, well, here he was, plopped in a chair by the front window sampling some cannabis called Enemy of the State.

He could tell right away, just by looking at it, that this was quality weed. He closed his eyes and took a sniff of the tight knuckle of dried bud, picking up a hint of a chemical scent, like cold metal, in the bouquet.

Miro had a finely-tuned nose for cannabis. He could distinguish between a garden variety hydroponic skunk and a high quality strain like Cherry Bomb—both of which smell vaguely like cat piss to the undiscerning—with a sniff. He could recognize Willie Nelson by its fresh garden scent, and tell if the Jamaican High Grade had been cured properly by noting the earth aroma that sprung from the bud as he rolled it in his fingers.

The color of the leaves and flowers told him the region and genetic lineage of the plants. The density of trichomes—the tiny silver hairs on the leaves—gave him an accurate measure of the THC content. He could tell if the plant had been raised outside in natural sunlight or under grow lights in a warehouse. He could detect subtle hints of mold on the bud and he could tell if the plants had been harvested too early—not quite reaching resinous maturity—or were past their prime, just by lighting up and having a taste. Which is what he did with Enemy of the State.

Miro exhaled a plume of acrid smoke, coughing a little—the herb was heavy in his throat—and looked around. The coffeeshop was modern, clean, almost corporate. Like a hip Starbucks with some kind of ambient techno soundtrack ticking in the background. There were a few people in the place, a quartet of British tourists who appeared to be Super Glued to their chairs, and some Euro-hippies who were passing a joint as they strung glass beads on strings, making necklaces and bracelets. Miro smiled at their industriousness.

He glanced out the window, at the rain, at the gray and shiny streets, and saw a young woman step out of a bookstore holding an umbrella. She flicked her wrist and the umbrella telescoped, snapping open like a parachute, like a condor taking flight, a kind of magic trick. She held it up, over a tangle of reddish curls, and crossed the street. She clutched a small package under her arm.

Perhaps, Miro speculated, *a book.*

He was surprised to see her walk toward him and enter the coffeeshop. He looked up at her, almost as if he knew her, as she stuck her umbrella in the umbrella stand. She put the package down on the bar near him, hung her coat on a chair, and smiled.

"I'll be right back."

She had an accent but Miro couldn't tell where she was from. He watched her walk to the counter and place her order. He couldn't help checking her out. She was beautiful, but not in a typical way, there was something atypically attractive and exotic about her green eyes and pale skin surrounded by a pile of amazing hair. Her prominent yet beautiful nose was punctuated by a piercing, a tiny diamond that seemed to be winking some kind of dot-dash code to Miro. He caught a glimpse of golden silk tunic peeking out from under the bottom of her wool sweater, the slash of color hanging down, just covering the round rise of her denim-covered ass.

She reminded him of a Chinese peony. He couldn't say why.

She came back to the counter carrying a coffee. That's when he noticed her boots. They looked incredibly mod, with a stylish, squared-off toe and a small heel. Miro realized that you just didn't see boots like that in Southern California.

She sat down near him, one stool between them, and looked at his joint.

"How's your head?"

Miro thought about it. He took a mental inventory of his mental health.

"Good."

"What're you smoking?"

Miro cleared his throat.

"Enemy of the State."

She nodded and stirred a sugar cube into her coffee. A thin cloud of milk foam floated on top and slowly turned the color of caramel as the spoon circled the cup.

"Is that a cappuccino?"

She shook her head.

"They make for me a style like you get in Lisbon. *Pingo.*"
The word resonated in Miro's brain.
"*Pingo?*"
"*Café pingo.*"
Miro nodded thoughtfully, then held up the joint.
"Would you like some? How can you resist a name like 'Enemy of the State'?"
"Okay."
Miro handed her the joint and struck his lighter. She put the joint to her lips—Miro couldn't help marveling at their plumpness and slightly off-kilter shape—and inhaled. She held the smoke in, expectantly, for a beat and then exhaled and handed the joint back to Miro. Even though he was completely baked, Miro wanted his lips to touch hers if only by proxy, so he stuck the joint in his mouth and took another hit. Somehow, the cannabis tasted even better this time.
"You are here for the Cup?"
Miro nodded. "You?"
She laughed.
"I live here. For a year now. I work at the Science Park."
"You're a scientist?"
She smiled at him. "I am."
Miro thought about that. He realized he'd never met such a cool-looking scientist before. Then he realized that *he* was a kind of cool-looking scientist, although more accurately he was a guy with an interest in certain scientific ideas and practices that led to better cannabis. He was, really, more like a gentleman farmer. True science, the hard-core molecular stuff, those super-duper-powered microscopes and pictures of genes and swirly double helixes were beyond him. Plants were much simpler.

As he pondered the divergent paths of gentleman farmers and professional scientists, somewhere in the back of his brain he realized that Enemy of the State could actually live up to its name.

He watched as she opened her package, the sound of the rustling paper somehow erotic and provocative in Miro's ears, and pulled out a book. Miro looked at the cover. *Um Deus Passeando pela Brisa da Tarde.*

"You're Portuguese?" He hadn't meant it to be a question.

She nodded. "You are American."

"Californian. Los Angeleno." He stretched out the "Angeleno," attempting to emphasize the Spanish of the pronunciation, but the soft "g" got stuck in his mouth like a wad of gum and flubbed off his tongue, making him sound like he had a speech impediment.

She smiled. "A very stoned Californian."

Miro shrugged. What could he say? It was true. He looked out the window, not sure how to continue the conversation, not certain he should, distracted by a delivery truck in the street and the pattern of the rain hitting puddles on the sidewalk.

"What does it mean?" For a heartbeat, Miro wasn't sure he'd asked the question out loud. He wasn't sure he'd meant to.

"A god taking a walk for the breeze of the afternoon. It's by Mario de Carvalho. I've always wanted to read it."

"I like that."

"You've read it?"

Miro shook his head.

"Taking a walk. For the breeze. In the afternoon."

Before he knew what he was doing he was standing, putting on his jacket.

"My name's Miro." He held out his hand, feeling instantly dorky and uncool, like a Junior Achievement student at his first business meeting.

Miro pondered the difference between flora and fauna. Unlike plants, people were unpredictable, they didn't always make sense somehow, even if they had plenty of water and nutrients and sunlight. People lied, they had neuroses, they played games, they were hypocrites. People would talk about community, they would say all kinds of stuff about living in harmony with each other and the Earth, but it was just to make themselves feel good about all the destructive things they did to each other and the planet. People couldn't really be trusted. Plants, on the other hand, were logical, they sunk roots into soil searching for food and water, they grew up into the light looking for sun for photosynthesis, they converted carbon dioxide into oxygen; they lived relatively straightforward, useful lives.

Miro appreciated the reproductive strategies of flora; unlike animals who dance and preen and buy each other cocktails and struggle to make small talk, plants bloomed and then waited for pollinators to arrive. Plants got it.

This Portuguese woman with her Portuguese book was making him feel discombobulated. Or was it the pot? He felt like he was going to fall over. Topple like a statue at an insurrection, do a face plant on the floor right in front of her.

She rescued him. She took his hand and gave it a squeeze. Her skin felt warm and soft and full of promise and his head instantly flashed with regret. Why exactly was he leaving? He watched her lips form a word.

"Marianna."

5

"DO YOU EVER get a boner when you're riding your bike?"

Elder Collison looked up from his prayer book, startled.

"What?"

Daniel sat on his bed, staring at his hands. He knew he was supposed to follow Collison's example, put on his pajamas and read scripture, but he'd found himself unable to sleep at night, paralyzed by hormones urging him to touch himself, and fear that God would see him and send him straight to hell. He'd spent a week now, lying awake, listening to the cockroaches scamper across the linoleum of their grubby studio apartment until the exhaustion of bicycling all day caught up with him and he'd drift off into a sweaty dreamless sleep. When he woke up, his testicles would ache like they'd been kicked.

He was uncomfortable talking about sex and his sexual fantasies with Collison, but he'd reached the end of his rope and he didn't know what else to do.

"You know, you see a girl on the street or you think about a girl and you know, you get a boner."

"That's when you need to pray the hardest."

Collison found prayer the answer to everything. He used the scriptures like an ostrich uses sand, as something to stick his head into at the first sign of danger.

"I tried that. I pray all the time. But it doesn't help. I still think about it."

Collison stood and walked across their small studio to the only real piece of furniture other than the rickety twin beds: a dresser made almost nonfunctional by repeated slatherings with vibrant red, green, blue, and apparently purple paint. He opened the top drawer and rummaged through a stack of pamphlets from the Church of Jesus Christ of Latter Day Saints before finding the one he was looking for.

"What's that?"

"A guide to self-control. Here. Let me read it to you."

Collison opened the brochure and began to read in a stentorian voice, trying his best to sound like the bishop at his church back home.

"One. Never touch the intimate parts of your body except during normal toilet processes."

"Gross."

"Two. Avoid being alone as much as possible. Find good company and stay in this good company."

"I'm with you, aren't I?"

Collison nodded thoughtfully.

"How about this one? When you bathe, do not admire yourself in a mirror."

"I don't want to do it with myself."

Collison looked up at Daniel, momentarily confused.

"I thought that was the problem. You're tempted to masturbate."

Daniel stood and paced.

"But I'm thinking about girls. Like that one we saw at the bus stop."

"What girl?"

"The Mexican girl? The one in the pink tank top. Didn't you see her?"

He stopped suddenly, a stricken look on his face. "Look!"

He pointed to his crotch. Collison looked over and saw the problem. Daniel had another erection. Daniel raised his hands in the air, trying to keep them as far away from his crotch as he could.

"I'm gonna burn in hell."

Collison found some strength in his voice. "Remain calm."

He quickly skimmed through the pamphlet as Daniel stared at his bulging crotch.

"Help me, Lord!"

The pamphlet admonished them to pray, to keep pure thoughts, to find strength in the scriptures and in the Mormon community. Collison scanned the suggestions, speed-reading for divine intervention.

"This might work."

Collison looked up to see Lamb slowly grinding his crotch against the wall.

"Elder Lamb! Daniel. Step away from the wall."

Daniel burned bright red.

"I can't help it."

"Here. Listen to this. 'It is sometimes helpful to have a physical object to use in overcoming this problem. A Book of Mormon, firmly held in hand, even in bed at night has proven helpful in extreme cases. In very severe cases it may be necessary to tie a hand to the bed frame in order that the habit of masturbating can be broken.'"

The two young men looked at each other. Daniel nodded.

"I don't know what else to do."

Daniel, fully clothed, the crotch of his pants pitched like a pup tent, lay down on the bed and let Collison tie his arms to the bed frame using their clip-on ties. Collison took to the task with ritualistic seriousness. He made sure that Daniel was not going to wriggle a hand free and touch his privates.

"I'll pray for you."

"Thank you. I'm going to need it."

Collison turned the lights out, letting Daniel lie there in the dark, his body on fire with sensation.

For Elder Daniel Lamb, being bound was a revelation. He had never dreamed it could feel so good. Excited, aroused, and restrained. He let impure thoughts race through his mind. He imagined women touching him, slowly unzipping his pants and stroking his penis. They put it in their mouths. They rubbed it between their breasts. Up and down, the imaginary women stroked and pulled, and sucked and rubbed his cock. No matter how much he wanted to touch them, he couldn't. He was tied to the bed. It was agony. It was ecstasy. It was enough to make him ejaculate in his pants.

After that he insisted on being tied to the bed every night.

6

To MIRO they looked like visitors from another time beamed into the middle of a nightclub in Amsterdam; wormhole-warped stragglers, casualties from the Summer of Love who carried a John Lennon song in their heart and wore the stink of patchouli like a badge of honor. They wheeled around the Cannabis Cup Expo preaching the holiness of cannabis, the seven lights of spirituality that matched the seven leaves of the plant. They used words like "epiphany" and "elevation" and "disestablishmentarianism." For them, cannabis was the peace-inducing herb that was going to save the world.

Miro hoped they were right—*it is an extremely useful plant*—and he respected what they had done in the past, they had created the culture, paving the way for people like him, but for an Angeleno raised on a healthy diet of post-punk cynicism, marijuana was less a spiritual pursuit and more of a business proposition. The plant was fun, fascinating, and with real medicinal value for sure, but he wasn't a hippie and he wasn't about to build a religion around it.

Given the nature of the convention he shouldn't have been surprised by the free-lovesters, but he *was* surprised by the international flavor of the event. It was like the United Nations of marijuana. There was a European Union of pot-heads from Spain, France, Holland, Germany, Italy, and England; hipsters from Japan snapping photos, Mexican growers seeking to open trade with Europe, Canadians in their snow-boarder vests and wraparound sunglasses, Brazilian samba stoners shuffling to a capoeira-cannabis beat, and a huge contingent of Americans. There were thousands of them. All the young dudes from New York, California, and points in between, shuffling along in groups of four, wearing hoodies, low jeans, and their baseball caps cocked in a gangsta lean. There were housewives from Oklahoma, farmers from Fresno, fans of the herb from Denver, Sacramento, Austin, Washington D.C. Every possible corner of the country was represented.

Miro was impressed. The Powerzone, a massive night-club that looked like it had once housed some kind of manufacturing, had been transformed into a flower power Disneyland, a counter-culture clubhouse.

The crowd was hip, happy, and had come to party. The vibe was warm and convivial, as if you were among friends.

If you enjoyed getting high, this was the place to be.

Miro checked out the exhibitors on the convention floor. There were booths selling glass pipes and bongs of every size and description, clothing made from hemp, laser beams, and political action groups working to legalize marijuana in various countries around the world. There were vaporizers, grow lights, fertilizers, and informational how-to indoor-pot-farming seminars.

Miro could easily pick out the few serious-looking cannabis wheeler-dealers. They might be dressed in T-shirts and jeans, but their intent was clear. They understood that cannabis was a business, a deeply lucrative endeavor, and taking home the big prize, winning the Cannabis Cup, would mean a financial windfall worth millions of dollars.

Miro wasn't after the money. It would be nice, sure, but he was looking for validation. He had theories about cannabis, and where better to put his ideas to the test than here, among the world's most sophisticated cannabis consumers, in a blind tasting against the world's best growers. This was the Olympics of weed, the World Cup of marijuana, and he hoped the outcome would be like the Paris wine tasting of 1976 when the Californians took home the gold. One of his experiments, a strain based on a theory he had about wild plant genetics, had turned out exceptionally well. It was, if Miro said so himself, the best cannabis he'd ever smoked and a political statement against over-hybridization. Miro was for a return —albeit controlled—to the state of nature, to the vibrant, original, old-school type of cannabis plants that were called Landrace strains.

If he prevailed in this head-to-head—no pun intended —competition with the best cannabis breeders in the world, he would break into the top echelon and could sell his seeds to growers everywhere. He could change cannabis the way Floyd Zaiger had changed the stone-fruit industry.

This was the big time. Although there were plenty of dedicated professional cannabis growers in Los Angeles, only a few branched out and tried to create hybrids, and those that did stuck to tried and true combinations, spinning out variations of Santa Cruz Kush. All the others had become home-grown skunk weed supermarkets, specializing in a kind of standardized hydroponic product that was solid, but nothing special. The gangs that had moved into weed sales were more like Wal-Mart or Costco—what they offered was cheap and plentiful, but it wasn't the highest quality and some of it was outright crap.

Miro had built a clientele of smart, well-to-do people who appreciated the finer things in life. He could claim professional athletes, rappers, record producers, studio executives, movie stars, and a whole cast and crew list of directors, editors, and screenwriters as fans of his cannabis. They were the same people who paid top dollar for artisanal cheeses, heirloom vegetables, single-malt scotch, Cuban cigars, and organic wines. They were well-heeled hipsters who wanted to know that they weren't just smoking weed, but were enjoying a rarified, singular experience. Humboldt County Sensi might be good enough for most people, but Miro's fans considered themselves *cannasseurs,* pot snobs, *ganjaficionados.* And because of California's humane and liberal laws, all they had to do was claim a medical condition—general anxiety or restless leg syndrome—flash their prescription cards at the door of one of the cannabis clubs that carried his brands, and they could purchase his delicious, exotic cannabis legally.

But there was one glitch in his plan. Miro needed a coffeeshop to sponsor him. He couldn't just sashay up to the judges and tell them to check out his weed. He needed someone to represent his cannabis, and he needed them by midnight tonight.

It wasn't as easy as it sounds. The well-established coffeeshops had affiliated seed merchants like DNA Genetics, Sensi Seeds, Barney's, and Greenhouse Seeds, whose booths were piled with photos, info, and samples of their world-famous

Cup-winning hybrids with names like Big Buddha Cheese, Hawaiian Snow, Great White Shark, Super Silver Haze, Super Lemon Haze, Chocolope, and Martian Mean Green. These were Hall of Fame names in the cannabis business and, all combined, these growers and coffeeshops had won dozens of Cannabis Cups. It wasn't in their interest to help someone who might sell to—or worse, become—a competitor.

That left Miro with one or two unaligned coffeeshops who might, if they liked his strain, sponsor him. That's why he'd come to Amsterdam. There was one coffeeshop in particular he'd heard about that had caught his eye. Miro had been paying attention to rumblings across the internet, postings on various Web sites, and discussion groups about some beautiful and obscure strains available at a small coffeeshop outside the central district. The coffeeshop went by the name Orange and had two strains of hash entered in the competition.

Miro found a folding table in the far corner of the exhibition hall. A small, laser-printed sign read ORANGE COFFEE-SHOP, NETHERLANDS.

Sitting upright behind the table, almost at attention, was the owner of the coffeeshop, a tall and lanky, blond-haired and blue-eyed man in a black leather jacket. A line of six perfectly arranged Pyrex beakers filled with precisely cut samples of hashish stood on the table. He looked more like an avant-garde architect or a neurosurgeon than a coffeeshop owner.

"Guus van der . . . ?" Miro hesitated. "I'm sorry, I can't pronounce your last name."

The man reached a long, thin, perfectly manicured finger up and adjusted his designer eyeglasses, pushing them up his nose. He blinked at Miro through what had to be the thickest lenses Miro had ever seen. Miro smiled.

"It's van der Gijp."

Miro extended his hand and the Dutchman shook it.

"I'm Miro Basinas. From LA. I sent you an e-mail?"

Guus stared at Miro without blinking for what seemed an impossibly long time.

"The Californian."

"Yes."

"Call me Guus. No hard 'g.' Guus. Like an owl talks."

Miro blushed. "Your English is perfect."

"As is my Italian."

Miro nodded, he shifted from foot to foot, unsure what to say. Guus tilted his head forward and looked over his glasses at Miro. Miro noticed how blue the Dutchman's eyes were; they were almost periwinkle.

"Remind me. Why are you here?"

Miro took a deep breath, told himself to relax; he didn't know why he felt like this was some kind of job interview and then realized that, in a way, it was.

Miro had a simple business proposal. If Orange would sponsor Miro's cannabis, he was willing to give them a one-year monopoly on the strain, in Europe.

"I have a few hundred seeds. So you could grow them here and, obviously, make as many clones as you like."

He watched as Guus considered his proposal. Finally the Dutchman looked at him.

"It's a generous offer, but my coffeeshop is known for hashish. We have the best in the world, that is not disputable." Guus shook his head. "I'm sorry, but I don't think it will work with me."

"Don't you want to try it? At least have a taste."

Guus adjusted his glasses.

"I'm sorry. Like I said in my reply to your e-mail, any cannabis would have to be very special to interest me."

"It's the best."

"Every grower thinks his cannabis is the best."

With that Guus turned away from Miro, leaving him standing there. Miro walked off, losing himself in the crowd on the convention floor.

7

SHAMUS NORIEGA was only half Salvadoran. His father was an Irish merchant seaman turned construction worker turned bartender turned Latina impregnator turned deportation victim who was sent back to Cork when Shamus was only five. He'd promised to send for his family but once he was gone, he was gone, like he'd fallen off the face of the Earth. Shamus and his mother—a twenty-three year old from San Salvador—never heard from him again.

That left her to single-parent young Shamus in the tough east-side LA neighborhood of Highland Park. While most of the boys his age got into gangs like the Highland Park Aves or the Toonerville Rifa—even the fucking Filipinos had the Pinoy Real—nobody wanted to have anything to do with a redheaded freckle-faced kid named Shamus.

It was, in retrospect, a mistake. Unwanted by the gangs and unsupervised by his hard-working mother, he did what any kid would do, he became a complete fuck up. A gang-banger without a gang.

He liked to think of himself as a Ronin, a samurai without a master, the ultimate freelancer. He wasn't afraid to take on the *cholos,* the cops, or anybody else that got in his way. He got his ass handed to him on more than one occasion but by the time he dropped out of high school he was, by all accounts and general consensus, a 100 percent genuine badass and a thorn in the side of the legitimate criminal operators on the Eastside.

As Shamus gained a rep and started to carve out a mini Eastside drug-selling empire, the gangs took notice. At first they just wanted a cut, a little taste of the business. But Shamus knew that if he showed any weakness, if he paid any commission, tax, or tribute, they'd bleed him to death, so he politely told them—all due respect—to go fuck themselves.

After that, it wasn't like the gangs needed to convene a board meeting to decide what to do. The Toons tried a classic drive-by ambush, but this attempt backfired, leaving a couple of dead Toons splattered along a residential street in a funky part of the city called Frogtown. Shamus wasn't the kind of kid to run and hide, so he responded by impaling the head of the Toonerville jefe's brother-in law on top of the jefe's mailbox in Atwater.

Shortly thereafter, a compromise was worked out between Shamus and the local gangs and Shamus became the controlling force in the Eastside marijuana market. He left all other drugs, gambling, immigrant smuggling, extortion, and prostitution alone and in return the gangs allowed him to import weed from Mexico and wholesale it to a network of dealers.

When the laws changed and medical marijuana outlets began to spring up all over the city, it became essential for these stores to have a reliable stream of affordable cannabis. Shamus—who had educated himself by reading books like

Who Moved My Cheese? and *The Seven Habits of Highly Effective People*—decided that the smart thing to do was to align himself with this new, legal, operation. That's how he became a major supplier for a chain of medical marijuana dispensaries called Compassion Centers. The guy who ran the Centers was a *pendejo,* but he paid really well and the work was almost legal, like the real job his mother always wanted him to have.

...

Shamus caught his reflection in his living-room window and couldn't help taking a moment for some spontaneous grooming. He ran his hand across his tightly shaved head. It was smooth and hard. Just like him. He ran his fingers down the sides of his reddish goatee, flattening the loose hairs. He smiled and checked between his teeth for any signs of debris, any loose strands of *carne asada* that might've gotten stuck in his grill.

Damon, a chunky Caucasian with a shaved head, sat on the black leather couch, rolling a joint.

Damon looked around. It wasn't much of a place, really. There was the couch, a glass coffee table, a couple of black leather chairs, and a couple of floor lamps—all of it taken from a furniture warehouse in the middle of the night. No rug. No pictures on the wall. It was like a living room in Sparta or some shit.

Shamus made a face, his expression a mix of horror and disgust, as Damon licked the papers, running his tongue up and down the joint like it was some kind of baby-back rib and he wanted to get every last drop of sauce.

"What are you doing?"

Damon looked up at him.

"Rollin' it tight, man."

"Can't you use a machine?"

Damon just shrugged. "Nobody ever complained about my rolling before."

Shamus sighed and shifted his legs.

"It looks like you're suckin' the motherfucker off, *cabrón*."

Damon sniffed, defensively. "You're welcome to roll your own."

Damon fired up the joint, inhaled, and held it out to Shamus. Shamus grunted and walked out of the room toward his bedroom. Damon took another hit off the fatty and then called out to Shamus.

"What the fuck're you doing, man? Don't you want any?"

Shamus didn't answer, so Damon followed him back into the bedroom. Damon had only been back there once before, to help him move the dresser around. It was the only room in the house that had a picture on the wall: a framed poster of the emerald Irish countryside with the words "County Cork" printed across the bottom in faux-Gaelic type.

Shamus stood in front of his closet, buttoning his shirt. He waved the joint away.

"Not before business."

Shamus was wearing khakis and a pale-blue dress shirt, looking like he'd just stepped out of a Macy's ad. He glared at Damon.

"Why you gotta dress that way?"

Damon checked himself in the mirror.

"What way?" Damon thought he looked sharp, rockin' a powder blue Puma tracksuit with immaculate Paul

Rodriguez Hat Rod Nike SBs and a big chunk of bling dangling from his neck.

"You look like a drug dealer."

Damon didn't look Shamus in the eye; instead he fidgeted with his necklace, a hunk of 21-carat gold shaped like a marijuana leaf with his name "Damon," scrawled out, in the middle in a curlicue of canary diamonds.

"Fuck, man. I *am* a drug dealer."

Shamus shook his head.

"You really want to look like a dealer, start wearin' an orange jumpsuit that says 'county' on the back."

Shamus was trying to school his helpers. He couldn't even call them assistants because, like, they offered little in the way of fucking assistance, but they did lift shit for him and drive him around, so "helpers" seemed right. He wanted them to be a little smarter, to not look like poster boys for probable cause.

The doorbell rang. Shamus opened it to reveal Guillermo, a muscular twenty-two year old. His other helper. Shamus liked Guillermo. He had potential. He wasn't as stupid as Damon but Guillermo also dressed like he was some kind of member of a hip-hop posse or character on Sesame Street. Like Damon, he was Caucasian, but he had hard-looking, deep-set eyes and close-cropped black hair that made his face look like a flocked skull. Guillermo wore a chunky nugget of gold and diamonds shaped like a giant letter "G." Maybe that's how they could tell each other apart.

They bumped fists as Guillermo strutted into the house. Damon gave a nod and held up the burning joint.

"Want a hit? Diamond Kush."

Guillermo shook him off and looked at Shamus.

"Time is tight. You ready?"
"Almost."
Shamus walked into the kitchen, opened a cupboard, and pulled out his gun—a .45 caliber Glock 30—and stuffed it into the waistband of his jeans behind his back, draping his shirttail over it.
"*Vamanos.*"

...

The three men walked out into the evening side by side, rolling in a kind of slow-motion strut, all menace and flow, Shamus in the middle, like how gangsters are supposed to look. All they needed was a soundtrack.

Damon beeped the white SUV open and they piled in.

Shamus was proud of his car. Riding high above the traffic, snug in his hand-tooled leather seat, screened from the world by tinted windows and air conditioning, with a bass-throbbing, beat-kicking track blasting from the five-thousand-dollar car stereo, Shamus felt invincible. It was even better that he didn't have to drive. Damon took care of that.

Damon reached into the compartment between the seats and pulled out a DVD entitled *Saffron vs The Fuck Machine*. The cover featured a topless woman holding boxing gloves in front of her breasts and the words "Full Contact! No Holds Barred!"

"It's too early for that shit."

"It's never too early for pussy, dude."

Shamus reached for a different disc and fed it into the dashboard system. The machine whirred and suddenly a scene of Al Pacino, his nose caked with pure Peruvian marching powder, his hands holding a huge assault rifle, appeared on the dashboard screen and on little TV screens embedded in the backs of the front seats.

Damon groaned.

"Oh man. Fuckin' *Scarface*. We always watch this."

"I got *Dawn of the Dead,* the original version."

"No."

"*Shaun of the Dead*? It's funny."

"I hate zombies."

"*Godfather II*?"

"Forget it."

Damon sulked. Shamus glanced in the rearview to see Guillermo calmly checking the load in his Beretta nine millimeter.

"This okay with you?"

Guillermo looked at the screen. Al Pacino was still raging.

"Yeah. Whatever."

Shamus didn't like to watch porn before a meet. Porn was distracting. It got your hormones pumping, it made your body and mind hot when you need to be cool. You find yourself in a tight situation, when you need to be on top of things, and all you're thinking about is the girl-on-girl action you just watched in the car. That's the kind of thing that could get a motherfucker killed.

Sometimes it was okay, like when you're kicking back, drinking beer with your friends and all you're gonna do is stretch out on your bed and let some *chica* suck your cock. Then it's fine. It's appropriate. But when you're on your way to buy a few hundred pounds of dope from some ferocious

Arrellano Félix cartel-style *culeros,* well, it's better to stay in the moment.

You'd think that after years of being in the business he could relax. But Shamus didn't trust the cartel. Why should he? Someone might put a bullet in him just because they wanted to impress somebody. The *vatos* were always trying to impress each other. Always vying for promotion. Who was the baddest, the most loco. Shamus didn't have time for that brand of bullshit. School, prison, jobs, gangs, it was all about following the fucking rules and doing what some asshole told you to do. Life was too short. Even working for the Compassion Center was a drag sometimes, but at least he didn't have to go to an office.

...

They pulled into an out-of-the-way cul-de-sac near the LA river in Frogtown. The barrio wasn't called that because a lot of French people lived there; it had earned the name because when it rained, thousands of little frogs would come hopping out of the river onto the streets. Perhaps this sign of the apocalypse was what kept the area low density—filled with light industry and car-repair shops—perfect for drug drops, executions, and other activities that required a discreet yet urban environment.

Shamus scanned the area; there were a few homeless people camped out in nylon tents and huts made out of cardboard boxes and shopping carts. The usual. Not far away, he saw a man with an easel and canvas, working on what looked like a painting of the LA river at sunset. Shamus wondered if the artist would put in the old tires, beer cans, dead dogs, and assorted plastic shit that floated around in the river or if he'd paint some kind of idealized version.

Shamus admired the LA river. The city had taken something wild and paved it over in the name of flood control; they had sterilized it, buried it under tons of smooth concrete, and turned it into just another freeway in a city of freeways. They thought they'd fixed it, but the river had other ideas. It didn't just lie there, it fought back. Shrubby trees had sprouted in cracks in the cement and forced their way up, followed by bushes and reeds, and soon all the native plants had returned. The plants brought back the frogs, turtles, ducks, cranes, herons, hawks, and eagles. It was a real river again. It was nature's way of saying "fuck you" to the city.

"I fucked this chick last night. Tight little pussy."

Shamus turned and looked at Damon. "Yeah?"

Damon nodded. He was stoned, mouthing off.

"I was at this bar in Hollywood, man. And she was fine, really Westside, you know what I'm sayin'?"

Shamus heard Guillermo snort.

"What'd she want with you?"

"She wanted my full ten inches."

Guillermo laughed out loud. "So she didn't want your dick? Is that what you're sayin'?"

Damon spit on the ground.

"Shut up and let me tell the story."

Shamus looked at Damon. He didn't say anything. He wasn't going to encourage him but maybe if he told the story now he wouldn't try and tell it to the guys from Tijuana.

"So what happened?"

"Well you know how that upscale pussy likes to play it. You know? They get you to buy 'em top shelf firewater all night and then they give you a kiss and go."

Guillermo looked at him.

"That's a great story, man. You should write a fucking book."

"No, man. The story ain't over. I slipped a little gift into her cocktail. Took her back to her crib and banged it out, baby."

Damon held up his fist for Shamus and Guillermo to bump. They declined.

"You gave her a roofie?"

Damon spit again, his cottonmouth kicking in big time.

"Shit man, she was beggin' for it."

It was not the first time that Damon had gone out and drugged some woman before raping her. This bugged Shamus. Usually he took a kind of "live and let live" philosophy, but this got under his skin. He thought women, particularly mothers, should be protected. He realized that one of these days he'd have to have a talk with Damon about it.

. . .

A brown panel van pulled into the cul-de-sac and parked next to the SUV. Two men, Luis and Gonzalo, both in their mid-thirties, both dressed like furniture movers, climbed out of the van and stretched. Shamus lifted a hand in greeting as Luis went around to the front of the van and launched a stream of piss into the bushes.

Gonzalo nodded at Shamus.

"Hey, Irish."

"Nice drive?"

Gonzalo shook his head.

"The *pinche* traffic, man. It took us five fucking hours to get here."

Luis came over, wiping his hand against his pants.

"Next time maybe you could meet us in Santa Ana or something."

Shamus nodded.

"Yeah, sure."

Luis threw open the back door of the panel van to reveal a hundred brightly colored piñatas.

That's how it worked. The border patrol would crack open a piñata or two, looking for drugs. They were too lazy to open all the piñatas and too distracted to notice the false bottom in the panel van that held a cargo of five hundred pounds of fresh Mexican skunk weed.

While Shamus and Gonzalo went over to the SUV to exchange money, Damon, Guillermo, and Luis popped open the false bottom and began moving the bricks of weed from the van into the SUV. This all happened quickly and with little conversation. Even though they did this exchange once a month—five hundred pounds might seem like a lot but the Compassion Center's customers burned through it quickly—they weren't friends and there was no collegial atmosphere. When they were done with the transaction they went their separate ways. They didn't go out for tacos and *chelas,* they didn't socialize. The Mexicans didn't talk about their lives or their families or the struggles of their favorite soccer team, Chivas de Guadalajara—in fact, Shamus didn't even know their last names, and he made sure they didn't know his. The exchange was fast, discreet, and virtually anonymous.

Medical marijuana co-ops had originally been set up so that each member could legally grow up to ten plants. Then they were supposed to sell the plants to the co-op and that's how the dispensaries got inventory. With a small, mom-and-pop type ganja grocer the plan worked great, but with a chain of dispensaries like the Compassion Centers, demand quickly outstripped the ability of a few members to grow ten plants at a time. So even though the Compassion Centers were legal, they were forced to purchase their cannabis from large-scale, illegal growers.

As the swap was taking place something caught Shamus's eye. He turned and saw the artist by the river watching them.

"We good?"

Gonzalo nodded.

"*Hasta la proxima.*"

Gonzalo and Luis got back into the panel van, this time with four brown grocery bags filled with hundred-dollar bills stuck in the secret compartment, and drove off.

Damon and Guillermo got into the SUV. Shamus looked at them.

"Start the engine. I'll be right back."

Shamus cut through a gap in the fence and walked toward the painter. The artist must've sensed he was in some kind of trouble because as Shamus drew near he held up his hands, which held a brush and a color-smeared palette.

"It's cool, man. No worries. I didn't see anything."

Which meant he had. Shamus put two bullets into the man's chest. The painter dropped, instantly dead. Shamus went over and gave his body a shove, rolling it down the embankment into the river. He turned to leave and then stopped and took a moment to look at the canvas. It was pretty good, really, a depiction of the scene at dusk, the sky a vibrant pink and purple over the jungled-up riverbed. Shamus carefully picked the painting off the easel. It was still wet and he didn't want to smudge it. This, he realized, would look nice in his living room.

8

IRO SPENT the afternoon getting rejected. The other coffeeshops unaffiliated with seed companies had either already entered a strain or declined to even taste his cannabis based on some kind of anti-American prejudice.

Miro had even talked to one of the cup officials in the hopes that they would consider his strain without a sponsor. That request was turned down.

Miro didn't know what else to do so he entered the coffeeshop called Orange and saw the lanky Dutchman named Guus sitting in the back corner drinking tea and reading a copy of the day's *De Telegraaf.*

Miro walked up to him.

"Just try it."

Guus didn't look up from his paper.

"Please."

Miro took a small glass jar out of his jacket pocket. Inside was a good-sized knuckle of dense jungle-green bud, the leaves radiant with trichomes and specked with saffron-colored blooms.

"If you don't like it, no problem. I'll leave. But I came to Amsterdam to enter the competition and, for fuck's sake, just have a taste. I can't get anyone to even try it. It's like they've all got some big attitude about it because I'm from California."

Guus looked over his paper, slightly annoyed.

"I would hate for you to get the wrong impression of my city."

Guus picked up the jar and unscrewed the lid. He sniffed the bud.

"Tropical fruit?"

Miro watched as Guus broke off a chunk and crushed it in his fingers, giving it another sniff before putting it in a grinder and crushing the bud into smaller bits. He reached for a vaporizer sitting nearby. Guus packed the ground leaves carefully into a glass container and connected it to the vaporizer's heat element.

As the vaporizer heated the leaves, Guus indicated that Miro should sit with him. He took a plastic tube and began to gently draw air into his lungs. He was obviously an expert at this, careful not to suck too hard—too much air and the weed would ignite. That was the point of the vaporizer, it heated the leaves and evaporated the THC in the bud, turning it into a gas without actually burning anything. The theory was that it gave you a pure hit of the active ingredients and it was easy on the lungs.

A fine mist rose off the heating herb and wended its way down the tube and into Guus' lungs. Miro watched as the Dutchman held it in for a beat, then exhaled a plume toward the ceiling and looked at Miro.

He had a curious look on his face—perhaps a reaction to the rollicking scamper of THC rushing into his brain—that caused Miro to smile.

"You like it?"

Guus held up a finger, shushing Miro, and took another hit.

He exhaled and smiled at Miro.

"Very smooth. Everyone always says to me, Sativa. Always Sativa. They want the energy high. But too much energy is not the answer. I believe a balance is necessary. This is very nicely balanced."

Guus plucked the cluster of bud from the jar and studied it. He took a small magnifying glass out of his jacket pocket.

"Do you mind?"

"Please."

Under magnification the bud looked like an alien rain forest: dark green mountains covered in spiky spiderweblike trichomes and a sticky coat of resin. Guus put the bud back into the jar and looked at his fingers. A silvery residue coated the tips.

"What is it?" he asked.

Miro smiled.

"I have some theories about overhybridization. How if we keep overprocessing and inbreeding the plants we're going to end up with Velveeta, you know? Like the cheese?"

Guus shook his head. "Cheese?"

"Overprocessed and boring. That's what I'm saying."

Miro took a big hit off the vaporizer and almost immediately felt the effects. His eyes glazed and everything in the coffeeshop became a little shinier than it had been before. He realized that he hadn't paid any attention to where he was; he had been so intent on convincing Guus to sponsor him that he hadn't noticed the coffeeshop at all. But now, as Guus ground up some more of the bud and began rolling it into a joint, Miro looked around. The coffeeshop wasn't like the others he'd been to. It was groovy. Not hippie groovy but that kind of retro-fifties groovy that was popular in the seventies. Danish modern furniture mixed with odds and ends, bowling-pin-shaped lamps and skeletal room dividers and goofy advertising billboards like the kind they put on bus benches. Brazilian Tropicalismo music floated in the smoky air.

Miro watched some hipsters on the other side of the room passing a massive spliff. He turned and saw an attractive young woman behind the counter. She was laughing as she brewed a pot of herbal tea. Her teeth were white and seemed to sparkle as she smiled. Her eyes were an intense hazel. She was looking at him.

Guus held up an expertly rolled joint.

"I want to see how it smokes."

Guus lit the joint and took a long, luxurious inhale. He released a plume of smoke and looked at Miro.

"I think you are a little bit genius."

Miro shrugged. He felt good, not overly stoned, lucid yet filled with a sense of general all rightness with the world. Then there was this gleaming quality in everything he saw. Miro moved his neck and felt his shoulders. He realized that he was deeply relaxed, almost as if he'd popped a muscle relaxant.

"Why do you say it is like cheese?"

"It's not like cheese. Well, maybe it's like an artisanal cheese from France or something. It was just a metaphor."

Guus handed the joint to the young woman with the hazel eyes and sparkling teeth.

"I was referring to processed cheese. There's too much inbreeding going on. The hybrids they're selling here in Amsterdam, they're like the little retarded cousins of the original plants."

Guus stared at him intently, as if he couldn't tell if Miro was joking or not.

"Stop talking about cheese."

Miro nodded, suddenly feeling awkward, as if he'd insulted the Dutchman.

"Sorry."

Guus smacked his hand down on the table with enough force to cause a nearby bong to wobble.

"You are correct about one thing. A lot of the cannabis they sell at the other shops is inferior. That's why I don't sell it. They have nothing as good as this."

He pointed to the remaining bud in the test tube. "This is something special."

Miro leaned forward, excited. "I wanted only wild, Landrace strains. So I went to Northern Thailand. It took me a few weeks, but I eventually found a small community of farmers near the Cambodian border who grow potent cannabis for their own uses. It was undiluted, pure, old-school Thai *sativa*."

As Miro was telling this, the girl with the hazel eyes and sparkly teeth took another hit.

"*Ce goût de mangues.*"

Guus laughed. Miro looked at him.

"What did she say?"

"She says it tastes like mangoes."

"Exactly."

Miro smiled at the girl, then continued. "I took some seeds back to my laboratory and grew the wild Thai plants."

"This is wild Thai?"

Miro shook his head.

"I took a similar trip to the Big Island of Hawaii. Do you know it?"

Guus shook his head. "I've never been to Hawaii. But I like macadamia nuts."

Miro nodded. "They are tasty."

The girl flashed Miro a thumbs-up.

"You like it?"

She nodded. "Wow. Wowee."

Guus laughed. "She likes it a lot."

Miro smiled.

"So, on the Hilo side. The rainy side. I isolated a strain of wild Hawaiian Indica. Someone must have left it growing in the national park since, I don't know, the sixties."

Guus thought about it. "So that's what this is? Wild Thai and wild Hawaiian crossed?"

"Not quite. First I crossed them, creating an F1, then I crossed the F1s to create an F2, and so on until I had grown a perfect F6 mix of my wild plants."

Guus took a sip of tea.

"Although the taste and quality of buzz was there, it still wasn't performing as I'd hoped, so I went back to create an unstable F1 and crossed that with a Haze and Brazilian F1 I had experimented with to increase the trichome content and give it some stability. Then I used my F6 as a parent and began again."

Guus nodded. "What's it called?"

Miro sat back and smiled.

"I named it Elephant Crush. You know, after the elephants in Thailand. But if you enter it in the competition we can call it Orange Crush after your coffeeshop."

Miro was startled when a lean gray and white cat suddenly leaped up on the table. The cat glanced at Miro, then purred and allowed Guus to scratch its head before it slunk over and sniffed the vaporizer. Guus smiled. "Even Viola likes it."

Guus looked at Miro. "She keeps the mice out of the hash."

The cat began to groom herself. Miro looked across the table at Guus. The Dutchman was stoned now, his face screwed up in a warped expression of whimsy. He had come to a decision.

"I like the Elephant Crush. Viola likes the Elephant Crush. So I will sponsor you."

Guus leaned in conspiratorially. "And I think we will win."

9

I T WAS AFTER service at their local Church of Jesus
Christ of Latter Day Saints that Daniel asked to have
a meeting in private with the bishop. He didn't
want to talk to anyone but a combination of guilt and
Collison's insistence that he needed help gave him no choice.
Collison was happy to wait; there was a Mutual—a social
mixer for teenagers—taking place in a meeting room, and the
promise of ice cream and pie was enough for him.

Daniel followed the bishop, a tall handsome man with
gray hair and steel-blue eyes, into his office. The office was
spare and utilitarian, like the office of a high school guidance
counselor. A few plaques and diplomas—and the American
flag in the corner—imparted a reassuring authority to the
folding metal chairs and linoleum floor.

The bishop pointed to a chair.

"Have a seat."

Daniel sat down and looked at his hands. The bishop
settled into his chair, all high-backed and comfy looking
leather, and looked at Daniel.

"This is about sex, isn't it?"

Daniel nodded.

"Have you been touching yourself?"

Daniel shook his head. Being here, talking to a stranger about sex was the last place he wanted to be.

"Good."

Daniel cleared his throat.

"It's just . . ."

For some reason his voice cracked.

"It's just that when I wake up in the morning, well, there's like . . . some kind of goo in my underwear."

The bishop smiled.

"That's as it should be."

Daniel was confused.

"I don't understand."

The Bishop leaned forward and folded his hands together, ready to do his job, to give spiritual guidance to a troubled young person.

"You have feelings. Sexual feelings. Don't you?"

Daniel nodded.

"When you see a young woman, do you feel the sap rising within you?"

"Yes."

"That is as it should be. Think about a tree. Tall and strong. It is filled with sap, that's the tree's blood, its life force."

The bishop pointed at Daniel.

"You have the same force within you. The force of creation. It's a powerful force."

Daniel nodded again. "I'll say."

"But you must control this force and wait to use it at the proper time."

"I understand all that. I just wonder if the goo is a sin."

The bishop smiled.

"No. Not at all. Your body is like a machine. A goo-producing factory if you will. Every now and then the factory produces a little too much. So while you're asleep it does a little practice delivery to get rid of the excess inventory."

"So it's practicing for a time when I'm married?"

The bishop nodded.

"But don't practice the delivery yourself. You've got to cherish your sap. That's what makes you strong."

10

THE FOOD WOULD not stop coming. Just when he thought he couldn't eat another bite, a new dish would appear. Guus had wanted to eat a *rijstafel* to celebrate getting the Elephant Crush entered in the competition, so here they were, in a sleek and modern Indonesian restaurant being presented with course after course after course. Miro and Guus had already devoured fried crabs, a fragrant lobster soup from Java called *bobor kraton,* sizzling grilled lamb *sate* with some kind of peanut sauce, fish in a sweet-sour jackfruit sauce, and a pungent beef stew called *dendeng.* Now they were presented with a blazingly spicy prawn soup called *udang blado.* The names of the dishes conjured up images of characters from *Star Wars* movies, not the original trilogy, but the crappy ones that came later.

Not that Miro wasn't enjoying the food, it was delicious. The spices excited his cannabis-enhanced taste buds, warmed his stomach, and made his nose run. A bottle of crisp Sancerre was perched at the ready in an ice bucket like a cool French fire extinguisher. But there was so much food, he could've hosted a dinner party.

Miro was startled to hear a loud American voice break through the low murmur of the restaurant. He turned and saw four men sitting at a table on the other side of the room.

Guus stopped spooning soup into his mouth long enough to ask him a question.

"Someone you know?"

Miro nodded.

"Someone I've met before. He owns the Compassion Center chain."

"What?"

"Medical marijuana stores. He has, like, eight or nine around LA. They all look the same. Same menu, same furniture. The employees even wear uniforms. His name's Vincent something."

Guus laughed and a half-chewed prawn jumped out of his mouth. He popped it back in and continued chewing.

"Vincent Starbucks."

Miro laughed. "I'm always suspicious of logos on clothes."

Miro didn't like the Compassion Centers. For starters he didn't think they were particularly compassionate; they were more corporate than anything, they bought in bulk and sought exclusives from growers, paying below-market prices whenever they could. It was like trying to make a deal with Wal-Mart. You either played by their rules and took their prices, or they'd try to put you out of business. Miro preferred the cannabis clubs and herbal co-ops he dealt with. They were nice people, little mom-and-pop shops and cannabis boutiques, that served a wide range of clientele, some of whom had actual medical problems like cancer and AIDS and glaucoma and needed cannabis. The Compassion Centers, on the other hand, cultivated an upscale clientele from Brentwood, Santa Monica, and Beverly Hills—

the kind of people who had botox treatments more often than they smoked marijuana.

Miro took a sip of wine.

"I wonder who he's with."

Guus smirked. "That's easy. Across from him is Arjan, the owner of the Greenhouse and Greenhouse Seeds. I don't know the other two."

Miro couldn't help himself, he stared. Greenhouse Seeds was the New York Yankees of the Cannabis Cup, dominating the competition every year and winning over thirty Cups for their various strains of Sativas, Indicas, and hashish. Arjan was the self-proclaimed King of Cannabis.

"I wonder what they've entered. It'll be good, you can count on that."

Guus leaned forward. "We'll beat them."

"You think?"

Guus nodded.

"If I didn't think so, I wouldn't have entered."

A black rice pudding studded with jackfruit and coconut shavings arrived at the table. Guus drained his glass of wine and then began shoveling the pudding into his mouth. He looked up at Miro, who was watching Vincent and the King of Cannabis.

"This pudding is fantastic."

...

Miro and Guus waddled out of the restaurant and into the street. It was cold; a damp foggy chill that seemed to cling to everything had descended. Miro flipped his collar up for the hundredth time since he'd arrived in Amsterdam and reminded himself that he really needed to buy a scarf and a hat. The raw air didn't seem to bother Guus, he let his scarf dangle nonchalantly in front of his unbuttoned leather jacket.

Guus turned to Miro. "I need to walk. If I sit down, I fear I will rupture."

Miro nodded. "I could use a stroll."

...

They walked for a while, two stoned and satiated men, one deep in a kind of gormandized, pigged-out coma, the other freezing his nuts off.

After a few blocks they turned a corner and entered the De Wallen section of Amsterdam. The streets were narrow and dark, the few streetlights that bounced off the wet cobblestones provided a kind of upside-down illumination that made the faces of the people passing by look vaguely ghoulish. In some spots men stood huddled together, talking in hushed voices, buying and selling narcotics. Other men walked alone, their faces clenched tight against the night air, moving quickly down the street.

Miro noticed that the block was lined with small shops, although there wasn't any signage, just scantily clad women standing behind large windows affecting seductive poses, one after the other after the other under red lights. They looked like plants lined up in a nursery. He turned to Guus.

"We're in the red-light district?"

Guus nodded and smiled.

"If you want to partake in carnal pleasures, please, it is permitted."

Miro shook his head.

"Not my thing."

Guus laughed.

"It's not why I came this way. There is a church here that I want to see."

"A church?"

"It has a very famous organ."

...

The lights were still on inside the old church, illuminating the massive arched windows and sending a diffuse glow out into the fog. Guus stopped and tilted his head. Miro was about to say something when the first wisps of organ music floated out of the building. They stood there for a few minutes as the organ pumped and rattled and chirped and sang like it was squeezing the life out of a flock of angels. Guus smiled and said, "Messiaen." He sat down on a bench and listened.

It was classical music, that was all Miro knew. Although it didn't sound like any classical music he'd ever heard before. The music was dense and strange, like a jungled-up fever dream.

Miro didn't feel like sitting down; the last thing he wanted was damp pants. He was already shivering. He saw a sculpture and walked over for a closer look. It was a bronze of a woman standing in a rectangle meant to resemble a door frame. She was posing provocatively, wearing large Weimar Republic dominatrix boots, her hands on her hips. The inscription on the plaque said, "Respect sex workers all over the world."

Miro walked back to where Guus was sitting. He looked out at the canal where a few houseboats were moored, smoke rising from their fireplaces as they rocked gently on the water.

The music stopped and Guus let out a sigh.

"Beautiful. It almost makes you believe in God."

Miro turned toward him.

"You believe in God?"

Guus stood, suppressed a burp, and shook his head.

"I don't know anything. But do you really think you created Elephant Crush by yourself?"

11

IRO COULD HEAR the clap of a snare drum; he could feel the thud of the bass in his chest even though he was standing on the street outside the building. He let a cold Dutch drizzle fall on him. He didn't care. He was too nervous to go in. The cannabis had been smoked, the jury had deliberated, the votes had been counted, and they would be announcing the winner of the Cup after the band's set. It was too much for Miro. So he paced the sidewalk.

Guus gave him a pat on the shoulder.

"Relax. You have to trust."

"What does that mean?"

"It means, my American friend, that the judgment is out of your control. You did the best that you could, now the judges will do the best that they can. We will see what happens."

It was true. But that didn't make Miro feel any less nervous.

There was a buzz going around the convention floor about some amazing weed. Because it was a blind tasting—every strain was given a code name—Miro didn't know if they were talking about the Elephant Crush or if there was another, even better cannabis entered. What if Greenhouse Seeds had come up with another remarkable strain like Super Lemon Haze? Maybe Barney's, the other big coffeeshop, had developed another G13 Haze, or someone else had discovered some rare gem, a once-in-a-lifetime cannabis. Miro had spent over two years, putting his life on hold as he sunk all his money and time into developing Elephant Crush. What if he lost? What if he was wrong?

Guus laughed at him. "I'm going inside. If you have a heart attack call one-one-two and they'll send an ambulance."

Miro watched as Guus shouldered his way through the crowd, back into the hall. He thought about following, thought about joining the throng and grooving to the reggae beat inside, but realized that would only make him more nervous; he was in no mood to groove so instead he decided to take a walk around the block.

He hadn't gotten far when he heard a familiar voice behind him.

"If you are looking for the breeze of the afternoon, you're too late."

He turned and saw Marianna, the beautiful Portuguese scientist, standing in front of a wine bar holding her umbrella.

Miro smiled. "Hi."

She offered her hand and he took it, giving her a warm handshake, trying not to grin too much.

"Aren't you supposed to be at the conference?" She raised her umbrella so that he could stand under it with her.

"Yeah. I guess. I'm too nervous."

"You're nervous? Or stoned?"

"Nervous. I have a strain entered in the competition."

He watched her face shift, like she was reassessing him.

"You are one of the geneticists?"

Miro nodded.

"Kind of. I'm a botanist. I even have a degree to prove it."

She smiled.

"Well, come have a glass of wine with me. It is also made from plants."

Miro wasn't going to be as dumb as he had been last time. He followed her into the wine bar.

It wasn't like he had never had a girlfriend before. He'd had a few. One of them had even lasted a couple of years: they'd met in college and, after graduation, they'd moved to LA together. She was the one who initially got him interested in marijuana. He'd always been a weekend smoker but she was a real connoisseur and introduced him to the wide world of distinct strains and styles of cannabis. He sometimes wondered if he would have ever put the *pluot* and the idea of perfect cannabis together in his mind without her influence. With his skill as a grower and her love of quality reefer, you'd think they would've been a perfect match, but Miro had always felt like he was an accessory in the relationship. He occupied a kind of support position between her bong and her vibrator. Just another pleasure gadget.

After that he dated. Had a few flings. A couple of times he fell into starter relationships but those only lasted a few months before the woman would begin to realize that he was more committed to his plants, to his scientific endeavors, than to "them," and they'd invariably complain about the dirt under his fingernails and the smell of organic fertilizer in the kitchen.

He thought maybe he needed to date someone who worked at a nursery, maybe a garden designer or landscape architect; someone who shared his passion for plants.

He wasn't sure how the Portuguese scientist fit into the scheme of things but as he sipped a glass of ruby-plum Cortes de Cima Incognito, looked into her shining green eyes, and watched as her delicate hand swept a loose curl back behind her ear, he forgot about plants and strains and competitions. He let the wine glow in his stomach and her accent fill his ears.

He learned that she was an information scientist, a kind of super-high-tech librarian, and that she was living in Amsterdam for two years working on a special project funded by the European Union. She had two older sisters; one was a doctor and the other was a graphic designer. He asked about her accent and learned that if he spoke Portuguese, her accent would tell him that she was obviously an *alfacinha,* a native of Lisbon. She'd graduated with honors from the Universidade de Lisboa and done her graduate work at the University of Chicago. She didn't like rock music but she adored Tropicalismo from Brazil.

Miro had never met anyone like her before. He could've sat in the wine bar listening to her for hours, but then it occurred to him that he'd been there too long already.

"Fuck."

"What?"

"We've got to go."

Inside the hall the air was thick with ganja smoke and the crowd was pulsing to some old-school drum and bass mixed by a DJ on the stage. The DJ somehow mashed up a mambo marimba riff with the guitar break from the Gang of Four's "At Home He's a Tourist" and a chewing-gum jingle. Miro felt his nerves return. His mouth went dry and his heart pounded in his throat as he and Marianna burst into the room.

As his eyes adjusted he saw Guus standing with a group of people in the far corner. They appeared to be having an animated discussion and were passing around a huge spliff.

Guus saw Miro and waved. Miro realized he was holding Marianna's hand—although he couldn't say when that had happened—and juked his way through the crowd toward Guus. He had almost made it to the other side of the crowd when suddenly the King of Cannabis himself threw his arms around him.

"Your weed is out of sight, man. Congratulations."

Miro nodded. It was hard to hear in the din of the mash up so Miro communicated by bobbing his head up and down.

"Come by the Greenhouse later and we talk."

Miro nodded some more.

The King patted his shoulder, turned to go, and was swallowed by the crowd. Miro looked at Marianna. She was smiling, enjoying the scene. That made him extra happy.

Miro turned back toward Guus and that's when he saw it. Guus was holding it up above his head with two hands. A bronze trophy that looked a lot like the mythical holy grail. It was the Cannabis Cup.

12

I F, AS MANY great religions believe, there is an afterlife, an eternity of blissful reward filled with goblets of ambrosia, rivers of wine, angelic singing, and seventy-two virgins, then the after party for the Cannabis Cup was its own kind of Heaven.

By the time they got there, Miro was so stoned that he was having an out-of-body experience. It might have looked like he was slumped across the corner of a couch like an old coat, cradling his trophy in the crook of his arm like a newborn, but his mind was somewhere else, zooming along the ceiling of the nightclub in a part of Amsterdam called the Old South, hovering over the Franco-Algerian reggae band from Marseille—the singer rapping in Arabic—zipping over the clusters of stoners huddled around various bongs and water pipes. His consciousness or essence or spirit or whatever you want to call it flitted among the dancers, zoomed over the bar, and boomeranged outside and back. Miro felt slightly queasy; he wasn't really accustomed to these kinds of transitory corporeal experiences, but then he'd never been this baked before.

As he held the Cup in his hands, it dawned on Miro that he'd never won anything in his life. Not even a spelling bee or a kickball game. Miro understood what it must have felt like when Floyd Zaiger bit into the very first *pluot*. How sweet it must've tasted! Now he could understand how those Olympic athletes and Oscar Award winners felt when they accepted their trophies. With one simple announcement, he was launched into the stratosphere, acclaimed one of the best, the top dog, a gold medalist like Usain Bolt or an Oscar winner like Meryl Streep. He had spent thousands of hours reading and researching, tending plants with care, tasting and refining, always hoping that his ideas would somehow manifest in greatness. And now he was vindicated, validated, victorious.

It didn't hurt that winning also meant his plants and their seeds were now worth millions of dollars.

...

At one point he saw Guus dancing his way through the throng, trying desperately not to spill the three beers he was carrying as various people—their arms flailing in some kind of spastic kung-fu flower-petal dance—pinballed around him. Miro saw himself half-gassed on the couch and realized that Guus was headed toward him. It was then that he noticed Marianna sitting on the couch next to him.

Guus set the beers down and Miro re-entered his body. Miro blinked and saw Guus wagging a finger at him.

"Too much Elephant Crush."

Miro grinned. It was an uncontrollable, stupidly-wasted grin.

"Cannabis Cup–winning Elephant Crush."

It sounded like a voice coming from somewhere else, as if a ventriloquist was sitting on the other side of the room pulling a little string in Miro's back, making his mouth move. Guus smiled and raised his glass in a toast.

"To the Elephant Crush!"

Marianna joined them in the toast and the three clinked their glasses. She smiled at Miro.

"I now see why you won."

Miro grinned and sipped the beer. It was cold and foamy, slightly bitter and slightly sweet. It was, he realized, an ingenious beer. The beer was like a masseuse who knew just where to push; it excited all the various areas of his tongue, from the filiform papillae at the tip that sensed sweetness to the ones at the back that were sensitive to bitter and salty flavors—his tongue was being turned on by this beer. It felt like his tongue was having sex with the beer.

Miro was interrupted by a familiar face. It was Vincent, the owner of the Compassion Centers. He was signaling something with his hands, miming what looked like talking on the phone.

"Let's have lunch. In LA."

Miro smiled and flashed Vincent a thumbs-up. Vincent returned the gesture and walked off into the crowd. Guus leaned forward.

"We will be hearing from all the coffeeshops now. Everyone wants the winner."

Miro smiled. "But you have the exclusive."

Guus let out a discreet belch.

"I do. But you can, of course, sell it to whomever you want in your country. I think it could be good for America. Maybe they will stop making wars."

Miro started to laugh but caught himself when he realized that Guus was totally serious. Besides, he was too stoned, too happy, to get into the political intricacies of a vast and populous country like the United States. And who knew? Maybe the Crush could change the world. Maybe he would win a Nobel Peace Prize. Why not?

They were interrupted by several other growers, fans, and well-wishers.

As Guus fielded the congratulations, Miro reached for Marianna. She looked at him, her eyes completely glazed over from the herb. When their hands touched Miro felt a jolt of sensation. Like the beer on his tongue, her skin was communicating with his skin, sending deeply encoded animal bursts that coursed through his nervous system and triggered some kind of glandular secretions, some primeval brain chemistry reactions that started his body whirring like an amorous supercollider. The power of it startled him. He couldn't tell if it was the pot or her, but he'd never felt this way before.

She smiled at him and leaned over to whisper something in his ear. Miro felt her warm breath on his neck, the sunshine in her accent.

"Do you want to get high and go to bed?"

Miro laughed.

"I'm already high."

...

Mark Haskell Smith

They started kissing in the cab. Her moist tongue darting into Miro's mouth and exciting him, making him hard. She was soft and warm and smelled like lavender. As they kissed Miro snaked his hand into her velvet coat, under a woolen sweater, past a hanging garden of necklaces, between a gap in her silk blouse, and reached beneath her T-shirt to find a small firm breast waiting for him.

Miro didn't remember much about how they got back to the hotel, into the room, and under the covers, yet somehow that's where they ended up. He couldn't tell you how their clothes fell from their bodies and ended up mingled in a heap on the floor. All he could recall was their naked bodies coming together, somehow fitting perfectly in a soft and slow coupling, surprising him, as if it were the first time.

After the Bullet

13

ELDER DANIEL LAMB prayed like a motherfucker. Not that he'd ever use that particular word in a conversation with God. He wouldn't use that particular word in a conversation with anyone. But here he was, standing on the street, praying harder than he'd ever prayed before. Pleading with God so intensely that he was sweating, his fists clenched together into a white-knuckled mouthpiece, his body trembling with the power of his transmission, pleading with God to spare the life of the poor man lying on the grass.

The field strength of his prayers took him by surprise, making him feel as if he'd become some electro-humming altar-boy antenna broadcasting directly to the cosmos.

God is goodness and love. Surely He would hear him and spare this man's life. He wouldn't let someone die senselessly. Unless, of course, God had other plans.

Daniel looked up from his prayers and watched as the paramedics intubated the blood-spattered body on the ground.

Collison grabbed his arm.

"I think I'm gonna be sick. I never saw a dead person before."

Daniel turned and looked at his partner. Collison *did* look like he might vomit. His face was sweaty and red, a roll of neck fat bulging out, leaping over the buttoned-up collar of his white shirt.

"Really. I'm gonna hurl."

"Take some deep breaths. Loosen your tie."

"I gotta sit down."

Collison crumpled to the sidewalk and let out a groan.

Daniel looked up, away from his fallen colleague, to see the paramedics sliding the man into the back of the ambulance. For a brief, tiny second, Daniel made eye contact with the victim.

"He's alive. His eyes are open."

"People die with their eyes open. I had a cat once and that's what it looked like. She had her eyes open."

Collison followed this statement with a gut-churning moan and a loud *kack*ing gag, then vomited onto his lap. Daniel stepped back, away from the sludge, as Collison convulsed and *urp*ed again, coating his pants.

"You okay?"

"I don't think so." Collison groaned again and then flopped over and curled up fetal in his own vomit.

Daniel looked up, needing help. He saw a mangy-looking dog lapping blood off the grass where the victim had been. The dog's dirty white fur was turning brown, stained with gore. There were a couple of cops around, detective-looking guys.

Daniel waved to them.

"Hey! Help!"

A big Asian detective with a shaved head turned and started jogging over to see what was wrong.

Daniel turned to reassure his partner and noticed that tears were streaming down Collison's face. The detective looked at Collison, then turned to Daniel.

"What's wrong?"

Collison, his tears carving little gullies in the vomit on his face, looked up at Daniel.

"I don't think I can do this anymore."

And that's when Elder Collison had a nervous breakdown.

14

SHAMUS ROLLED the window down to try and get a better view of what was happening at the other end of the street.

"Slow the fuck down."

He craned his neck, trying to see what was going on.

"What're we doin' man?"

"I wanna see if he's dead."

Damon slowed down but he didn't look happy about it. He slouched, like he was afraid someone was watching him. He pulled a bandanna out of his pocket and mopped the sweat on his forehead.

"C'mon man. You got him. I saw him drop."

Shamus turned and glared.

"I want the kill."

Shamus liked to keep track of the people he killed, not necessarily their names or what they did or if they had a family or anything, just the cold stats. It was like how they keep track of baseball players with runs batted in and slugging percentage. Shamus had his own stats. Heads bashed in and plugging percentage. It had been almost a month since he had plugged the painter in the LA river and he had been feeling the itch to shoot somebody. Either that or beat some asshole senseless. Lucky for him, this errand had come along at the right time.

Shamus turned back to the street. He wished he had binoculars so he could see if the motherfucker was dead or not. He watched the cops run around like they actually knew what they were doing. He saw the locals, the little old ladies from Hermosillo and Manila, gathering and gawking. This was way better than their Pinoy soap operas and telenovelas on Telemundo. A smattering of hipsters—Shamus assumed they were all unemployed screenwriters—stood off to the side, whispering to each other. They would probably use this scene in their next big project.

"They'll see us."

"So?"

"So, like they're not supposed to."

Shamus shook his head, disgusted, as he watched the paramedics do their thing, wasting taxpayer money trying to save a dead man.

And then there were the two squirrelly-looking Mormon dickheads standing there praying for the asshole with the bullet in his chest.

"Look at those fuckers."

"The cops?"

"Those fucking Mormons."

Damon mopped his face and looked down the street.

"They came to my house once."

Shamus looked at Damon.

"You fuck 'em?"

Damon didn't know how to respond to that.
"Can we go now? This isn't cool."
Shamus nodded.
"Drive on, bitch."

15

THERE WAS NO pure white light at the end of a tunnel, no warm and fuzzy greetings from his long-dead ancestors, and no ghostly hovering above the doctors as they worked frantically to repair his damaged body. As far as near-death experiences go, Miro's was anticlimactic.

Not that it was some kind of cakewalk. They almost lost him: his blood pressure dropped at one point, and the doctors had to shout excitedly—a stream of coded references to solutions, drugs, and other medical wonders followed by the word "stat." They had to zap his heart with defibrillators. The young doctors liked to think they were on a television show. They rubbed the paddles together and shouted "clear!" It made them feel like superheroes.

...

Daniel stood in the waiting area of the emergency room and did what people do in waiting rooms. He waited.

He had sat in the back of the ambulance and watched as his mission partner was strapped to a gurney and given a strong sedative to put a halt to what had become a never-ending stream of tears and nonsensical babbling. They'd slid Collison right next to the gunshot victim and they had all piled into the ambulance.

At first Daniel thought Collison was speaking in tongues. But how can you tell? He'd never heard someone speak in tongues and wasn't sure that incomprehensible yammering was proof that Collison was filled with the Holy Spirit. *Was this the miracle of Pentecost?* Maybe Collison's gibberish was touched by the divine, but mostly it sounded like baby talk, babble and grunts and flying spittle.

Every now and then a profanity would spark from Collison's mouth like he was some kind of short-circuiting Tourette's patient. Collison called for his mommy. He wanted to fuck her.

Daniel was scared for him; he'd never seen a mental breakdown before, and was relieved when the paramedic had, mercifully, restrained Collison's hands and doubled up on the dosage.

...

Daniel looked at the other people in the waiting room: a little girl with measles, a guy freshly detached from his thumb, an incredibly fat man wrapped in a foul-smelling bedspread. Daniel didn't feel like preaching to them. They didn't need to hear about the Book of Mormon or the Church of Jesus Christ of Latter Day Saints. They didn't need him to comfort them, they needed real help.

Daniel walked over to the water fountain and took a long, lukewarm drink. He wondered if he was somehow to blame for Collison's condition. Would the church elders hold him responsible? Partners were supposed to look out for each other. What would he tell them? That the mission had been difficult? Weren't the missions supposed to be difficult? Isn't that the point?

Daniel saw the detectives from the crime scene talking to a couple of EMT paramedics. He went up to them.

"Hey. Did that guy make it? The guy who got shot?"

The detective, the big one with the shaved head, turned and looked at him.

"He'll live."

Daniel felt a rush of adrenaline. His body felt light, energized; his prayers had been answered and now the power and the glory of God was flowing inside him.

"It's a miracle."

The detective made a sour face.

"It's dumb fucking luck."

16

THEY WORE dark blue uniforms with the letters LAFD emblazoned across the front and little patches that indicated they were emergency medical technicians: paramedics, first responders. They saw a lot of blood and guts and shit; sometimes they saved lives but mostly they dealt with heart attacks, car accidents—those were always gross—and gunshot wounds, in that order. It was Los Angeles. Lots of people, lots of cars, lots of guns. Shit was bound to happen.

Ted was waiting to hit the trifecta—guy has a heart attack while driving, rear ends some hothead suffering from road rage who jumps out of his car and shoots him—he figured it was only a matter of time.

While Fran worked in the back of the ambulance to secure the gurney and catalog what meds they'd used to subdue the hysterical Mormon boy, Ted sat in the front with a clipboard, finishing off the paperwork.

Fran turned and looked at Ted.

"I thought they wore special underwear."

Ted looked up from his papers.

"What?"

"You know, like magic underwear."

"Who?"

"The Mormons. They're supposed to wear underwear that protects them from evil. Looked like Fruit o' the Loom to me."

Ted shrugged. "I'm not very religious."

Fran locked down the last of the drawers and slid into the driver's seat.

"Rambo Taco?"

Ted winced at the mention of the roach coach with its spray-painted mural of a muscle-bound warrior wearing camouflage and holding an assault rifle displayed on its side. It was supposed to look like Sylvester Stallone in the movie *Rambo,* and it did, kind of. But Ted wasn't sure what Rambo had to do with tacos. He didn't remember the movie that well but wasn't Rambo a post-traumatic-stress-disorder sufferer? A Vietnam vet on a one-man vendetta against a corrupt sheriff in Oregon? What did that have to do with quesadillas?

"We had Rambo Taco yesterday."

"Yeah, and you said they were good."

Ted remembered he'd been up all night dealing with repeater burps that tasted like hot grease and chilies.

"I can't do it today. What about the place Escalante told us about?"

"The car wash?"

"The little café by the college."

Fran considered it. Ted knew that mentioning Escalante —a rotund and affable fireman known not only for his fine firehouse cooking but for his culinary judgement in general— was a plus. But Fran didn't seem swayed by this.

"I really want a taco."

"He said they had meat-loaf sandwiches."

The mention of meat loaf seemed to change Fran's outlook.

"And cupcakes."

Fran started the ambulance.

...

Ted watched as Fran polished off a coconut cupcake, washing it down with a bottle of Coke.

"How can you eat all that sugar?"

Fran looked at him.

"Because it's real sugar. This is a Mexican Coke. Not that corn syrup crap. Real sugar's good for you."

Ted wondered why he was partnered with Fran. You would think the LAFD would find people who were, at the very least, gastronomically compatible. Fran wouldn't know how to spell gastronomic. She was a community college dropout from the Valley who'd ricocheted through a series of mindless minimum-wage jobs before running off to join the army. She'd been trained as a medic, gone through tours of Afghanistan and Iraq and, if you believed her, she'd seen more than her share of action.

Ted had been a comparative literature major at UC Santa Barbara. He'd written articles for the student paper: mostly reviews of reggae concerts, a front-page story about the annual joint-rolling contest, and a hard-hitting series exposing corruption in the Ultimate Frisbee world championships.

Joining the Los Angeles Fire Department as a paramedic was a logical choice for Fran, part of her natural trajectory, but Ted still didn't know why he was doing it. It was almost like a joke that had gotten out of hand. His parents wanted him to be a doctor but he wasn't good at math so he had applied to train as an EMT, got accepted and now, well, here he was. Not that he minded. It was the most interesting job he could think of.

Ted watched as Fran strutted up to the counter to get a second cupcake. He had to admit that she was attractive, with a handsome face and short brown hair that could look boyish or pixyish depending on her mood. Her body was tight, strong from pumping iron at the firehouse gym, and she moved with the rigid posture of a prison guard. She had nice breasts and an ass that could've been used in the *Buns of Steel* infomercials. Ted had never really paid much attention to her looks until they were at a bar with some firefighters and Fran had drunkenly risen to the challenge of a wet T-shirt contest, pitting herself against a hot blonde from the LAPD. As her tight jeans clung to her ideal ass and her T-shirt became transparent, Ted became the envy of his colleagues.

But Ted wasn't involved with her and he wasn't interested in getting involved with her. Even if he found her physically attractive, their differences kept him from making a move. Fran's tour of duty in the army had turned her into a discipline freak, a belligerent throwback to the days before mandatory sensitivity training. Ted was, by nature of his upbringing, already sensitive.

Fran sat back down with her second cupcake. She took a bite, the frosting sticking to her nose. She looked at Ted.

"Next Mormon we get, let's strip 'em and see if they got the magic underwear."

17

"THIS IS BULLSHIT, man."

As Damon struggled to lift a ten-gallon container holding a lush and leafy cannabis plant, guano-rich dirt spilled out onto his bright white sneakers.

"Fuck this. We should've hired some fucking Mexicans to do this."

Shamus watched as Damon frantically tried to brush dirt off his fancy new shoes.

"What the fuck're you doin', man?"

"You know how much these cost? I can't let my kicks get dirty."

Shamus picked up a cardboard box filled with glass jars. The jars were labeled in some kind of scientist code and contained a variety of buds and seeds. Shamus looked at Damon and shook his head in disgust.

"Stop being such a little bitch and get this shit in the van."

Guillermo came into the room carrying a mature plant, one that looked close to blooming, with large blossom-studded *colas* at the ends of the stalks.

"Look at these beauties. There's a bunch more, too. Dude's got almost a hundred plants."

Damon set his container down and brushed dirt off his track pants, carefully inspecting them to see if they were smudged. He looked at Shamus.

"There's a bunch of baby clones in the other room. I'll get them."

Damon walked off. Shamus and Guillermo exchanged a look. Guillermo had to laugh.

"Long as I can smoke some of this shit, I'll carry whatever."

Shamus grunted and walked out the back door carrying the box of glass jars. He slid it into the back of the truck and looked around, scanning the area for witnesses. Shamus didn't like people testifying against him; they should mind their own fucking business. But he couldn't have picked a more perfect night for a robbery. It was dark, there were no lights on in the house next door, no streetlight, and only a half-moon in the sky—not enough to give someone a look at what they were doing. For all anyone knew, someone was moving out.

Damon carried a flat of small plants and plopped it into the back of the van with a loud thud. Then he began to brush the dirt off his tracksuit.

"I should've worn some motherfuckin' overalls. Who knew this asshole was the farmer in the dell?"

Shamus looked at him.

"This weed won the Cannabis Cup. That makes it the best weed in the world. You should show some respect."

Damon looked at the plants, considering what Shamus was saying.

"I'm still takin' his CDs."

...

While Damon and Guillermo loaded the rest of the plants into the van, Shamus took a look around the house.

Two bedrooms had been turned into organic farms with grow lights suspended from the ceilings and big CO_2 tanks circulating air; one room was some sort of laboratory area with microscopes and some sorts of miniature gardening tools lined up on a table; the rest of the house looked like it was decorated by a professional. That or the guy was gay. There were lamps and sofas and a coffee table that looked like that modern shit, like stuff you'd see on TV. Shamus had to admit that it looked pretty sharp. Not comfy—you couldn't veg out on that couch and watch the Dodgers or anything, you'd probably kill your back—but it looked nice. Even better was a large framed poster, some kind of crazy picture of a squirrel putting nuts into a tree. The squirrel was saying "Nuts to Winter" in a big cartoon voice bubble.

Shamus liked the squirrel picture. He took it down and loaded it into the back of the van.

18

THE PAIN WOKE him up. A searing throb of raw nerves emanating from the center of his body and radiating outward in all directions. He couldn't feel his legs or his fingers or even the dryness in his throat. It was all just pain. Pure, crystalline, undeniable.

Miro's eyes blinked open; the world looking gauzy, like his brain had been replaced by cotton fluff. He blinked again and his vision ratcheted into focus. A young guy was sitting in a chair next to his bed, reading a book or something in the dim sunlight that filtered through the curtains; some doofus wearing a white short-sleeved shirt and a retarded clip-on tie. A fresh-faced teen with a military haircut.

The kid jumped out of his chair.

"He's awake."

There might've been some commotion. The light in the room shifted. Maybe the door opened and someone entered. The kid stepped closer; he was grinning like a salesman, like some kind of freak.

"I've been praying for you."

His words didn't compute in Miro's brain. Praying? It didn't make any sense. Miro fell back on a default response.

The same thing he would've said to a Hare Krishna in an airport, a rabbi at the Wailing Wall, or the pope at the Vatican. He moved his dry, chapped lips and wheezed out two profound words. His first words since his flirtation with death.

"Fuck off."

Then his eyes closed and he was out. Swallowed up in the gray waves of freshly administered narcotics and a deep desire to sleep.

...

"Any idea who did it?"

Miro looked up from his hospital bed; it had been a day since he found the Mormon in his room and he was now sitting up, able to talk and consume some of the lukewarm nutrients the hospital provided. He saw a pair of detectives standing in the doorway flashing their badges, looking dour.

"I'm Detective Cho. This is Detective Quijano. We're with the LAPD."

Then, as if to clarify something, he added, "Northeast Division."

Miro squinted at the two men. One of them seemed familiar: the big Asian guy with his shaved head and mustache, he was the guy with the coffee breath who'd talked to him after he'd gotten shot. That was Cho. The other detective, Quijano, a youngish Latino guy, was eating a carrot stick and reading a text message on his cell phone.

"I don't know who did it."

Cho took out a notepad while Quijano pocketed his cell phone and leaned against the door frame. Quijano chomped the carrot stick and then pointed to Miro's chest.

"The doc said the bullet hit you just right; another inch to the side it would've nailed your heart, an inch to the left it would've severed your spine. You'd be dead or you'd be fishin' your shit out of a baggie for the rest of your life. You're a lucky man. You know that?"

Why is it that the police make you feel like you did something wrong, like you deserved the crime that happened to you? The police have a funny understanding of karma.

Quijano took another carrot stick out of a small plastic baggie and resumed chomping. His posture reminded Miro of a famous cartoon rabbit.

"I would've been luckier if the bullet had missed."

Quijano grimaced as if someone had stepped on his toe. He apparently didn't appreciate a snappy comeback.

"I guess whoever took a shot at you is gonna want to come back and finish the job. You better start wearin' a vest, numbnuts."

Miro scowled; he didn't like being called numbnuts, even if, at present, he couldn't feel that part of his body.

Cho pulled up a chair. He had a different Hawaiian shirt on than last time; this one had elephants and palm trees patterned all over it. Miro had a momentary flash of paranoia. *Elephants? Does he know?*

"Of course you know who's behind this. You know you know, and I know you know, and the last thing I want is for you to go all gangbanger on me and try to get revenge on the guy who did this to you."

While it was true Miro could make an educated guess as to why someone had tried to kill him—the drug business being a somewhat notoriously cutthroat field—he honestly didn't know who was behind it.

"Do I look like the gangbangin' type?"

The detective stared at him, appraising him as if trying to gauge his potential for violent retribution, his capacity for vendetta.

"Do you know why you were shot?"

Miro shrugged, instantly wincing in pain as he realized that even the slightest movements caused an unpleasant shifting of nerves and tissue in his body.

"I was in the wrong place at the wrong time."

The detective sighed and sat back in his chair. He brushed his fingers over his mustache.

"Don't be a dick, Miro. You think you can fix this? People want you dead. And I know why they want you dead."

Miro looked at the detective and blinked.

"Why?"

Miro watched as Cho folded up his notepad.

"I'm an amateur astrophysicist. I know, it's strange for a cop to be into that but, you know, I'm an interested person."

Cho sat there, waiting for it to sink in but all Miro could think was that it was totally weird for there to be an astrophysicist detective.

"What do you know about string theory?"

Miro realized that he wasn't really sure what was going on. Was it the drugs in his IV? Was he dreaming? He could tell he was in a kind of high-tech hospital room. The lights were muted and there were a lot of blinking, beeping monitors around. Miro felt the needle in his hand; he could see the clear plastic tube rising up into the air and connecting to the saline drip. There was some oxygen feeding into his nose through a looping tube, and little adhesive disks stuck to his chest and wired to machines. He could also feel a numb pain gnawing at his torso, like there was a rat stuck inside his body trying to find a way out. He could taste the painkillers and antibiotics in his throat and his breathing was ragged, like a hot half-breath.

It all seemed pretty real. So why was the cop asking weird questions?

"What?"

"String theory. You know? Some nerds figured it out. They took out the assumption that particles are points."

"Particles look like points to me."

"But what if they're not? What if they're strings?"

Miro didn't know what to say. The detective smiled and leaned forward.

"Well, I'll tell you what those nerds said. They said that the strings hook everything together. They unify all the natural forces in the world."

The big detective took a business card out of his pocket and laid it on the table next to Miro.

"Everything's connected. There's a reason you got shot and it's because you're up to something. Am I right so far?"

Miro didn't answer. He watched the big detective in the Hawaiian shirt stand and walk toward the door. He turned and looked at Miro.

"I'm going to find out what it is. Then we'll have another chat."

19

RECOVERING FROM a life-threatening bullet wound turned out to be more boring than Miro could ever have imagined. The hospital room was designed to be dull, with its ceiling-bolted television, hotel blinds over the window, and a kind of drab industrial greige-colored paint on the walls. There was a bouquet of cheap flowers and a "Get Well Soon" card from his parents on the table next to his bed and that, as they say, was about it.

There was nothing but noise on the TV and the painkillers wouldn't let his brain concentrate enough to read a book, so he spent a lot of his day staring at the perforated acoustical tiles on the ceiling above his hospital bed. He quickly discovered that if he stared up without blinking long enough, his eyes would cross and the field of dots would separate and become three-dimensional. Depending on the amount of Demerol and other painkillers in his system, patterns and shapes—sometimes faces—would emerge out of the dots. It was the indoor equivalent of seeing shapes in clouds. Good times.

Sometimes he thought about the scientist in Amsterdam. *Marianna*. He wondered what she was doing. He wished he'd gotten her phone number or an e-mail address, some way to contact her. But he hadn't, and he didn't know why. But he'd think of her and try jacking off, hoping it would give him a few minutes of enjoyment, but his body wouldn't cooperate. Healing was, apparently, more complicated than you'd think.

Because he was bored, Miro found he not only tolerated the young Mormon's daily visits, he looked forward to them. Daniel never preached or proselytized. He'd just keep Miro company, read him articles from the newspaper or from magazines left lying around the waiting room; sometimes he'd bring Miro an apple or banana to eat. But mostly he peppered Miro with questions. What's it like to be with a girl? What does beer taste like? Is coffee really bad for you? How come it's okay to drink Pepsi and not Coke? At first Miro laughed; he figured most eighteen-year-old boys would already know the answers to these questions, but the more time he spent with Daniel, the happier he was to help him.

...

A nurse, her smock dotted with a patterned print of friendly teddy bears, opened the door.

"Are you up for some visitors?"

"As long as it's not those cops again."

The nurse held the door open as Miro's friends Rupert and Stacey entered the room. Miro smiled at Rupert, who looked like some kind of hobo skate punk with his scruffy beard and ridiculous habit of wearing shirts on top of shirts with a T-shirt on top. Rupert's girlfriend Stacey was dressed like a thrift store kook, in a vintage 50s sweater set over tight turquoise capri pants and pink Converse sneakers. Her arms were covered in tattoos, as if she'd taken Rupert's idea of lay-ering to its logical conclusion.

Rupert pulled a chair around and plopped his heavy body into it. Despite years of eating a vegan diet he was still twenty-four pounds overweight—Rupert attributed this to his genetics, but Miro believed the excess poundage had more to do with Rupert's robust alcohol intake. Rupert tugged at the scruff on his chin and looked at all the tubes going into Miro's body.

"How's it goin' Daddy-O? They give you anything good?"

"The thrill of morphine wears off sooner than you'd think."

"Can't they mix it up?"

Miro smiled.

"I'll ask."

Miro looked at Stacey, who stood behind Rupert like she was hiding, as if she were afraid a bullet wound could somehow be contagious. She adjusted her thick-rimmed glasses —the kind Italian movie stars made famous in the sixties— and ran a hand through her short, blonde, stylishly asymmetri-cal hair. She looked at Miro.

"I hate hospitals."

Miro didn't care much for hospitals, either. In fact, he'd prefer that he wasn't in one at all.

"Any news from the outside world?"

"Oh, you know," Rupert said, "the usual. Bands keep selling out."

"Who sold out?"

"Giant Rumpus. Silvertone. They all got written up in the *Weekly*."

Rupert said this with a disgusted shake of his head. Selling out was one of Rupert's pet peeves. He believed that whenever a band or an artist attained even a small amount of success they should be immediately repudiated and shunned. In other words, you were cool until you were popular. Then you sucked. Unless, of course, it was Rupert's band that made it. Then he could change the system from the inside.

Miro smiled.

"Good for them."

Rupert scratched his beard.

"Art versus commerce, man. Free market triumphalism."

By "free market triumphalism" Rupert meant that whatever the general public embraced—pop music, gangsta rap, and imitation alternative rock—was, in fact, unadulterated crap. Miro decided to change the subject before Rupert started ranting.

"Did you go by my place?"

Rupert hung his head and looked at the floor.

"Dude, I hate to be the bearer of bad tidings, but your place got trashed."

"How bad?"

"Bad."

"What's that mean?" Miro looked at him and cocked an eyebrow. Rupert shook his head.

"Don't expect to get your deposit back."

Miro groaned. It wasn't easy to find a place in Los Angeles and he'd lucked out when he'd discovered the tidy little house near the LA river. It was on a quiet street—speed bumps placed every twenty yards enforced that—lined with bungalows and small homes filled with a mix of working class families, retirees, and hipsters searching for cheap digs. It wasn't anything fancy, just a modest tract home built during the boom of the late forties, but it had a patio and a little garden in the back. Miro had been slowly furnishing it with cool fifties furniture that he found at various junk shops around town. He wanted to give his home a Palm Springs vibe, a cocktail sophistication.

"What about the glass jars?"

Rupert shook his head.

"The seeds are gone, dude."

Miro blinked. He'd almost expected it. But the systematic trashing of his home confirmed his worst fears. Like Detective Cho had said, the bullet wasn't random, it was an assassination attempt; and somebody had stolen the Elephant Crush.

Miro wondered if any of the past winners of the Cannabis Cup had ever been shot at or killed. What if this was just one of those things the Cup committee didn't tell you about?

"Fuck."

Miro realized that while "fuck" was the best possible word to use, it was also a bit of an understatement. He'd invested almost all of his money in developing and growing the Elephant Crush and what little he had remaining he'd spent on the trip to Amsterdam. He'd been planning to recoup his investment when he sold the seeds. He did a quick calculation in his head and realized he only had a couple thousand bucks in his bank account. And even with his catastrophic-coverage health insurance plan, he'd be on the hook for thousands of dollars in hospital costs. He was broke. He tried the word again. This time putting a new emphasis on it.

"*Fuck.*"

Rupert tried to cheer him up.

"I saved some of your clothes. I got 'em at my house."

"What about the furniture?"

"They trashed everything. Sliced your couch. Broke your chairs up. Even smashed the toilet."

"They broke the toilet?"

"Like with a hammer, man."

Miro sighed. "*Fuck.*"

Rupert shot a look at Stacey, then turned to Miro.

"You can always crash at our place."

"Thanks. But my parents want me to stay with them while I recoup. I think I'll go up there and lay low."

"You think you'll be up for Coachella this year?"

Miro shrugged. Normally the three-day music festival in the desert was the highlight of his year. This was not a typical year.

"You never know."

"I'm really glad you're not dead, man."

It got quiet in the room. Miro didn't know what he should say. He was glad he wasn't dead, too, but that seemed like an obvious sentiment. One of the machines made a beep. Stacey finally broke the silence.

"I got a new tattoo."

This was not a surprise. Stacey got a new tattoo almost every month. In fact, she was either bandaged or scabby so often that she'd had to quit her job at a restaurant—apparently even customers in Los Angeles could only take so much open wound with their lunch—and lately she'd been working as a cashier at the local Whole Foods grocery store.

"Do you want to see it?"

Miro lied. "Of course."

Stacey walked close to Miro's bed, but not close enough to where there could be actual contact, turned around, and lifted her shirt. Sure enough, running along her lower back—just above her waistband—was a beautifully rendered, though still slightly raw, tattoo of a dozen teeny frolicking pug dogs chasing each other, sniffing the ground, playing leapfrog, and generally gamboling across her back.

"Pugs?"

"We had pugs when I was little."

Miro squinted. He thought it might be the drugs, but looking closely, he noticed that one of the dogs was different than the others.

"This one's taking a shit."

Stacey laughed.

"Isn't she cute?"

20

ANIEL SAT ON his bed eating a *carnitas* burrito he'd picked up from a nearby taco truck. The burritos he got in Los Angeles weren't anything like the ones he'd eaten in Idaho. These were simpler, spicier, and tastier. There was no sour cream, diced tomatoes, lettuce, or shredded cheddar. LA burritos were intense.

He was tired. The trek from his apartment to the hospital was one long uphill slog on his bike. The ride back, a breakneck downhill race through traffic, was nerve-wracking. He'd arrive home smelly, exhausted, and rattled from a series of near misses with minivans piloted by soccer moms who blindly careened through the streets, yakking on their cellphones while their kids played video games in the backseat. Like they'd somehow managed to put wheels on a family room and turn it into a murderous steel rectangle.

Then there was the mental exhaustion. He was at a loss; he honestly didn't know what to do. Ever since his partner's nervous breakdown Daniel had found himself at loose ends. No one from the LDS told him what to do, where to go, or what would happen next. There was no news of a replacement for Elder Collison, no word of a new assignment, nothing.

Daniel had called a few times, checking in and trying to figure out what the plan was but they always put him off. They were working on it. They'd let him know.

Daniel wondered if Collison had ratted on him, told the bishops about his shameful urges and how they had to tie his hands to the bed every night. Had the church given up on him? Was this isolation some kind of punishment?

Maybe he was supposed to spend every day in the hospital helping Miro recover. Maybe that was God's plan. After all, it had been his prayers that saved Miro's life. Now Miro was his responsibility, his mission. God was showing him a path. All he had to do was walk down it.

Daniel shoved the last bit of burrito into his mouth—a sploop of meat grease and salsa popped out the bottom of the burrito and stained his white shirt—and wadded up the wrapper. He steadied himself and tried a three-point shot into the trash bag. The foil bounced off the side of the bag, sending a couple of cockroaches running for their lives, and hit the floor. He swallowed and lay back on the bed.

Daniel liked Miro. Miro gave him straight answers. There was no evasion, no doublespeak, no reference to the Bible or the Book of Mormon. Daniel could ask him anything, even questions about girls, and Miro would give him an answer. Daniel appreciated that Miro offered no judgment, no invoking of Heaven or Hell or his duties here on Earth, he just gave him the facts.

The only time he'd seen Miro hedge was when he asked him what he did for a living. Miro had hesitated and then said he was a gentleman farmer. Daniel knew some farmers in Boise and there was no way that a guy like Miro worked on a farm. Daniel figured that he probably did something seedy, like worked in the music business or for an Internet company, but that was okay with him. It only made Miro cooler.

Daniel went into the bathroom and brushed his teeth. He'd shower in the morning.

He came out of the bathroom, turned off the lights, and lay back down on the bed. He kept his clothes on, just like the pamphlet had told him to, and, very carefully, stuck his hands through loops of clip-on ties tied to the bed frame. He tugged, the slipknots pulling the loops tight around his wrists, closed his eyes, and waited for the sensations to begin.

21

VINCENT WAS OPPOSED to the legalization of marijuana. He didn't support NORML or the US Marijuana Party or any of those "legalize it" groups. He didn't listen to Peter Tosh, or any other Jamaican music for that matter. As far as Vincent was concerned marijuana was as legal as it needed to be. All anyone had to do was visit a doctor, feign insomnia or some kind of anxiety disorder, and walk out with a little card that allowed him or her to shop at one of his Compassion Centers and purchase the finest cannabis that money could buy. The system was controlled. It worked. And it was legal enough.

Vincent didn't understand why these marijuana activists were rocking the boat. The antiprohibition movement would undermine dedicated professionals like himself; true legalization would destroy his empire of compassion. The thought of a Los Angeles studded with coffeeshops like Amsterdam made him shudder. There was already too much competition, with legit herbal co-ops popping up in every strip mall in the county, not to mention the hundreds of millions of dollars that changed hands in illegal dealing.

Vincent had actually donated thousands of dollars to a conservative Republican candidate who was vocal in his opposition to legalization. Not only that, but he wanted to see law enforcement redouble their efforts in the war on drugs. It amused him that this Christian Conservative from Newport Beach didn't have any problem taking campaign contributions from a cannabis collective. Vincent donated to lots of politicians, he gave to Democrats, Republicans, Libertarians, and Greens. As long as they were committed to keeping cannabis illegal—unless you had a doctor's prescription—it was fine with him. It was just good business.

Vincent had started making a list and courting people who were hip and wealthy and respected for being on the cutting edge of whatever was cool—hipsters with disposable incomes who might want to invest in his plan to expand the Compassion Center chain across California and into some of the other states where medical marijuana was legal. He had plans to spread into New Mexico, Oregon, Washington, and maybe Michigan, and to open a flagship branch in Amsterdam. Why should the Dutch make all the money? Once he was established as the number-one provider of reliable, high quality cannabis, he'd take the company public. An initial public offering on the NASDAQ would make him millions.

It wasn't a new strategy. He wasn't raising the bar or breaking new ground. It was the same business plan that Wal-Mart, Starbucks, Krispy Kreme donuts, and Baskin-Robbins had used. It would be a carefully considered expansion, the company growing by finding prime locations in productive areas. By purchasing inventory in volume, Vincent was able to control the profit margins and could, if there was a competitor already established in the area, go about underselling the existing cannabis club, stealing their clientele, and forcing them out of business. And if Vincent couldn't drive them out of business with lower prices and free bongs, he'd do it the old-fashioned way: have the police hassle their customers, get the city council to file zoning violations, bring in Franchise Tax Board audits, or connect them to organized crime and let the Feds raid them. That's what the political donations were all about. You got to pay to play.

Vincent had read a few books about branding, tipping points, and the flow of information. His goal was to turn the Compassion Centers into the biggest brand in the world. That's why his employees all wore colorful polo shirts with the Compassion Center logo on them. That's why he needed the store in Amsterdam. Winning a few Cannabis Cups would turn his company into a worldwide name brand like Barney's or the Greenhouse.

The Internet was already buzzing with rumors and stories about Elephant Crush. Every stoner in the world was dying to try it and a few dealers had begun trying to pass counterfeit versions. It had become a cause célèbre.

Vincent had already told a few of his potential investors —the cool TV producers with their hit show and seven-figure overall deal at Paramount, a club DJ turned record producer, a couple of famous actors known for giving large sums to Democratic candidates, and a yoga instructor with a reputation for teaching his most flexible and predominantly blonde female students a few private asanas in the privacy of his home—to get ready, that he was working on getting it, that he would give them the honor of being the first to taste the

Cup winner. That kind of VIP treatment—who doesn't love having an exclusive—would help him raise enough capital to fully fund his ambitious business plan. If he succeeded he'd be rich, he'd be famous. He'd dethrone Arjan as the King of Cannabis.

Vincent had always been attracted to the trappings of the stylish and groovy. He was well-groomed, with a manicured goatee and a fashionable haircut. He wore expensive clothes, favoring artsy T-shirts or tight sweaters, pants that looked like they might belong with a suit but were stretchy enough that you could do yoga in them, and cool shoes. Always the coolest shoes.

When it was fashionable to drive a Hummer, he did. But lately he tooled around in a Prius. Despite his fondness for sushi, he'd recently decided to eat only vegan because his personal Pilates trainer had recommended it. You want to be a success you've got to look and act the part.

His psychiatrist had helped him understand this desire. She had helped him frame it, put it in perspective. If you grow up surrounded by mediocrity, by friends and family that have no aspirations beyond the barbecue grill and watching football on TV, then it is understandable that you might find yourself rebelling. And what better way to rebel than to become extremely successful doing something illegal? Even if he failed and went to jail, he'd become infamous in his family, notorious in the sleepy suburb of Redwood City. He wouldn't be just another guy sitting on his ass rooting for the 49ers.

His shrink had suggested that he be more "authentic" and not worry so much about following trends or be so concerned with style. She suggested that he needed to dig deep and find the things that made him truly happy. Vincent tried to explain that these seemingly superficial things did, actually and on a deep level, make him feel good. When she suggested that it made him seem like a sociopath, he didn't know if that was a compliment or not.

But there was more to him than that. He actually enjoyed selling weed. He was the man, the source, the secret provider of highs, experiences, and good times. What's wrong with that? He made money and people felt good about the products he provided. He had his passion. He wanted to be the best and he was prepared to be ruthless if he had to.

His shrink approved of his passion to be the best. She had him read inspirational biographies by business leaders, politicians, and professional athletes. He would visualize, manifest, and make daily positive affirmations. She outlined it in terms of what she called "progressive goals for life-long success." Once he was satisfied with his business and career, then maybe he could turn all his energy and desire into improving his inner life. Vincent agreed. He was beginning to think the three-times-a-week visits with the shrink were really helping.

...

Vincent sat back in the rattan chair and squinted at his guests. Two of the aforementioned investors—the TV producers, shaggy men in their late twenties who were so wealthy that they dressed like impoverished teenagers—slouched in their seats across the table from him. They were silent investors in Vincent's business, young and rich and sitting on top of a serious amount of disposable income. For sure they didn't spend their money on clothes: they lounged like bored skate-boarders at the mall, in distressed and torn cargo pants and jeans, and ironic vintage T-shirts, believing that their world-weary poses conveyed some kind of hipster sophistication. Despite the affected air of disinterest they were actually excited, anxious to hear what Vincent had to say. They had come to Vincent's office because he had promised them big news. They sat expectantly, slumped in exotic rattan chairs, surrounded by antique furniture from Thailand and a grove of potted tropical plants.

Vincent, like the consummate salesman he was, was in no hurry to tell them the news; he wanted to take his time, let the suspense build.

"I think the tea's ready."

Vincent took the small ceramic teapot and carefully, almost ritualistically, filled three small raku teacups.

"Green tea from the Yame region of the Fukuoka Prefecture in Japan. They say the climate there produces the best leaves."

Vincent watched the two men sip their tea and pretend like they could tell the difference between top-notch green tea and horse piss.

"Nice."

"Awesome."

Vincent smiled. "So what's new?"

One of the producers, the one with the closely trimmed facial hair, leaned forward.

"I bought a Murakami."

Vincent was impressed.

"A painting?"

The producer nodded.

"Superflat series."

"Cool."

The other producer ran his hands through his meticulously unkempt hair and sighed.

"I bought one of those new Toyota hybrids with the solar cell embedded in the roof."

Vincent nodded his approval.

"Very green of you."

"I guess. Chicks seem to dig it. But I gotta tell you, I miss my Porsche. I really do. But, you know, global warming an' shit."

The bearded producer leaned forward and spoke softly.

"So, c'mon Vince, what's this about the Cannabis Cup?"

The other producer chimed in. "Yeah, man. What the fuck's up with this Elephant shit? We heard it was, like, totally impossible to acquire."

Vincent smiled.

"Nothing's impossible."

The producers grinned.

"You got it?"

Vincent flashed his Clorox-white teeth at them.

"I'm getting it. Probably in the next week. And you two will be the first to try it."

The two TV producers sat back in their chairs and looked at Vincent with undisguised admiration.

"Dude."

Vincent smiled, his lips pulling into an extremely self-satisfied smirk.

"I'm thinking about opening a Compassion Center in Amsterdam."

22

I T WAS TIME to go. The flowers by his hospital bed were dead. It had started with a dusting of pollen on the table, followed by a few dropped petals, and slowly built to a crescendo as gravity exerted its force and the blooms fell apart. Now the bare stalks had begun to droop like Twizzlers in August and the water in the vase was emitting a faintly swampish stink. The nurses had wanted to throw them out, but Miro liked them. They were kind of inspiring in a way. Even as death and decay settled in on their stalks and leaves, they were still beautiful somehow, they were still flowers. It was life. And life was something Miro had a newfound appreciation for. Like him, the flowers had been cut in their prime. Snipped from their roots, dropped by a bullet. But unlike the flowers, Miro had been given a second chance.

Sometimes, when he lay there feeling his heart beat and listening to the static rasps coming from his punctured lung, Miro felt that there must be a reason he'd lived. He didn't know what that reason might be, but he figured that maybe there were forces operating outside of normal human existence pulling strings, keeping him alive. Like possibly there was a God who had answered the Mormon kid's prayers, or perhaps he had good karma, or maybe, like the detective had said, he was just really fucking lucky.

Now he was feeling restless, his energy coming back, his body healing faster than anyone had expected. It was a good thing, too, he was tired of being in the hospital, creeped out by all the technology, the shiny needles and clear plastic tubing, the stainless implements and disposable gloves, the smell of betadine. The constant drip of liquid into his veins had become a slow crawling torture. There were times when he wanted to yank all the tubes and drips and needles out of his body and flee.

Miro appreciated the efforts of the doctors and nurses, all the technology, the highly specialized care, and the spectrum of antibiotics that had kept him alive and initiated his healing. He really did. But it was time to go. His crappy insurance company had made that clear. It was okay with him, though, he'd rather chill somewhere with edible food. The hospital food was appalling: the salty broth, the unidentifiable chunks of meat, the pale wisps of slightly rotted lettuce, the over-boiled potatoes, the scrambled eggs that looked like desiccated cat barf, the sausages stinking of grease. No wonder everyone was on narcotics.

What the hell he was going to do, well, that he hadn't decided. Sometimes he felt angry, outraged and pissed off, like he needed to whip up a vendetta, find out who had ripped him off and bring down the fiery wrath of the destroyer. But he knew he wasn't a warrior, at least he had no prior experience with weapons, vendettas, or bringing down any wrath of any size. Ferociousness was not his thing. In fact, he hardly ever lost his temper. Still, he wanted to do something. He couldn't let them get away with it. There had to be some justice. He felt sure of that.

Miro wondered what Floyd Zaiger would do. Would he just roll over and let someone steal the *pluot* from him? Of course he didn't *know* who'd done this to him. As far as he knew he had no enemies. So where did that leave him? Floyd Zaiger could go to the cops. Miro couldn't really do that without implicating himself in illegal shenanigans.

Besides, he hadn't heard from the two detectives since their visit to the ICU a week ago. Miro assumed that whatever strings were connecting them to his case had yo-yo'd them off in another direction and they were now too busy to bother with him.

...

"So, you're leaving?"

Miro nodded.

"They're kicking me out."

Daniel looked worried.

"That's not right."

Miro shrugged.

"Doctor's orders."

"So what're you going to do?"

"I'm going to stay with my folks, up the coast, for a few days. Until I get my strength back."

Miro noticed that Daniel was looking at the floor, unable to look Miro in the eye.

"What's wrong?"

"Nothing."

"I can tell something's bothering you."

Daniel heaved a sigh.

"I don't know what to do."

"What about your mission?"

"I don't think I want to be on a mission anymore."

Miro smiled.

"Maybe your mission's changed."

Daniel liked the sound of that.

Miro got an idea.

"You like burritos?"

"Love 'em."

Miro took a pen and some paper off the bedside table and jotted down a name and a number.

"Call this guy. He'll give you a job."

Daniel took the paper and studied it.

"What kind of job?"

"I have a friend who owns a taco truck. He's always looking for help."

23

DETECTIVE CHO WAS not having a good day. He'd been dragged out of bed at the crack of dawn to go wade around in the shit-clogged muck of the LA river after some crack-of-dawn health-freak triathlete noticed a body decomposing in the weeds. Cho was one of the Northeast Division's lead criminal investigators and so the honor and privilege of an early morning wade in an open sewer fell to him.

His wife wasn't happy about it, either. She had made plans to go to a Pilates class with her friends and he was supposed to give their fifteen-year-old son a ride to the charter school he attended. The early a.m. call only prompted yet another argument about his refusal to retire and take a cushy corporate security job. To top it off, Cho had a head cold, a real wet one. He'd already blown his nose raw and gone through a packet of tissues, but he felt like he could stuff a couple tampons up his snout and even that wouldn't stop the mucus from flowing out of him like a faucet.

The front pocket of his Hawaiian shirt stuffed with tissues, Cho sipped hot tea from a Styrofoam cup as he stood in front of a group of officers and ran down the basics of the case. Body found in river. Apparently, as best anyone could figure, someone had shot him. From the look of it, the body had been in the river for a month, maybe longer.

The bug guys were on their way. They would break out their little nets and jars and wade around capturing maggots and looking at what kind of bugs had nibbled what part of the carcass. Now there was a career Cho didn't understand. You put two of the creepiest things you can think of together and make it your job? What kind of freak does that?

Cho turned away from the other officers and sneezed. His tea jumped out of the cup and scalded his fingers. It was just that kind of day.

Cho sneezed again and thought about his next step. The protocol was pretty standard, stuff he'd done hundreds of times. He'd order a ballistics test on the bullet they'd recovered from the dead guy. He had the guy's wallet, empty of everything but his California driver's license. Cho read the name out loud.

"Barry White."

Quijano looked over at him.

"Like the singer?"

Cho nodded.

"You think he's a gang guy?"

"His name's Barry. I don't think he's gonna be runnin' with the Toons."

Cho sneezed again and reached into his pocket for a tissue as two clear streamers of mucus festooned his upper lip.

"That's disgusting. You should cover your mouth."

Cho nodded. It *was* disgusting. There was no denying it. The more he blew his nose, the more snot came out. He filled tissue after tissue.

Quijano put his hand over his face and moved a few feet away from Cho.

"I'll run a check against the missing-person reports. Then I guess we go by the victim's address. Deliver the bad news."

Cho nodded. "I need an Advil." He turned and walked toward a couple of EMT paramedics who were hanging around.

...

Ted handed the snot-nosed detective a couple of acetaminophen and a decongestant.

"Get some rest."

The detective nodded, started to say something, then changed his mind and walked off. Fran and Ted stood in front of the ambulance and watched him skulk back toward the crime scene. They'd been called when the body was found but it wasn't like they could do anything. They didn't really deal with people who were already dead. Especially people who'd been dead a long time.

Fran started humming a song, one of those insipid pop ballads like the kind they sing on American Idol, the kind of song that's more true-love propaganda than music. Ted didn't know what song it was. Of course he'd heard it a thousand times before, but now it would be stuck in his head all day like a viral infection. He wished Fran liked hip-hop. Nobody hums a rap song.

Ted looked out at the river with its clumps of broken concrete and scabby palm trees, crime-scene vehicles, police cars, and coroner's van. Ted never liked it when they got to a call and found a DOA. It was a bummer. He watched as an SUV arrived and pulled in alongside the police cars.

A man got out and started pulling on thigh-high rubber boots.

"Looks like the bug guys are here."

He turned to look at her.

"Didn't you go out with one of them once?"

Fran made a face.

"Are you kidding? Can you imagine fucking one of those guys? Gross."

Ted had to admit he couldn't imagine fucking a forensic entymologist, but he didn't think he needed to answer Fran's question.

"You wanna get a coffee?"

Fran nodded and climbed into the ambulance.

...

They rode in silence for a few blocks. Ted looked out the window, watching the morning traffic coalesce, seeing kids on their way to school. He saw a lone skateboarder, a tall teenager with his long dark hair flowing in the breeze, go flying down a hill.

"Look at that kid go."

Fran turned to look and saw the kid crouch down and jump up, hopping over the curb. The skateboarder's school backpack bounced around on his back.

"In my day we walked places."

Ted had to laugh. It wasn't that Fran had said anything funny. It was the way she said it. As if there was some kind of morally superior way to transport yourself to school in the mornings.

Ted watched the skateboarder turn his head to check out a young Latina mother pushing her baby in a stroller. The front wheel of his board must've caught a crack or divot in the sidewalk because one second the guy was cruising, looking cool, checking out a hottie, and the next he was doing a face-plant into the street.

Ted turned to Fran.

"Stop."

...

Detective Cho leaned his head against the window of the burnt-sienna colored Crown Vic and closed his eyes. He didn't want to look at his partner. Quijano had a penchant for putting some kind of goo in his hair that made it black and shiny and smeared back like he was moving fast even when he was sitting still. It reminded Cho of an anime character, like in those Japanese cartoons his kids were always watching. Normally it didn't bother him, but today it made him feel slightly dizzy.

Cho felt Quijano's hand on his shoulder.

"You okay?"

"I'm just waiting for the cold medicine to kick in."

That was the truth. He wanted the decongestants to start decongesting, the painkiller to start easing the achy feeling he had all over and he wanted whatever would stop his runny nose to stop the ridiculous drip. It occurred to him that the decongestants and drip stoppers might actually be working at cross-purposes.

"You should go home, get some rest. That's what it means when you've got a cold. Your body needs rest."

Another truism. Quijano was full of 'em. That was the problem with the younger generation, they traded in clichés and reliable standbys. Clichés and platitudes and common expressions had become marketing slogans; even the expression "thinking outside the box" was probably trademarked and copyright registered to some marketing guru somewhere. It was like they'd put a gigantic, invisible box around the box that you're thinking outside of, so you're never really outside the box, you're just in a bigger box, a box so gigantic that you can't see it, so you can't begin to think outside it. It gave Cho a headache. He wanted nothing more in life right now than to curl up on his big soft bed and fall asleep. But that wasn't what they were doing. They had a body. Now they had to verify who he was, what had killed him, and, if they were lucky, why. Once he knew why, he could figure out who had done it. That's how it worked.

...

Ted reached behind him for a first-aid kit as Fran hopped out of the vehicle. The skateboarder was obviously injured— blood was gushing out of his nose and it looked, from the way he was holding it, like he'd broken his arm—but he stood up and tried to wave them off.

"I'm okay. Really."

Fran shook her head.

"Sit back down. Take it easy."

But instead of letting the EMT assist him—and talk about response time, this was, like, five seconds—the teenager turned, leaving his backpack and skateboard on the sidewalk, and ran as fast as he could down a side street.

Ted came up to Fran as she stood there, watching the kid run.

"What did you say to him?"

"Nothing."

"You think he's illegal?"

Fran shrugged.

"Who gives a flying fuck?"

Ted picked up the backpack and skateboard and tossed them in the ambulance.

"I bet I can find the name of his school on his books. We can drop it by for him."

Fran shook her head.

"There you go with that bleeding-heart thing."

"The kid needs his books."

"Then he shouldn't have run off."

...

Fran sat in the ambulance and watched as Ted walked into the Starbucks. Why anyone would pay five bucks for a cup of coffee was beyond her. Especially when there was a Yum-Yum Donut shop just down the street that made really good, always piping hot, coffee. But Ted liked his fancy espresso drink with hazelnut flavor and soy milk. He was a nice enough guy, she liked him, she really did, but sometimes he did stuff that was so, she didn't know what to call it. *Metrosexual*?

She reached around behind and pulled out the skateboarder's backpack. She was curious what kind of crap kids carried to school nowadays. Maybe there was a gun or something in there. Maybe that's why the kid had gone all Speedy Gonzalez.

But when she opened the backpack and looked inside she understood instantly why the kid had taken off running. Nestled between a three-ring notebook and an American History textbook, all packaged up in a couple of large Ziplocs, was a giant bag of marijuana.

24

THE WHITE PICKET FENCE needed a coat of paint and the grass was slowly turning brown but the yard was neat and the hibiscus bushes were in bloom. The small, two-bedroom, ranch-style house was painted gray and white, a couple of lawn chairs were parked on the front porch, and an old screen door slouched on its hinges as if it was drunk, leaning on the sturdy, periwinkle-blue door behind it.

The house fit in with the rest of the neighborhood. It was as bland and characterless as every other ranch house on the street and that's exactly the way it was supposed to be.

If you were ever invited inside, if you knew the couple who lived there—Bernardo and his wife Blanca—you might notice some discreet fortifications. The periwinkle blue door was actually steel, reinforced with a special door frame and hinge that were built to withstand sustained attempts to kick it in; the windows were all shatter-proof glass and the ones in the backyard had steel bars over them; and there was a small armory of shotguns, automatic rifles, flak jackets, and gas masks in one of the bedroom closets. These improvements were not made to enhance the resale value of the home but were there because the entire basement and attic of the innocuous house had been converted into a massive indoor marijuana farm capable of accommodating—with seedlings sprouted in the shed behind the house—almost one thousand plants in various stages of maturation. Shamus had thrown the grow-house operation together quickly, converting a building that he had been using as a storage facility into a viable greenhouse, using the equipment they'd stolen from Miro's home. The entire house had been converted into an Elephant Crush farm. Fortunately, Bernardo had grown up on a ranch outside Guanajuato and had worked as a gardener for a rich lady in Beverly Hills when he first came to the United States, so he knew a thing or two about plants, fertilizers, and all the other shit farmers need to know about.

Even though Shamus had a key to the house, he knocked and waited for Bernardo to open the door. It was, after all, the polite thing to do and he didn't want the neighbors to think that he was anything more than a friend or distant relative of the couple. Guillermo and Damon stood behind him. Guillermo had a bored look on his face like he'd prefer to be almost anywhere else, while Damon actually tried to play it cool.

When the door opened the smell of skunkweed and tropical fruit hit Shamus's nostrils and caused him to sneeze. He scowled at Bernardo.

"Turn on the filters, *ese*. This place stinks."

Bernardo, a surprisingly diminutive man who was also an excellent car mechanic who specialized in diesel engines, shook his head.

"They're on, *jefe*. It's my wife's cooking that smells so bad."

Bernardo looked over at Blanca who, in turn, gave an exasperated snort and threw her dish towel on the floor as she stomped out of the room.

"*Mira.*"

The men followed Bernardo through the well-kept living room, the kitchen, and down a flight of stairs to the basement where hundreds of plants were growing, like a small forest, under dozens of grow lights. The whirr of the irrigation pump was complimented by the hum of fans as CO_2-enriched air was circulated through the room.

Damon gasped when he saw all the plants.

"Fucking A. This is the shizzle."

Guillermo grinned and leaned in to get a closer look at the massive *colas* sprouting off the plants.

Bernardo fiddled with the system, checking to see that water and nutrients were flowing evenly. Shamus stroked his goatee.

"We're like, what? A month away?"

Bernardo nodded. "We've got a few big ones that are almost ready, I think they're days away. The clones need more time."

Damon's cell phone went off, bleating some kind of hip-hop ringtone that Shamus didn't recognize. Damon looked at him apologetically.

"Sorry. I gotta take this."

Damon answered his phone, turning his back on the other men.

Guillermo was leaning in, whispering something to one of the taller plants. Shamus looked over at him.

"What the fuck're you doing?"

Guillermo shrugged.

"You're supposed to talk to them. I read about it in the newspaper. It makes them feel good."

"They're fuckin' plants, man."

Behind him, Shamus detected something in the way Damon was speaking into the phone. It was a kind of urgent panic. It was fear.

Damon snapped his cell phone shut and turned to Shamus with a worried look on his face.

"We lost a package."

25

ARIANNA STARED at the doctor.

"Positive?"

The doctor, a young and extremely tall Dutch woman, nodded.

"Positively positive."

Marianna hung her head.

"*Filho da puta.*"

The doctor reached down and patted her on the shoulder.

"If it makes you feel any better, you're completely healthy."

Of course Marianna knew she was pregnant. She didn't need the test result to tell her that. She felt it in her moods, her swelling and sensitive breasts, and the sudden looseness in her joints, like someone had untied the strings inside that kept her body from falling apart. She could see it in her suddenly robust appetite and her newfound aversion to cashews. And she had never been so tired.

She had tried to deny it, naturally. Blaming the early morning nausea on the stress of her research project. Attributing her shifting moods—from jubilant to melancholy in sixty seconds or less—to some kind of homesickness for Lisbon. She craved *bacalhau* and roasted potatoes, and her mother's garlic and bread soup. She wanted to drink wine from her homeland, a tart *Vinho Verde* or a rosy *Tinta Roriz*. But in the back of her mind she knew.

The timing was bad. She was right in the middle of a special project for the bio-informatics think tank at Science Park Amsterdam, but then being pregnant wouldn't really get in the way of her work; she sat in front of a computer all day.

She wasn't a religious person by any stretch, even though she'd been raised Catholic; she was a spiritual person, a person who believed that there were things that happened for reasons that couldn't be codified or understood by science, and it never occurred to her to have an abortion.

She thought about the baby's father. What did she know about him? She knew he was American, but realized she didn't know his last name. Was Miro a common name in the States? She knew he was some kind of botanist in Los Angeles, knew that he'd won the Cannabis Cup and that he'd been involved in some kind of business deal with the owner of Orange. She knew all this but she didn't really know what kind of man he was. How would he feel about being a parent? How would he feel about her?

She had felt something different with him, a kind of connection that she hadn't felt with any man before. What had caused it she couldn't say. Because she was a scientist her rational side sometimes clashed with her spiritual side; she had convinced herself that true love and the idea of a soul mate was just a fantasy concocted by poets to explain pheromones and other biochemical phenomena that caused humans to attract mates. But despite this pragmatic and completely reasonable, rational approach to love, she had a nagging feeling that there really was something special about Miro. Why she had let him leave without getting his e-mail address, she couldn't say. Maybe it was because she was afraid that they would make hollow promises to be in touch or meet somewhere again and it wouldn't happen. Or maybe it would happen and it wouldn't be the same. She didn't want to live on false hope. Isn't it better to remember the magic than to discover that the magic is gone? Maybe their few days together were everything they were supposed to be.

She'd logged in online and found the Web site for Orange. She moused around and found Guus's e-mail address. Now that her condition was a medical certainty she was going to write Guus and get Miro's phone number in America. Marianna had carefully considered her options. She wasn't going to ask Miro for anything, she was fully prepared to take responsibility for the child, but she thought, as a courtesy, he ought to know.

Marianna walked along a canal, one hand holding her briefcase, the other on her belly, as if suddenly conscious that she had to protect the new life inside her. She stopped and entered a café she knew—one that had free Wi-Fi—and ordered a cup of peppermint tea. She sat at a table and pulled out her laptop. She wasn't sure what to say to Guus. What if he wanted to protect Miro? What if he never responded? She thought of various approaches and strategies but ultimately opted for the truth.

...

Now that he had won the Cup, Guus was receiving samples sent from seed developers and growers from all over Europe. He packed his bong with a tight cluster of a new strain he'd been sent from a grower in Hamburg. The German grower was trying to get as pure an Indica wallop as possible; he wanted to develop a strain that would knock you on your ass and keep you there. It didn't have the uplifting, euphoric quality of Elephant Crush but sometimes you just want to get flattened, KO'd, completely baked. His plan was to call it Mohammed Ali.

Guus sparked his lighter and, in honor of the ganja from Deutschland, said, "*Setzen sie ihren phasers, um zu betäuben!*"

He sucked down a long, heavy hit, held it, and then exhaled a plume of thick oily smoke up toward the ceiling of his coffeeshop. He felt the air pressure in his eyeballs drop, his ocular barometer registering the incoming storm of THC moving toward his cerebellum. He grinned.

Some kind of liquid techno trickled out of the speakers in the coffeeshop and the music made him smile, it made him crave one of those chocolates that are filled with liqueur, a nice hit of framboise locked in a dark chocolate box. That would be so good right now. Or chocolate cake and an ice-cold glass of milk.

He was thinking about having another hit, of getting really crispy, when his laptop chimed. He clicked on a link on the screen and opened his e-mail. When Guus read Marianna's message, he couldn't help himself, he let out a low moan that sounded a lot like something Keanu Reeves might say.

"Whoooa."

26

"**W**HAT DID YOU DO to my car?"

Miro looked at the spot where Rupert had jacked his iPod into the space where the radio used to be. A spaghetti tangle of wires hung out of the gaping hole in the dashboard.

"Listen to how good it sounds."

Rupert spun the wheel on his iPod, hit play, and instantly some kind of strange music began blasting inside the car.

"What's this?"

Rupert grinned.

"Ethiopian jazz."

Miro nodded. Of course it was Ethiopian jazz. He turned and looked out the window. They were driving up Highway 101. Passing through Oxnard. A car dealership built to look like a fake pueblo passed by in a blur of balloons, steel, and red-tile roof on the right, an outlet mall—selling crap at low, low prices—stretched out on the left.

Miro pointed to the destroyed dashboard.

"You could've asked."

Rupert smiled.

"Don't worry. I'll put it all back together when you want this baby back."

Miro had to admit the music did sound good, the speakers in the back pumping and flexing to the odd African beats. The volume was high enough to cover the rocker-rattle of the big diesel engine—converted to run on vegetable oil—of his 1975 Mercedes-Benz 240D. A large metal can of veggie oil, donated by a local Japanese restaurant, clunked in the backseat whenever the car turned. It was eco-friendly and Miro loved that the car's exhaust smelled like tempura.

Rupert turned down the volume.

"What're you gonna do?"

Miro thought about it. What was he going to do?

"I'm not sure. What would you do?"

"I'd hire a bunch of ninjas to go and, like, *shuriken* their ass. Or put out a hit, man."

"I don't even know who did it."

Rupert raised an eyebrow and looked over at him.

"Really? Dude? You don't know? You don't have an inkling?"

Miro shook his head.

"Take a stab. A wild guess. A shot in the dark, no irony intended."

Miro thought about it.

"I guess it must've been someone who was at the Cup."

Rupert nodded.

"Okay. That narrows it down from two hundred million to what?"

"Couple thousand? Maybe."

Rupert stroked his beard thoughtfully. "That's a lot of *shurikens.*"

Miro felt a surge of agitation.

"Look, if I knew who did it, I'd do something about it. Okay?"

Rupert smiled. "That's the spirit."

"I'm not joking. I won the fucking Cannabis Cup. I shouldn't be treated this way. I should've got a ticker-tape parade down Main Street."

"Now you know how Rambo felt."

"What?"

"Comes back from Vietnam, nobody cares. People hate him. He goes renegade on them."

"I didn't see the movie."

"Fuck the movie, dude. Read the book."

Miro changed the subject.

"How's the band? What's happening?"

Rupert bobbed in his seat. He liked nothing better than talking about music, specifically *his* music.

"We're hoping to do Sunset Junction this year."

"That'd be cool."

"But I might have to find a new keyboard player."

"What's wrong with Laura?"

Rupert shrugged.

"First she was on heroin and everything was fine. I mean, not fine, like, you know, like that's a healthy choice, but then she got clean and now she wants to quit the group."

"Why?"

Rupert looked at Miro and sneered.

"She wants to do something with her life."

Miro didn't know what to say to that. Miro knew lots of people who didn't do anything at all. He didn't understand how they could afford to live in big fancy houses in Los Feliz, he didn't know how they could hang out all day, smoke expensive ganja, and then go clubbing all night. Sometimes he thought everyone in Los Angeles had a trust fund. Everyone but him.

"Yeah, well, that's kind of a noble thing, you know. Doing something with your life. Helping people."

Rupert laughed.

"She wants to make money. She got a job at one of the big agencies in Century City. She's going to be a talent agent."

Rupert's face screwed up in a cross between scorn and betrayal as he tugged on his scruffy beard.

"Fucking sellout."

They drove in silence for a bit, Rupert stewing about his keyboard player's departure, the iPod shifting from Ethiopian jazz to obscure Nigerian pop to bootleg B-sides from Cabaret Voltaire's 1981 tour of the former Czechoslovakia. Miro would've liked to listen to a little reggae, maybe something old-school like Toots & The Maytals or the Abyssinians. He would've liked to smoke a joint, too, but his lungs were still in the process of healing. The last thing he wanted to do was laugh or cough or sneeze. It was a shame, really, because he was going to spend a few days with his parents and around them it always helped to be stoned.

...

An hour later the old Mercedes was bouncing down the pocked driveway toward Miro's parent's small cottage near the beach in Summerland. It was a cute place, with a kind of faded bohemian vibe, as if years ago the place had been jammed with groovy cats and chicks who'd danced to Booker T. & the

MG's and spilled cheap red wine on their rayon shirts while they were making out on the beach. Miro had never spent the night there. His parents had sold their little Spanish house in Glendale and moved to this beach community a few days after Miro had started college. Like they couldn't wait for him to get out of the house. In retaliation Miro had only gone to see them a few times and never for more than a couple of hours.

Miro's parents had visited him once in the hospital, making sure he was alive, then returning to their work. They were both modestly successful artists—hence his name, after the Spanish painter Joan Miró—who spent most of their time painting or working with big blobs of clay in the various parts of the house they'd converted into studio space. Miro knew this meant he was going to be commandeering the couch in the living room until he was strong enough to go back to Los Angeles, find a place to live, and figure out how the hell he was going to get back into the cannabis-breeding business without getting killed.

...

His mother was busy making falafel—dropping little clumplettes of mashed chickpeas and herbs into hot oil—while his dad wrestled with a bottle of pinot grigio.

Miro slumped on the couch, he was really tired, while Rupert got the tour of the various studios and works-in-progress. Miro's father somehow got it into his head that he should paint a backdrop for Rupert's band for when they performed. Miro's jaw dropped when Rupert, sucking down half a glass of wine in a couple gulps, nodded enthusiastically and said, "That would be awesome." Miro cringed. It was only partially from watching his father try to be a hipster; the majority of the cringe—a good 75 percent—was reserved for the usage of the word "awesome." Miro wasn't a linguist or an lexicographer but he didn't have to be to know that "awesome" was the most awesomely overused word in the English language. Sometimes when he got stoned Miro would rant about it. How many things in this world justify the use of a word that means "a cross between dread and veneration"? Certainly not an MP3 download of an obscure power trio from Sweden or a pair of clunky shoes found in a thrift store. "Awesome" was supposed to describe the feeling you would have if you came into contact with God or if you were in the presence of something truly miraculous, not, as it was commonly used, to describe a reality-TV show.

Miro wondered why it bothered him so much. It was just a word.

27

"**Y**OU'RE NOT GOING to get one of them Westside bitches to let you assfuck her. You could cover her with diamonds and pearls and the bangingest bling money can buy, but you won't get in through the back door. They just don't do that, man."

Damon was listing the advantages of date raping unconscious women for the teen skateboarder—whose arm and shoulder were now wrapped in a sling—as they sat in the SUV across from the fire station. Shamus sat in the backseat, keeping his eye on the station, drumming his fingers absentmindedly on his knee.

"Knock 'em out, man, you can stick it anywhere you want. Sleeping Beauty always puts out."

They'd been sitting there for about an hour. Shamus knew the shifts changed in the late afternoon so he figured the EMT chick would probably change clothes and go home. He wanted to teach her a lesson, convince her that harassing his couriers was a bad idea, or, if that didn't work, he'd just fucking kill her. He wasn't sure yet what he was going to do. He figured he'd play it by ear.

The skateboarder sat up in his seat.

"That's her. And that's my backpack."

Shamus squinted out the window and watched as the paramedic, now out of uniform, climbed into a police car driven by a young, uniformed officer.

"She's taking the shit to the cops."

Shamus waited until the squad car rounded the corner, then he opened the door and turned to the teen.

"Get out."

The kid bailed out of the SUV as fast as he could. Damon looked at Shamus.

"We follow them?" Damon asked.

Shamus nodded.

"She's got my shit."

The fact that she hadn't already turned the product in to the police was a surprise, but maybe that's what she was doing now.

...

Fran sat in the passenger seat of the squad car, the skateboarder's backpack stowed on the floor by her feet. She looked over at the driver. He was young, a rookie, but he had a body-builder's physique and that made him a total stud in her eyes.

"You've got some serious guns," she said.

She was referring to his rock-solid biceps. Officer Bill Bennett turned to her, winked from behind his sunglasses, and flexed his right arm.

"Give it a squeeze."

Fran did. The solid mass sent a shiver down her spine.

"What can you bench?"

He ran his tongue over his lips.

"Three fifteen."

"Not bad. For a rookie."

Bennett smiled at her. He was handsome in a sandy-haired linebacker kind of a way and he knew it.

"Turn here."

"Here?"

Fran nodded and the squad car left the road, a street that ran parallel to the freeway, and turned onto an old fire road near the foothills.

"Park right over there."

Bennett threw the car into park and flicked off the ignition with a flourish as a cloud of dust swirled up around them. He turned to face her, leaning forward to give her a kiss. Before he could, Fran deftly clicked a pair of handcuffs around his wrists and locked his hands to the steering wheel. He looked at her.

"Hey. I thought . . ."

Fran kissed him, hard on the lips, jamming her tongue deep into his mouth, letting him know who was in charge. She broke from it and looked him in the eyes.

"I do the touching."

It took Officer Bill Bennett a full ten seconds to process this information. This, he realized, was not going to be your usual romp in a car.

Fran kissed him again and, as she did, she unzipped his pants and fished his cock out of his uniform.

It was a well-known secret in the Northeast Division Police Department that Firewoman Fran enjoyed having sex with police officers in their squad cars. The male members of the force even had a special call code for when they'd be giving her a ride home.

What was less well known—the officers were embarrassed to talk about this—was that she usually handcuffed her lover so that he would be properly restrained. She would be in complete control; she touched you, you didn't touch her. She was dominant, you were submissive. Those were the rules. The only guy who ever tried to reverse roles on her found that she was somewhat expert in Brazilian jiujitsu and quickly put him in a submission hold until he, well, submitted. She still fucked him and, despite the bruises on his neck, he had to admit he'd enjoyed it, too. You wanted a piece of Fran, you had to do it her way. If she wanted her nipples sucked, she'd stuff them in your mouth. If she wanted you to eat her, she'd sit on your face. When it was time for you to come, she'd make you come.

Fran saw it as doing something good for the world. She was an anti-missionary-position missionary. She forced the officers to stop thinking like cavemen, to drop the dominating man-on-top cliché of sex. A little restraint, a little discipline was good for the soul. Sometimes it's better to let someone else drive.

The men hardly ever complained, although they all wanted to give her tits a squeeze before they dropped her off at home. She let them. It must be a guy thing.

Fran never invited men into her house. She never met them at a motel or at their "bachelor pad." Where was the fun in that? She didn't know why, but for some reason she was unable to have an orgasm during regular old-fashioned missionary-style sex. She could fake one. She'd mastered that art in college, wailing and screaming, shouting and hooting like she was strapped to a mechanical bull. But she never came. For some reason she couldn't climax unless she was in a squad car, with her partner handcuffed and whimpering underneath her, she needed to be dominant. And when that happened, well, it just rocked her world.

...

Shamus and Damon had seen the squad car turn off the main street and onto the abandoned fire road. When it pulled over and parked under a clump of trees, they drove past—not wanting to blow their cover—continued up about a quarter mile, then turned around and parked.

It was dark now, the sky having burned indigo in the west before falling into a black ambient haze. The dull glow of light pollution blotted out the stars, making it feel like they were under some kind of protective dome, a snow globe filled with motor oil.

It only took about ten minutes of sitting still for Shamus to lose his patience. He got out and crept down the road to see what was going on.

Damon sat in the car, watching Shamus's back disappear in the darkness. He'd smoked a joint about an hour ago and it didn't take long for tendrils of paranoia to begin creeping into his consciousness. He didn't want to be here. These were law enforcement officers. You don't fuck with cops. That's just stupid. Like if you go up and whack a hive of Africanized honey bees with a stick, you're gonna get stung.

Damon felt the crotch of his new tracksuit—this one was sweet, bright yellow, with cream-colored triple stripes down the sleeves and legs—creep up his ass. He sat up and tugged at the pants, attempting to unwedgie them from his ass crack. This is the kind of shit that happens when you have to sit in the car for hours and hours. Damon hated waiting. It made him feel like a motherfucking chauffeur. Why couldn't he be the one to go slinking off into the night to see what was going on? It was always the same. He waited in the car while Shamus and Guillermo got to do the fun stuff, whatever it was. Makin' deals, beating on some numbskull's head, slingin' shit, breakin' fingers; whatever needed to be done, they got to do it.

He turned up the stereo, pumping some old-school rap through the expensive speakers. He had a whole collection of the stuff, people like Kurtis Blow and Eazy-E, groups like the Furious 4 + 1 and Public Enemy—these were vintage rappers, people who knew how to rhyme about more than just their bullshit shopping sprees. Not that there's anything wrong with Louis Vuitton.

Damon half expected to hear gunshots, half hoped that the gunshots would be the police killing Shamus. Then he could be the boss. That would be sweet. And why not?

Damon pulled a bandanna out of his pocket and mopped the sweat off his forehead. Yeah. Once again. Sweating like a pig on a spit. He was beginning to realize how stressful it was to spend his days in the company of a homicidal maniac. The stress showed in the sheets of perspiration pouring off his head, in the tightness in his chest, and in the throb of his adrenal gland deep inside his head. It was like a panic attack that never quite got to attack. It was like a panic stalker, just lurking in the back of his head, haunting him, like a shadow stroke. Even the weed wasn't relaxing him like it used to. His mom had given him a pamphlet from her doctor. *Stress Is a Killer!* Damon went down the list of warning signs and could check them all. According to the pamphlet, he needed to make a career change.

Before Damon could figure out where to send his résumé —several years experience as flunky, gopher, sidekick, and bagman—Shamus opened the door and slid into the passenger seat.

"Okay, Tweety Bird, let's go."

Damon winced. Just because he looked sharp in his tracksuit didn't mean Shamus could mock him.

"See anything?"

Shamus nodded.

"She's sucking his cock."

"What?"

Shamus nodded.

"On our dime. He's supposed to be on patrol, protecting and serving and he's getting his knob polished. I don't know why the fuck I pay taxes."

...

Fran gripped Officer Bennett's erect penis tightly in her right hand. It was sticking up through the fly of his pants like a big pink mushroom. Fran looked up at him. He was gasping, mouth open. He had a frightened, pleading expression.

"Why are you stopping?"

Fran grinned. *Men are so easy to control.*

"Because I'm gonna fuck you now."

She sat up and slid out of her pants and panties and mounted him, his cock sliding into her easily, smoothly. She wrapped her fingers through the steel grill that divided the front seat from the rear to get some leverage and keep her ass from banging the steering wheel and began to thrust up and down on him.

Officer Bennett groaned. Fran stopped, grabbing his face roughly in her hands and squeezing his mouth.

"Don't you dare come until I tell you to."

He nodded.

"I'll try."

Fran started thrusting again, pushing down hard against him, feeling his belt buckle and mace canister against her inner thigh, her left knee scraping along the grip of his handgun. Occasionally the dispatch would come over the radio, calling out code numbers and directing officers to various addresses. Apparently someone's Lexus had just been stolen in the Galleria's parking structure.

She could feel an orgasm building inside her, the sensation expanding. She rode the tension until she came in a rush of serotonin to her brain, her muscles shuddering and contracting.

Officer Bill Bennett couldn't control himself. He followed, coming in a few uncontrollable thrusts and unintelligible guttural rumbles.

Fran looked at him and shook her head.

"I told you not to come."

"Sorry."

She laughed.

"I was just trying to save you some embarrassment when you go back to the station."

She got off him and pulled her pants on. Bennett looked down at his pants and realized what she meant. His crotch was drenched. It looked like he'd pissed himself.

...

Fran waved to Officer Bennett as she opened the security gate to her apartment complex. Like the others, he had to cop a feel as she was getting out of the car, but then, as he squished her boobs like he was giving her an examination, he asked her out on a date. *Men just didn't get it.* Going on a date was the last thing Fran wanted to do. But sometimes guys thought that she had sex with them because she wanted to be their girlfriend or mistress or something. As if they had something special that other men didn't. *God gave you all the same equipment.* People always say that women are the sappy ones, waiting for Mr. Right to come save them from their lives and make everything fireworks and roses, but men were just as deluded. Fran didn't understand why you couldn't just have sex without any strings attached. You know? Have some fun. Why did guys always have to ruin it by asking for dates?

Fran walked across the courtyard toward her apartment. The building had probably been really cool when it was built in the fifties but now it looked like an old folk's home plopped on a quiet side street just south of Glendale. There was a biomorphic-shaped pool in the center of the U-shaped complex and a half dozen chaise longues were scattered around it, their cheap aluminum frames deformed from years of abuse. Despite the patina of algae and probable traces of urine in the water, Fran was happy to have the pool. It got hot in the summer and the air conditioning in her place just couldn't keep up with the rising misery index of the valley in August.

Fran unlocked her door and entered her small, stuffy apartment. She walked past the two beanbag chairs and the one floor lamp that comprised her entire living room set. An oil painting of Jesus and his disciples standing by a windswept shore hung in the middle of the wall. Fran wasn't religious but her born-again Christian mother had gotten it for her as a housewarming gift and Fran had left it hanging. Besides, you had to look close to tell that it was the Son of God standing there; from a distance it looked like a bunch of hippies getting ready to smoke a joint. Anyway, it was better than the bare wall.

Fran dumped the yellow backpack on her kitchen table, opened the fridge, and grabbed a cold beer.

She walked into her bedroom, the one room with some actual furniture, and got undressed. Putting the beer down on the dresser, she looked at her naked self in the mirror. Damn, she looked good. Strong and lean and hard. She reached under her bed and pulled out a metal box. It wasn't anything special, no bigger than a briefcase.

Inside were two handguns—a Glock and a Colt .45 semiautomatic—that she'd acquired while in the army. Next to the guns was her special toy. She took it out and slid the box back under the bed.

Standing in front of the mirror she slipped her legs through the thong harness and pulled it up, tight, over her ass. The front of the harness made a small black triangle over her crotch. That's what she liked about it. It looked like pubic hair and made the ten-inch jelly dildo sticking out from it look almost lifelike. The strap-on was her security blanket, her teddy bear, the thing that she took to bed that made her feel safe and cuddly. She realized that people might think it was strange or kinky, but it made her feel strong and protected. When she was in the army she'd slept with a gun under her pillow; in civilian life she had her dildo. Maybe if she was married she wouldn't need it, she'd have her husband's cock to cling to. But she wasn't, so this would have to do.

In the mirror, Fran looked like a really buff and beautiful hermaphrodite with an erection. She admired herself, gave her cock a good squeeze, then slipped under the covers and turned on the TV.

There's nothing like drinking beer in bed while you watch TV after a hard day's work.

...

Damon had watched as the door to the squad car opened and the paramedic chick started to get out. He saw the officer inside reach an arm out and quickly grope her breasts before she stood up and closed the car door. He watched as she carried the yellow backpack toward an apartment building. She turned and waved and the squad car drove off.

"Let's bum-rush her ass."

Shamus shook his head.

"Let's see where she goes."

Damon took out his bandanna and wiped his face down. Tailing cop cars was not something he liked to do. In fact, if you asked him, the goal should be to keep as much distance between yourself and the police as possible.

Shamus slipped out of the car and trotted across the street. Damon watched as he went up to the security gate and peered through. He stood there for a moment—it seemed like an hour to Damon—then turned and jogged back to the SUV.

"She's on the first floor, right side, second apartment from the end."

Damon figured now would be a good time to argue against the plan, whatever the plan was.

"It's just a couple pounds, man."

Shamus turned and glared at Damon. More sweat erupted from Damon's forehead.

"What're you sayin'?"

"Like, we got hundreds of pounds of the shit. That's all."

Shamus looked at him and shook his head.

"It's the principal."

"She's just doing her job."

"She's a paramedic."

Damon didn't know what to say to that. He had to admit that it wasn't normal for public employees to take confiscated Schedule 1 narcotics home with them. Was it?

"So what do you want to do?"

"Go in there and get it."

There was something about the way Shamus said it that didn't sound right to Damon.

"Who?"

"You."

"Me?"

"Yeah."

More sweat. More mopping. Damon realized he needed another bandanna.

"Why me?"

"I thought you were Mr. B and E."

It was true. Damon had spent a lot of his youth jimmying doors and climbing through windows, but he was bigger now. Slower, stockier, sweatier. The fact that he was wearing bright yellow didn't help either.

"Well, yeah, I can get in there. But . . ."

Shamus looked at him.

"But what, motherfucker?"

Damon was smart enough to realize that it was time for him to do what Shamus told him.

"Okay, man. I'll do my best."

Damon climbed out of the SUV and walked, as casually as he could, toward the apartment complex.

. . .

Fran had fallen asleep with the TV on. That wasn't unusual. What was unusual was the intruder in her bedroom pressing a gun against her head.

"Don't fuckin' move. You scream and I'm gonna drop the hammer. Understand?"

Fran nodded.

"Where's the shit?"

Fran realized that her arms were trembling. She told herself to take a deep breath. *Stay calm. Relax and wait for the perp to make a mistake.* She noticed he was a big guy, stocky, and in some kind of bright yellow costume. Was she being robbed by Big Bird?

"I have some money in my wallet."

Damon dug the hard steel barrel of the pistol into her cheek.

"Don't make me fuck up your pretty face. I don't want your fuckin' money. Where's the shit you stole?"

This, she realized, was about the marijuana.

"On the kitchen table. It's all there."

She felt the perp relax. He let his full weight rest on the bed causing it to creak and list to one side.

"You like to get high?"
Fran shook her head.
"I was going to sell it."
The perp nodded knowingly.
"You should try it. Chill you out."
He pulled the covers down revealing her breasts. Fran watched as he stared at them. Then she saw him lick his lips.
"You got nice tits."
He reached over and began touching her breasts.
"These are real."
Fran remembered something from her rape prevention counseling. Keep them talking.
"You don't want to do this. Just take the pot and go."
Damon cocked the gun.
"Don't tell me what to do."
Fran swallowed.
"Okay."
"'Cos I think you like it."
Despite herself, she couldn't keep her nipples from responding. They became erect. She could tell that the perp was getting excited. His breathing changed, growing fast and ragged.
"You should stop."
She heard the perp chuckle.
"What did I tell you?"
"I shouldn't tell you what to do."
"That's right. Now don't fucking move."
She watched as he stood up and yanked his track pants down, keeping the gun in his hand. He had an erection.
"I never fucked a fireman before."

Fran didn't say anything. She wasn't about to beg this asshole for mercy.

He slipped under the covers next to her. Fran couldn't help it, she recoiled, not so much at his touch, but at the drops of perspiration falling from his face and head as he moved himself into a position to mount her. She tensed as he crouched over her.

"Open your mouth."

Fran did as he said, wincing a little as he took the barrel of his gun and pushed it into her mouth. He spread her legs with his knee and reached for her crotch. Then he froze.

"What the fuck?"

That was the moment she'd been waiting for. The second of hesitation when he discovered the strap-on she was wearing.

Fran grabbed the gun and deftly twisted it out of his hands while simultaneously doing a rapid sit-up and smashing her forehead into his face, breaking his nose. He flailed blindly, stunned by her actions. Fran twisted, rolling him over, and jammed the gun into his mouth. She felt the barrel knock out a couple of the perp's teeth on its way in.

"Give me a reason motherfucker. Give me a reason to blow your head off."

The perp stopped struggling. He moaned in pain. Blood was flowing freely from his crushed nose and bubbling up from his broken teeth and torn gums. He tried to say something. She thought he might be trying to apologize but Fran wasn't interested in an apology. She was just getting started. She grabbed his balls and gave them a hard squeeze. The perp bucked. She jammed the gun harder into his mouth.

"You like to rape? You think that's fun?"

The perp shook his head from side to side. Fran could hear him saying no, in a bloody gurgle.

"You ever been fucked by a fireman before?"

Fran let go of his balls and spit into her palm. She used the saliva to lubricate her strap-on. The perp's eyes widened in disbelief as she spread his cheeks and thrust the dildo straight up his ass.

The perp squealed in pain, his eyes rolling up into his head. Fran found herself completely turned on. Maybe the missionary position isn't so bad if you're the one on top. She began to fuck him as hard as she could.

...

Shamus didn't know what to think. He'd seen some kinky shit on pornos but he'd never seen anything like this. There, lit by the glow of the TV set, was the female paramedic on top of Damon, buttfucking him for all she was worth with a big strap-on dildo.

She was too busy jamming her cock into Damon to notice Shamus silently step behind her, raise his gun, and put two bullets into her back. She flopped down, dead before her head hit the pillow. But somehow, when her body landed on top of Damon it must've pulled the trigger on the gun stuck in his mouth, because it discharged, blowing the back of Damon's head into the soft down pillows. Duck feathers, or whatever it is they stuff pillows with, floated in the air.

Shamus stood there for a second, blinking, before realizing that someone must've heard the shots and he wasn't going to wait and see how long it took for the police to arrive. He went and retrieved the yellow backpack from the kitchen and started for the door. He stopped when he noticed the painting on the living room wall. It was some hippies, like Charles Manson or something, smoking a joint on the beach. Shamus liked it. It would look really good in his living room next to the LA river painting. He snatched it off the wall and left the apartment. He walked slowly, like any normal person, as he left the building.

28

HEN MIRO WOKE UP, he found that his mother had draped a blanket over him and left a cold falafel salad on the coffee table. Rupert was long gone.

He must've drifted off. He did that a lot lately. He'd blink, his eyelids snapping shut for a nanosecond, and then wake up hours later. The doctors assured him it was normal, that being quasi-narcoleptic was part of the healing process.

Miro stood, wrapping himself in the blanket like a shroud, and went to the window. He saw the black expanse of ocean, heard the crash of the waves. He looked up at the sky and was amazed at how vivid it was. Without the light pollution and dense haze of carbon fuel emissions in Los Angeles, he could see millions of stars, planets, even galaxies, stretching off into an unknowable infinity. It was so vast it made Miro shiver. It was awesome.

...

Detective Cho was starting to think his wife was right, that maybe it *was* time to retire from the force. Getting woken up in the middle of the night was unpleasant enough, but trying to wrest his brain from the over-the-counter half-nelson of a double shot of Nyquil and a fistful of Advil to investigate a double homicide involving a murdered LAFD paramedic mixed up in some kind of kinky sex with a known drug dealer was really more than he could handle. The homicide detective covering the night shift was out with the flu. Cho wondered what he had to do to get out of it. He had a cold. Didn't a rhinovirus count as a kind of flu? He made a mental note to send an e-mail to the police union about understaffing of detectives in the Northeast district.

The bizarre diorama he found in the bedroom—a dead female apparently sodomizing a dead drug dealer—was, cold medicine or not, hard to wrap his head around.

Cho ordered his men to seal the area. No press, no media. No nobody. The last thing he needed was a photo of this to leak out. You wouldn't find the chief and the mayor flashing their laser-bleached smiles at that press conference.

Quijano entered the room carrying one of those stainless metal coffee mugs that are guaranteed not to spill in your car.

"What've we got?"

Cho shrugged.

"Clusterfuck."

Quijano lifted the sheet and looked at the corpses. He put the sheet back down.

"Guess he was into pegging."

Cho blinked.

"What?"

"It's called pegging. You know? When you do what they were doing."

"How do you know this?"

Quijano took a sip of his coffee.

"I know a lot of shit. You just never ask."

Quijano turned and walked out of the room. Cho shrugged and followed.

In the living room, Cho noticed a young patrol officer leaning against the wall, his eyes tearing, his face green like he was about to vomit. Cho, who had somehow gotten accustomed to seeing human beings hacked, hewn, drowned, strangled, mangled, and otherwise turned into cuts of meat, went over to him.

"Officer Bennett, right? Are you okay?"

Bennett looked at Cho.

"I was just with her. I gave her a ride home."

Detective Cho had heard enough stories in the precinct locker room to know that that meant the officer's semen would probably be found on Fran's body when the autopsy was performed. Cho heaved a sigh and pulled out his notebook. It was going to be a long night.

29

MIRO WAS FEELING better and it was not a moment too soon. Another day of lying on the couch watching daytime television or reading another artsy-fartsy beatnik book from his father's library of legendary LSD-gobbling poets from the sixties was going to cause him to go postal. It was giving him too much time for reflection. He kept thinking about the Portuguese scientist, so he went to the local library and checked out the book about a god taking a walk for the breeze. He liked it, although he was surprised it was about political maneuvering between a magistrate and Emperor Marcus Aurelius during the end days of the Roman Empire as the people revolted and the Moors invaded. There was something funny about a scientist reading about people wearing togas. It made him like her even more.

Miro wondered why his parents never asked him anything about his life. They never asked him what he did or how he made money. Was it because they knew what he was doing? Or were they just too self-absorbed to care? As much as he hated to admit it, it was probably the later. He'd always felt as if he were some kind of afterthought. Years ago, when he was a freshman in college, his dad had turned to him and, apropos of nothing, said, "You're a survivor, I never worry about you." Which Miro took to mean, *Good fucking luck, kid.*

He wondered what they would've done if the bullet had caused some permanent damage, if he'd been paralyzed or turned into a vegetable. Would they wheel him out onto the beach for some fresh air? Would his mother spoon gruel into his mouth for breakfast? Or would they put him in a home? Let the state take care of him? Stop by once a year on his birthday to sing a song and complain to the nurse about his infected bedsores? Maybe they'd just leave him in the wilderness; say, "You're a survivor," and beat a retreat back to their boho beach bubble as the wolves circled.

Miro sighed. He loved his parents and he knew they loved him. Why did he feel neglected? And at his age, why did he care?

After a bowl of some kind of multigrain glop that his mother fixed, Miro borrowed his father's computer—his had been stolen when his apartment was trashed—and went online to check his e-mail. As he saw that he had almost two hundred messages—one hundred eighty seven of them spam —he realized that he hadn't even thought about his e-mail since he'd been shot.

He was happy to see several messages from Guus, checking in, wanting to know what was going on. Miro considered how he should respond. If he told him the truth, that the Elephant Crush was gone, what would happen? Would the Cannabis Cup committee give the award to another strain? Would Guus abandon him?

"Is that your novel?"

Miro looked up to see his mother standing behind him, wiping paint off her hands with a rag. Even though she was in her late fifties she still looked good. A testament to vegetarianism, daily yoga, and bimonthly applications of Miss Clairol. She was wearing her painting clothes, an oversized men's dress shirt, paint-splattered blue jeans, and some well-worn huaraches she'd bought on a trip to Mexico twenty years before.

The novel was the lie Miro used to keep his parents from bugging him. It'd been a great disappointment to them that he hadn't followed in their footsteps and become some kind of artist. They'd subjected the young Miro to all kinds of art and enrichment classes. He'd taken piano, modern dance, ceramics, sculpting, painting, vocal coaching, and drawing classes. Although being thirteen and spending a couple hours a week staring at naked girls in the life drawing class had been a thrill, he hadn't shown any artistic ability at all. When he decided to major in biology, his mother actually cried.

The idea that he might be working on a novel, the fantasy that he might have inherited some of their artist genes, gave his parents a thread of hope that they clung to. It never once occurred to them that a child raised in a home filled with artists, whose lives ran on a tightrope of feast or famine, might want to find some kind of financial stability when he grew up. It wasn't until he was in college that Miro realized his parents were vegetarian by choice and not because they couldn't afford meat.

"The novel got stolen."

"What?"

"After I got shot, my apartment was robbed. They took everything."

His mother's face fell, heartbroken.

"Oh, honey."

Miro tried to cheer her up.

"It wasn't that good."

"I'm sure it was brilliant."

Miro turned and looked at his mother, his expression suddenly serious.

"Mom? What would you do if someone stole your art? You know, if someone just came in here and took all your work?"

His mother looked at him and put her hand up to her face, thoughtfully stroking her chin.

"Well, I'd probably follow them to the ends of the Earth and get my art back. Then I'd pull their balls off with a pair of pliers."

She patted him on the shoulder.

"But that's just me."

. . .

Cho looked at the report and rubbed his eyes. On the surface, it was annoying. Three shootings, two of them fatal, all from the same gun. A watercolorist in the LA River, a paramedic with a strap-on, and a guy named Miro Basinas, a seemingly random dude out for a stroll. The only thing that connected them was the bullet. Or, more accurately, the gun that fired the bullets. That was the fact. In twenty-four hours that fact would become a statistic. The LAPD brass were obsessed with statistics. The chief loved nothing better than to stand in front of the press, the mayor grinning like an electroshock therapy patient by his side, and deliver a PowerPoint presentation consisting of charts and graphs and percentage points all showing the steady decline of murder, mayhem, drugs, and gangs. A couple of murders meant the percentage points ticked up. It would screw up all the graphs and charts.

Cho imagined the report going up a ladder, stopping at every rung long enough for the person above him to look at it and then drop their pants and take a big steaming shit. The turds would fall, slowly but surely, until they were raining down on his head. The higher the report went, the deeper the shit.

Cho took a sip of hot herbal tea, something his wife got from the health-food store, something with zinc and echinacea and loads of Vitamin C that she was convinced would help his immune system keep him from coming down with pneumonia. He opened a packet of artificial sweetener and dumped it into the tea, stirring it with a ballpoint pen, and realized the one thing he knew for sure: he was going to need a big fucking umbrella.

Of course, Cho was confident he could crack this. He'd solved more convoluted cases before, he just needed something to grab onto. He turned to his computer, opened a search engine, and typed in Miro's name.

What popped up on his screen made Cho laugh out loud. Quijano turned to him.

"What's so funny?"

"I love the Internet."

Cho hit PRINT and waited as a full-color photo from *High Times* magazine came out of the printer. The photo showed Miro holding a small trophy, above a headline that read ELEPHANT CRUSHES COMPETITION!

Quijano stood next to Cho and they read the article together. Quijano nodded his head in approval.

"Our boy's not such a loser after all."

Cho looked up at Quijano.

"Let's pick up some tacos and swing by his house. Then I want to talk to the EMT partner."

Quijano shook his head.

"Tacos aren't good for your cold."

...

Miro e-mailed Guus and told him everything that had happened and asked for his help. Guus replied almost instantly—Miro figured he probably stayed up all night—and said he would put feelers out and see if he could get any information. Guus was confident that the Elephant Crush would surface eventually. It had to. It was worth too much money. And once the weed was on the market, all they had to do was follow the money. Guus was confident the other coffeeshop owners would help; no one wanted to see a Cup winner killed. That wasn't what the Cup was about, man.

It cheered Miro up to think that even though they were separated by thousands of miles and nine time zones, he and Guus were still partners.

Miro e-mailed his friend Amin, a grower who lived in the hills above Ojai. Miro liked Amin, he was incredibly discreet and his methods, while slightly less reliable than a climate-controlled grow house, produced top-quality marijuana.

Amin would hike deep into the national parks, in the mountains surrounding Santa Barbara, and find small protected clearings for planting. He kept track of the locations with a handheld GPS device. He would spend days hiking and camping, searching for the perfect spot, ideally a south-facing slope—for the best sun exposure—near a stream or creek for easy irrigation, well off the beaten path, preferably inaccessible to all but the most experienced mountaineers. It was in these remote locations, the cannabis sproutlings planted in a seemingly random fashion so they blended with the natural flora—rows of manicured plants were easy to spot from the air—that Amin chose to raise his crops. Fertilized and watered regularly, his plants grew wild and abundant.

Amin knew everyone in the business and might be able to provide Miro with some info. He also had access to something Miro thought he might need.

It felt good to be doing something. Perhaps there was some karmic justice to be found in the universe after all. While Miro would be the first to admit that his life wasn't necessarily the most productive—he could've been working for a nonprofit, or volunteering, or making art like his parents—it wasn't like he was a bad guy. He wasn't profiting from the pain of others; he didn't exploit illegal immigrants or rip off the elderly. He didn't deserve to get shot. Although he had to admit it had given him second thoughts about his career choice. How many other jobs come with drive-by shootings? How many corporate salarymen have their homes ransacked? Do marketing managers worry about police interrogations?

He considered the possibility of doing something else. Maybe give up all this botanical stuff and join the ranks of corporate America, sign on with Microsoft or Google, one of those fun companies with high-tech campuses, executive gyms, and meditation rooms. But Miro liked plants. They were his thing.

Although he couldn't explain it to his parents—he didn't think they'd approve of his profession—Miro liked to think of what he did as a creative endeavor. He created new strains of cannabis. He was good at it, he liked cannabis, and he was providing an important service.

People weren't going to stop getting high. *It's always 4:20 somewhere.*

...

Cho looked at Miro's empty house. A couple of painters—chubby Guatemalan women—were inside painting the walls. It didn't strike Cho as particularly suspicious. You take a bullet, you might move, you might not be able to work. *Shit happens,* as they say. But that didn't mean he was going to quit looking for Miro.

Quijano climbed out of the car and waved to him.

"You want to go talk to his parents? They're up in Summerland."

Cho thought about spending a few hours on the 101 and shook his head.

"Let's talk to the EMT partner first."

30

"**H**OW ARE YOU feeling?"

"I don't know. I'm stunned, I guess."

"Shock is a normal response to tragedy."

Ted wasn't so sure about that. Shock is usually a normal response to trauma, broken bones, or blood loss. Shock didn't really describe what he'd been feeling since the fire captain had told him that Fran had been murdered in her apartment. Mostly he felt confusion. And rage. He was feeling a lot of rage. But he didn't know who to turn his rage on; there were no suspects, no culprits, no real explanation for any of it.

"Is it?"

The city-appointed psychiatrist looked at Ted and nodded solemnly.

"It's how the mind reacts."

Ted shifted on the couch. He wondered why, in the office of a psychiatrist who worked for the Police and Fire Department, there would be an overstuffed couch covered in the same chintz daffodil fabric that his grandma had on her couch. Was it supposed to be comforting? Ted picked up one of the needlepoint throw pillows scattered around the sofa.

The word "Relax" was stitched on one side. He saw another pillow that said, "One Day At A Time." The shrink leaned forward and handed Ted a box of tissues.

"Tissue?"

"No, thanks."

The shrink nodded, acting as if that was significant.

"It's okay to cry. This is a safe place."

"I don't feel like crying right now."

That was true. Ted cried at movies, he cried at his best friend's wedding, he cried on those rare occasions when the underdog won a gold medal at the Olympic games. He wasn't one to hold back tears for any kind of macho reason. He just didn't feel like crying right now. Fran's murder was bizarre. He couldn't get a handle on it. What the fuck had she been up to?

"Were you close?"

"She was my partner."

Ted watched as the shrink adjusted his glasses and scratched his beard thoughtfully.

"Partner. That's a significant word, don't you agree?"

Ted sighed.

"What do you want me to say?"

The shrink held his hands out, palms up.

"What do you feel like saying?"

"Can I go?"

The shrink stared at Ted intently, like he was some kind of bug in a jar. He jotted something down in his notebook.

"I'm going to recommend that they give you a couple of weeks off. You need time to process this."

Ted nodded. It was just as well; he didn't feel like working anyway. When he stood to leave the shrink removed his glasses and gave him an earnest, concerned look.

"Did you know about her, how can I put this . . ." He made an odd gesture. "Her sexual habits?"

Ted shook his head.

"She never mentioned it to me."

...

LAPD Detectives Cho and Quijones were waiting for him when he walked out of the shrink's office. They flashed their badges, acting all official. Not that they needed to identify themselves; Ted recognized them. Cho nodded, then took out a ratty looking tissue and blew his nose.

"I'm not going to shake hands. Head cold."

The big detective waved the tissue in the air as evidence.

"I appreciate that." Ted was being sincere. He hated catching colds. In fact, it was one of the few things that really bothered him; whenever someone came to work in the firehouse acting all heroic that they'd made it to work even though they were really sick, it made Ted want to take a fire extinguisher and pound their fucking face in. That's how much he didn't like catching colds. Why couldn't people realize that if they just stayed home until they were better the cold would stop. But then if people were considerate and took responsibility for their germs we wouldn't have epidemics, plagues, and herpes.

Quijones took out his notepad.

"We need to talk to you about your partner."

...

Marianna watched her breakfast spin down the toilet. *Nausea matinal* meet the Coriolis effect. Her doctor had told her it was normal; literally translating the English "morning sickness" to give a name to the hormonal, sea-tossed, lurch and gurgle that had made her empty the contents of her stomach into the toilet bowl every morning for the past few weeks. The doctor had assured her that this would taper off and eventually stop. But so far it hadn't. So far it had been one vomit-colored morning after another.

The weather had turned; the sky was clear and a crisp wind whipped her hair as she strolled down the street. There was a freshness to the air, it smelled clean and full of oxygen. She inhaled deeply, hoping the fresh air might help make her baby smarter or stronger. Marianna laughed at herself. Once she'd discovered she was pregnant she'd become some kind of health fanatic. She'd stopped drinking alcohol and caffeine, avoided smoke-filled bars and coffeeshops; she ate only organically-grown produce and hormone-free meats. Now she was trying to inhale pollution-free air.

She entered the restaurant, a smart bistro in the center of town, and scanned the room. She saw Guus, wearing his usual black leather jacket, sitting alone at a table, a German language newspaper spread out in front of him.

He looked up as she sat down.

"Pregnancy suits you. You look well."

Marianna smiled.

"I look hungry."

Guus handed her a menu and said, "I think we should go to Los Angeles this weekend."

Marianna gasped as she felt the baby give her insides a sharp whack.

...

Miro had borrowed his parent's car and, using his mother's iPhone for a GPS, had driven to the middle of fucking nowhere. At least it looked like the middle of fucking nowhere.

He'd turned off the main road and driven seventeen miles down a deformed two-lane—the pavement veined and warped by tree roots and years of neglect—to where a trailhead emerged from the woods. He hadn't passed another car or seen another person since he'd left Ojai.

Miro climbed out of the car and went to the edge of the woods to pee. He was standing there, watching his urine arc out into some bushes, when he heard a voice.

"You better hope that's not poison ivy."

Miro looked up to see Amin standing in-between the trees, dressed in camouflage with a bright red bandanna around his neck and his long scraggly hair tied up in a samurai top-knot. Amin was cradling some kind of military-looking rifle in his arms, like a Sandinista on safari. Miro zipped himself up.

"Subcommandante Marcos, I presume?"

Amin grinned.

"Yeah, baby. This season it's Zapatista-chic. Gonna design a whole line of revolutionary pret-à-porter in organic hemp."

Miro laughed.

Amin looked him in the eye. "I heard you caught a hot one."

"Any idea who did it?"

Amin shifted the rifle in his arms.

"No. But I got my peeps sniffin' around."

"You got my message?"

Amin nodded.

"Listen, Miro, are you sure you want to go there? Because trust me, once you do, you don't come back."

Miro shrugged.

"Do I have a choice?"

Amin leaned his rifle against a tree.

"You always have a choice. Don't think you don't. You could walk away from this shit right now. Start fresh. Grow a new strain. Shit, man, you might grow something even better."

Miro thought about this. Amin was right. You always have a choice.

"It's a deterrent. I don't want them to shoot me again."

Amin nodded and pulled a black handgun from behind his back.

"SIG Saur P229, forty cal. Go big or go home. That's what I say."

Miro hesitated for a second, then took the gun.

"Thanks."

Miro tried to stick the gun in his pocket, but it didn't fit.

"Jam it into your pants in back."

Miro looked at the gun, then turned to Amin.

"What if I shoot my ass off?"

Amin scowled.

"Have you ever fired a gun before?"

Miro shook his head.

"What kind of criminal are you?"

"I'm not a criminal, I'm a botanist."

"So I see."

Amin stepped toward Miro.

"Well, now that you're joining the ranks of us gun-toting outlaw farmers, I've got a surprise for you."

Amin swung a small canvas day pack off his shoulders and tossed it to Miro. Miro could smell the cannabis before he even picked the bag up off the ground. He opened it and saw two huge *colas*.

"Check the buds. Trichome city."

Miro pulled a *cola* out and held it up for a closer look. It was a dense group of buds, some just beginning to open, others tightly clustered. All of them were covered with tiny silver hairs—trichomes—glistening in the sunlight. Miro was astonished.

"Where did you get this?"

Amin laughed.

"You gave it to me, fool. Last time I saw you, you handed me a couple seeds and said 'try and grow these.'"

Miro vaguely remembered wanting to know how Elephant Crush would perform outdoors, but this was good news, this could be his salvation. If the plants were thriving he could grow some clones.

"I need to grab some cuttings."

Amin shook his head.

"This is it. I only had two plants and I harvested them."

Miro let out an audible sigh.

"Shit."

"It's nothing to get down about. Touch it. It's some crazy, sticky shit."

Miro gently felt the buds; they were sticky with resin, and when he looked at his fingers he saw they were covered with trichomes. It was such beautiful cannabis.

"This is all you got?"

"I kept a little for myself."

Miro smiled wistfully at Amin.

"This won the Cannabis Cup."

"So I heard."

Miro put the Elephant Crush back in the backpack.

"Can you show me how to use the gun?"

Amin nodded.

"Remember the Boy Scout motto?"

"Be prepared?"

Amin flashed him a quick two-fingered salute.

"Like a motherfucker."

31

ROLLING A BURRITO is harder than it looks. You have to warm the tortilla to make it pliable, pile on the right amount of ingredients—too many and you won't get a good fold, too wet and the tortilla will self-destruct—roll the tortilla over, tuck in the ends, and then wrap it tight enough so it won't fall apart yet loose enough that the salsa can circulate.

It had only taken Daniel a couple of days to get the hang of it and now he could roll a burrito with his eyes closed. He was fast, too. Lenny, the stocky Mexican who owned the taco truck, called him "Ramoncito" in honor of the speedy winger for Chivas. Daniel had tried to get Lenny to tell him something about Miro, but Lenny had the magical ability to be selectively unable to understand or speak English depending on who he was talking to or what he was talking about. Miro seemed to be involved in the business but he was never there. Lenny said he was a silent partner. A *socio comanditario*. That's all Daniel could get.

If being a Mormon missionary had been an exercise in being ignored, snubbed, sneered at, and ridiculed, working on the burrito truck was the complete opposite. People said hi. They smiled. They were happy to see him. The regulars learned his nickname.

Daniel felt loved. Like he was a part of something special. His burritos made people feel good. They brought happiness to their lives. Wasn't that part of his mission? To offer comfort to people in need? It occurred to Daniel that people didn't need dogma, religion, or special underwear; people needed a good burrito.

Since he still hadn't heard anything from his LDS mission sponsors and he'd stopped going to church, Daniel spent his free time at the library researching the history of the burrito. He was fascinated by the conflicting accounts, the legends and urban myths of the birth of the burrito. Some claimed the burrito originated in the sixteenth century, when Aztecs wrapped meats in tortillas as a way to make food portable for travelers, traders, and warriors. Others credited a man named Juan Mendez who, in Ciudad Juarez circa 1912, sold food from containers on the back of his donkey. He wrapped his meats in flour tortillas to keep them warm. Hence "burrito," which means "little donkey."

But to Daniel, the burrito seemed to be more than just a portable lunch. It was, in some strange way, similar to the Holy Trinity, the Godhead.

Three separate and distinct beings who are one in purpose.

In church Daniel had learned about the Father, the Son, and the Holy Ghost. On the taco truck he learned to fill a burrito with a different kind of trinity: grilled meat, rice, and refried beans. He wasn't sure how to classify the salsa, but he knew that to eat it, packed as it was with fiery habaneros, was to take a leap of faith.

Daniel thought that if God had put him on Earth to do good deeds, to fill people's lives with happiness, then perhaps God had put him on Earth to make burritos.

32

MARIANNA LOOKED at the laptop's screen. The temperature in Los Angeles was in the mid seventies. That was in Fahrenheit. She did a quick translation in her head and still decided she might want to take a sweater. It was weird that the United States didn't measure temperature in Celsius. They didn't use the metric system, either. Was it because they thought inches and miles were better units of measure? Or did they see themselves as iconoclasts? Maybe they were just stubborn. She didn't know many Americans and had never been to the States before. What kind of people don't use metric?

She took a sip of her mineral water—it was carbonated and the bubbles tickled her nose and helped settle her stomach—and thought for the thousandth time that she was making a big mistake. What if the Miro who lived in Los Angeles wasn't like the Miro she had spent a perfect weekend with? How would he react to the news that she was pregnant? Was he stubborn? Would he convert to metric for her?

...

"A little to the right."

Guillermo nodded and tipped the painting up an inch.

"Too much. Go back."

He adjusted it again and then turned to look at Shamus. "How's that?"

Shamus stood on the other side of his living room, studying the painting of the hippies on the beach. He smiled. It looked really good above his couch.

"*Bueno.*" Shamus clapped his hands together. He was happy. His apartment was really starting to come together. He had to admit that the paintings on the walls had made a huge difference. It wasn't until he'd actually hung the art that he realized the bare walls had gotten to him, made him feel like he was back in the O.H. Close Youth Correctional Facility in Stockton. But now, now it looked like home.

Guillermo sat on the couch. "Is that Jesus?"

"No, man. That's Jim Morrison."

Guillermo squinted at the painting.

"Oh, yeah."

"You ready to roll?"

Shamus tossed his car keys to Guillermo. Guillermo caught them and looked at Shamus.

"Where're we going?"

Shamus pointed to the backpack filled with cannabis.

"We gotta take this shit to the store."

"Shouldn't we wait for Damon?"

"He's dead."

...

Vincent had spent the morning sitting at his desk, trying to keep his eyes focused on an Excel spreadsheet blinking on his computer screen. Why did the Ventura store sell less bongs than the Hollywood outlet? Maybe all the customers were surfers and couldn't take a bong to the beach. Who knew? He decided he'd have to drive out to Ventura and get to the bottom of it. People forget how much work it takes to run a successful business. It's grueling. Not the fun part of hanging out with customers or taste testing the newest cannabis, not the part where you look at your bank balance and think, *How did I ever get so much fucking money?* It's the minutia, the mind-numbing details. There's inventory, making sure you've got product coming in that will sell; there's schedules to keep, making sure you've got someone behind the counter, juggling employees' requests to have days off here and take vacations there; there's sales tax to pay, withholding tax to calculate, property tax, business tax, and, if the desperate politicians in Sacramento got their way, a sin tax on the product itself—as if medicine was somehow connected with the idea of going to hell—and for all of it, for every single aspect that you had to think about, there were forms and forms and more forms. It was a Mobius strip of paperwork. Vincent had tried delegating. He had a bookkeeper, an accountant, and managers at each location, all responsible for as much of the drudge work as he could lay on them. But still, at the end of the day, he had to look everything over, double check for errors, lies, and outright theft.

But now was the fun part. Vincent stood in the middle of the room and let the clean smell of fresh paint fill his nostrils. A few workmen banged around on various cabinets and the counter that ran in front of the shelving units in the back. He looked at the color swatches the interior designer had given him and smiled. This was going to be the nicest, most up-scale Compassion Club yet. There were high-tech scales attached to a computer inventory system, a state of the art humidor to keep the cannabis from getting too dry, and beautiful lighting that made the buds look like diamond bracelets at Tiffany's, and it was all enclosed by soft plum painted walls, a plush sage-colored carpet, and a Bose sound system.

Vincent sat down in one of the plush leather smoker's chairs he'd imported from Spain and sighed. This was how marijuana should be sold, like rare wine or Cuban cigars.

But neighborhoods were still nervous about having dispensaries opening. The first few Compassion Centers didn't even have signs—you had to know about them, find the address online, to know where they were. Some areas were less picky and allowed him to put up a sign, either the Compassion Club logo or a simple green cross. But this store? Nobody would complain about this. This was the crème de la crème. This would be the model he'd use for future expansion.

Vincent realized that what this particular Compassion Center needed was a party, a gala, a grand opening. Something special to put it on the map. And if he could offer an exclusive preview of the current Cannabis Cup winner, well, that would be the cherry on top.

He pulled out his iPhone and dialed an event planner he knew.

...

Ted put the key in the lock. Fran had given him a key to her apartment a year ago when she went to Club Med in Ixtapa with an officer from the Orange County Sheriff's Department and needed her plants watered. Ted hadn't heard the particulars of how the vacation went, he just knew that Fran had gotten a sunburn and a series of wicked hangovers and that the deputy had assumed that daily oral copulation was part of the resort's all-inclusive policy. Whatever relationship Fran had with the deputy had ended in Mexico.

Ted turned the key, felt the bolt slide back, and opened the door.

Once he was inside he realized he'd made a mistake. The air in the apartment was alive with the smell of mold spores and the rusty tang of dried blood. Ted noticed that the large painting of Jesus and his disciples was missing from the wall— he could still see the outline where the painting had hung— but otherwise the living room looked exactly the same as it always looked: like no one lived here.

He walked into the kitchen and opened the refrigerator. It was what he expected. Beer and condiments in the fridge, a one-month supply of microwave dinners in the freezer. He realized that he'd never seen Fran eat an apple or a banana or a salad.

Ted took a beer and twisted off the top. He didn't know why he did that. He wasn't thirsty and it felt weird to drink a dead person's beer, but Fran would've offered him one if she'd been there. She would've wanted him to have it.

He suppressed a burp, waiting for some kind of sign or omen or something to give him the courage to go into the bedroom and look at the murder scene. He hadn't seen the photos or read the police report. They didn't share that kind of stuff with ambulance drivers and he didn't want to see it anyway. In his line of work he'd seen plenty of dead people. It wasn't one of the highlights of the job.

He went back into the living room and stared at the wall. Why hadn't the police said anything to him about the missing painting? Did they know it was gone? *Maybe it was a robbery that went crazy.* And what was all that talk about drugs? Fran didn't take drugs. At least she never talked about it to him and he didn't think it was something she'd get mixed up in. She was pretty straight for someone so kinky.

Of course, the police wouldn't notice a painting missing if they didn't know it had been there in the first place. This, he realized, was why he'd come to Fran's apartment. To look for things that might've been overlooked. Ted took out a scrap of paper and his pen and started a list. He wrote, "Painting of Jesus at the beach."

He put the beer down on top of the TV set and walked into Fran's bedroom.

It didn't look like how a crime scene should look, not like the crime scenes glamorized on TV. There wasn't any yellow "Do Not Cross" tape rolled around the perimeter, there was no moody blue light streaming through the miniblinds, and no soundtrack shimmering in the background; it was just Fran's bedroom. The only difference he could see was a couple of rusty stains on the mattress and powdery splotches around the bed and windows where the crime scene investigators had dusted for fingerprints.

Using the bottom of his T-shirt, Ted opened the top drawer of Fran's dresser. He pulled out a tube sock and put it over his hand. He didn't know why. He had nothing to hide. But then he thought he didn't want to contaminate the scene, he didn't want his prints mixed with anyone else's. Besides, what would he tell the police if they asked why he was in her apartment? He didn't have a good answer.

Using the sock like a mitten, he went carefully through Fran's dresser drawers. There was not a lot to discover. She didn't have any jewelry—he'd never seen her wear any—and all her clothes consisted of the dark blue of their EMT uniforms or blue jeans. She wore dark cotton socks and white cotton underwear, although he did find a couple of bright pink thongs. Maybe those were left over from the trip to Ixtapa.

Ted sifted through the medicine cabinet and the drawers in the bathroom. Fran didn't have a lot of makeup, certainly not as much as Ted's ex-girlfriend used to carry in her purse, but judging from a few half-squeezed tubes of cream, she suffered from the occasional yeast infection.

Ted found her birth control pills by the bedside table. He knew she was sexually active. It made him wonder why he wasn't. But he saw no evidence of kinky behavior. No tubes of lubricant, no anal beads or latex gloves. He'd never heard about her strap-on thing until the police told him.

Ted looked under the bed. He found a metal box and pulled it out. He knelt on the floor—there was no way he was going to sit on the bed—and opened it.

Inside were a couple of handguns, a few extra clips, and a box of ammunition. He wondered why the police would've left these here, then realized that they weren't illegal and they weren't part of the investigation, so of course they'd leave them. They were Fran's personal effects, after all.

Fran had never mentioned owning a gun but Ted wasn't surprised to find them. He supposed most single women living alone in LA had guns under their beds.

Ted pocketed the small Glock and the clips that went with it, closed the box, and slid it back under the bed. Ted wasn't prone to compulsive acts, and it wasn't something that he gave a lot of thought to until he got home; he just did it, as if he was responding to some primal impulse.

He left the apartment without finishing his beer.

...

The Pacific Surfliner rattled south toward LA, the ocean glittering obsidian out the right side, the lights of small seaside towns flashing by on the left, the buildings and people and their stories frozen in velocity-bound dioramas as the train hurtled past.

As he looked out the window, watching other people's lives flicker and fade, Miro felt his chest tighten, causing little twinges of pain to go pinging through his body. Things, it seemed, really weren't going his way. This wasn't how he'd planned his life. Not at all.

When he got back from seeing Amin, his mother informed him that a couple of detectives from the Los Angeles Police Department had come looking for him. There had been two more shootings, both with the same gun that shot him. The detectives had stressed to her that he wasn't in any trouble but they had some questions, there was some new evidence related to his shooting that they wanted to discuss. Miro made an educated guess and decided that this new evidence probably had something to do with his involvement in the cannabis business, and that was a subject he definitely didn't want to talk about with law enforcement.

But the news made his head spin. *Two more shootings? What the fuck was that about?* He was a gentleman farmer, a lay botanist. He wasn't a gangbanger or a *narcotraficante*. He was just a mellow guy who grew some herb.

But that's what it was about, he was sure of that. The Elephant Crush was the cause of all this mayhem.

The more he thought about it, the more it seemed to him that it wasn't just the cannabis business, it was business in general. These kinds of things happen all the time in the business world; pick up the paper and it's all hostile takeovers, bankruptcy, bailouts, layoffs, purges, strikes; the world of commerce was a vicious, violent place. Maybe Guus was right, America should smoke a little Elephant Crush, it would take the edge off.

Miro felt around inside his backpack and checked to see if he still had the gun. Not that he was going to go all gangsta on somebody. He wasn't stupid; he realized he was in over his head, and besides, he wasn't sure who exactly he was looking for. But if he had to mix it up with organized crime, with La Eme from Tijuana or the El Salvadoran MS-13 or the Crips and Bloods or Chinese Triad, whoever was behind this, well, what choice did he have? *They started it.*

He'd come up with a half-assed plan on the drive back to his parents' house. He couldn't even call it a plan, not really; it was more of a gambit, a ploy, a hail Mary. It was about as smart as poking an alligator with a stick to see if it's interested in eating you. But despite the utter stupidity of his scheme, he thought it just might work.

Miro watched another city flash by. *Is it La Conchita?* A tiny hamlet filled with strangers, people he'd never meet, people falling in love, suffering heartbreak, laughing and crying, their lives punctuated by occasional fatal mudslides.

Miro sipped some weak, soapy-tasting coffee from a Styrofoam cup. He'd bought the coffee at the train station in Santa Barbara. Now it was cold. But even when it was at its peak it wasn't anything like the coffee he'd had in Amsterdam. Miro remembered the last morning he'd spent with Marianna. He'd woken up to find himself entangled with her, his arms in her arms, his legs twisted through hers, holding on. She'd looked at him and smiled, said something in Portuguese— *Bom dia, good morning*—before kissing him.

They'd taken a shower together. Miro washing her, soaping her skin, feeling her small beautiful breasts, admiring how her body was lean and supple like a dancer's. He'd gotten excited doing that but they were both hungry so they dressed and bounded out of the hotel into the clear and sunny and cold Amsterdam morning.

...

There are thousands of taco trucks in Los Angeles. Some of them sell variations on the taco, like Korean tacos, which are regular tacos but with Korean barbecue and chopped up kimchi for salsa. But the really good trucks, with names like El Pique or La Estrella, were where the taco aficionados would congregate. Lenny's Tacos was one of these. Made of shiny metal and emblazoned with a cheerful cartoon of a fat man wearing a chef's hat and holding a platter of steaming *tortas,* it was parked in the same spot—a little side street just off San Fernando Boulevard—every day at lunch time and then on Eagle Rock Boulevard every night for dinner.

The truck did a brisk business at lunch: there was always a line of ravenous office workers, hungry day laborers covered in dry wall dust and mud, and hungover hipsters waiting patiently for their food. But for Miro the truck was more like an offshore bank, a place that laundered the cash transactions he received for selling his cannabis. The truck dealt in cash and whatever money it made during a busy day, Miro could add a few thousand dollars to the till, pay the taxes, give Lenny his cut, and take the rest out as taxable profits. A good taco truck is like a money-cleaning launderette on wheels.

Miro walked past the folding table covered with a bright oilcloth that was set up on the sidewalk as a do-it-yourself condiment center. It was laden with bowls of homemade salsa, fresh limes, cut radishes, sliced onion, and clumps of cilantro. Daniel had his back turned as Miro approached the truck.

"I hear you're the fastest burrito roller in the business."

Daniel turned and saw Miro standing outside the truck, grinning at him. Daniel couldn't help himself, he beamed.

"Hey! You're back."

Daniel came out the front door of the taco truck, took Miro's hand, and pumped it.

"You like the job?"

Daniel nodded his head in time with his hand pumping, making him look like a berserk oil well.

"I love it. The best job ever. Thank you so much."

Miro patted Daniel on the shoulder.

"I'm happy it worked out."

Daniel finally released Miro's hand.

"What about you? What're you doing?"

Miro shrugged.

"Just trying to get back on my feet. Find a place to live. That kind of thing."

Daniel didn't hesitate.

"Why don't you stay with me? I've got room."

At first glance, the idea of rooming with a young Mormon missionary struck Miro as about the craziest thing he could do, but then that was the genius of it. No one, not even the cagiest criminal on the street, would think to look for him at Daniel's.

"If it's not too much trouble."

Daniel beamed some more.

"Are you kidding?"

...

Later, they sat in Daniel's sad little apartment on a godforsaken strip of desolation along San Fernando Boulevard between Glendale and Burbank looking at each other. Miro noticed a couple of clip-on ties looped around the bedposts of Daniel's bed but decided not to mention it. Maybe it was a religious thing. Miro realized he didn't know very much about Mormons.

"How'd you find this place?"

The building next door was some kind of light industrial complex with frame shops and miniwarehouses; across the street were train tracks, chain-link fences trimmed with razor wire, and a large building that was, apparently, a business that imported Indian food products.

"We kind of inherited it from the missionaries that were here before. I like it. It's close to everything."

As far as Miro was concerned it wasn't close to anything. It was in another dimension, a sad new world of dirt and decay. The clanging of crossing signals and the hooting of a horn sounded as a freight train rumbled past, shaking the small room. Daniel cleared his throat.

"So, what do you really do? You're not really a taco truck owner, are you?"

Miro looked at Daniel, then lay back on the lumpy mattress that had once held Elder Collison's bulky young body.
He hoped the sheets were relatively clean.

"Why do you say that?"

Daniel sat up on his bed.

"Well, I don't know. Just because it doesn't seem like
you are."

"Yeah? What do I seem like?"

Miro stared at the ceiling; paint peeled off in scabs and
the wood underneath was stained a deep yellow from where
dog piss had leaked through from the floor above. Spiders
were nesting in the corners and gray strands of dusty cobwebs
dangled in the air. But it was better than looking at the floor.
Miro had noticed several large brown cockroaches scurrying
for cover when Daniel had opened the door, and the warped
linoleum in the kitchen was pocked with sticky black splotches
of unknown origin that made a sucking sound when you
stepped on them. Miro hoped they were just pieces of really
old chewing gum. All in all, the apartment was tiny, dumpy,
and smelled vaguely of rotting cabbage, but it was where he
needed to be.

Daniel looked at the floor.

"Something cooler, I guess."

Miro laughed.

"I don't know how cool it is."

"So, what do you really do?"

Miro didn't see any reason to lie to the kid.

"I grow cannabis."

"Cannabis?"

"Marijuana."

Daniel nodded. He didn't seem surprised.

"That's illegal."

Miro shrugged.

"Not if you have a prescription from a doctor."

"Really?"

Miro nodded. Then he said, "I'm surprised you don't smoke it."

"Me?"

"Why not? It's a plant. God must've put it here for people to enjoy. The laws against it are just political bullshit. I thought you guys didn't follow laws made by men."

"Those are Jehovah's Witnesses."

Miro laughed. He caught the fear in Daniel's voice.

"Don't worry. I won't smoke any in your apartment."

"Is that why they shot you?"

"I imagine so."

"Do you know who did it?"

Miro shook his head. "It will all be revealed in time."

"Now you sound like a Jehovah's Witness."

Miro was surprised.

"I do? I thought I sounded more like one of the characters from *Star Wars*."

"And then what are you going to do? You know? When all is revealed?"

Miro thought about it.

"Fuck if I know."

33

"WITH FAITH and diligence it will guide you through the wilderness."

That's a lot to ask from a bicycle but Miro had to admit the Liahona—built for LDS missionaries and named after a compass in the Book of Mormon—was a surprisingly good bike. The derailleur shifted smoothly through the gears and the bike flowed downhill through turns without a shudder. It was a rock-solid machine. Even though he felt like a complete dork wearing Elder Collison's old missionary outfit, Miro found himself enjoying the ride.

It was strange how a white, short-sleeved shirt and clip-on tie could transform you. He no longer looked cool or hip or edgy or anything like that. Now he looked like a great big nerd, like a computer geek from the days when Fortran was the lingo, one of those guys who builds rockets in his basement, a dude who knows how to use a slide rule but couldn't find a clitoris in the dictionary.

It wasn't much of a plan but he wanted to send a message to the people who'd ripped him off. You're not the only one with Elephant Crush. He was hoping that it would force their hand, make them announce to the world that they had it, too. Or they might just come after him and try to kill him again. That was a possibility. That's why he needed a disguise.

When he'd looked in the mirror he'd had to admit that this was about as incognito as he'd ever been. It had been Daniel's idea; he'd given Miro Elder Collison's clothes and bike and even the little plastic name tag that you pin on your shirt. The fact that Collison's clothes didn't fit made Miro seem even more authentic. The shirt billowed around his body like a sack and the pants were too short in length and way too big in the waist so they were baggy and crumpled while simultaneously revealing the bleached white tube socks at his ankles.

They rode as a pair. Daniel had insisted. That's the missionary way. Miro had warned him that he might not like what he would see and it could be dangerous—law enforcement was always a concern and there was, obviously, someone who wanted Miro dead—but Daniel was adamant. A solitary missionary might get a second look, but together they wouldn't raise an eyebrow.

They rode along Santa Monica Boulevard, the signs on the storefronts changing from Spanish to Spanglish to Korean to Armenian to English to Russian and then back to English as they moved westward.

Eventually they stopped, locked their bikes in front of a gay bookstore, and walked around the corner into a nondescript shop with a sign that said, "West Hollywood Herbal Cooperative" in small letters on the frosted-glass door. Daniel stopped in front when he saw a little green marijuana leaf decal on the window. He recognized it from all the drug-abuse-resistance-education lectures he'd sat through in high school. He knew that marijuana was bad.

Miro turned to him.

"You might want to wait outside."

Daniel looked hurt.

"Why?"

Miro thought about it.

"I don't know. It might offend your religious beliefs."

"I'm not judgmental. Those are the fundamentalists."

Daniel followed Miro in, expecting to find a den of skeevy-looking Manson followers, all crazy eyes and tattoos, discussing human sacrifice and the violent overthrow of the U.S. government in a fog of noxious smoke while black-light posters burned psychedelic on the walls and some kind rocked-out guitar solo buzzed over the speakers. He was not expecting to see an elderly couple—the man suffering from Parkinson's, she from glaucoma—or the woman in her late forties, her head covered with a scarf to hide that she'd lost her hair in chemotherapy. He wasn't expecting people in wheelchairs, people with eating disorders, AIDS patients, or insomniacs with dark purple bags hanging under their eyes from lack of sleep. There were a couple of people who didn't look obviously afflicted with medical problems but they didn't look dangerous, either. They looked really normal. Daniel also wasn't expecting the low murmur of classical music, or the way the place looked like someone's living room with couches, chairs, and lamps.

Judging by their reaction, the people in the co-op weren't expecting to seeing a couple of Mormon missionaries, either.

As they entered, an older customer wearing a T-shirt that proclaimed him a proud Democrat raised his hands in a gesture as if he were pushing them back out.

"Take it outside. I don't want to hear it."

BAKED

Daniel hesitated, he didn't want any trouble, but Miro just smiled at the man and wagged his finger.

"Don't judge."

An attractive woman with a giant mass of dark curly hair —piled up on her head and straining against a red scrunchy— jumped up from behind the counter when she saw them.

"Miro! You're back!"

"Hi, Barbara."

She gave him a big hug. Then she turned her eyes on Daniel.

"Have you joined a cult or something?"

Miro laughed.

"This is my friend, Daniel."

Barbara extended her hand and Daniel shook it. He noticed that she wasn't wearing a bra under her loose blouse and he watched her breasts wobble beneath the thin cotton as she pumped his arm up and down. It shocked him how warm and strong and fleshy her hand felt in his. He didn't know what to say. He hadn't ever touched a woman like her— an attractive woman who wasn't a relative or a member of his church or a teacher at his high school.

Daniel looked at Barbara, then looked at the floor. Miro laughed. Daniel wasn't sure if he was laughing at him or with him, but he wasn't sure it mattered. Finally, words formed in his mind and he got just enough air from his lungs to propel them out of his mouth.

"Hi."

"Hi."

Barbara turned to Miro.

"I thought you retired after the, um, you know."

195

Barbara bit her lip in a way that made her look slightly embarrassed yet sexy.

"The bullet?"

"Yeah. Ouch. I was worried about you."

Miro grinned and patted his messenger bag.

"How can I retire? I have the Cup winner and I'm going to give you an exclusive."

...

It was raining but Marianna didn't care. She let the rain pelt down on her as she dragged a small suitcase out to the taxi. So what if she got a little wet? There was no way she was taking an umbrella to California. The driver popped the trunk and Marianna hoisted her suitcase and plopped it in. She was traveling light; just a few items of clothing, her passport, and her plane ticket.

Guus opened the back door for her and she bundled in, strapped on the seatbelt and, as the taxi took off, let out a sigh. She still wasn't convinced that this was the best idea. But then, what else could she do? She had to talk to Miro face-to-face.

Guus patted her knee and smiled.

"If you like we can go to the La Brea Tar Pits."

She looked at him. She was so focused on what she had to say to Miro and how she felt about it—her emotions shifting and changing several times a day—that she hadn't considered that they might go sightseeing.

"What?"

"There are lakes of molten tar in Los Angeles. Right in the middle of the city. I've always wanted to see them."

Marianna laughed.

"Why would anyone build a city around a lake of tar?"

Guus shrugged.

"It's an interesting place."

...

Detective Cho scrolled down the Web page on his computer screen and clicked on a window. He watched a video showing the Cannabis Cup being awarded. Except for the lilt of reggae drifting in the background and the absence of tuxedos and gowns, it was kind of like any award ceremony you might see on TV. The winner was announced and a European guy with an accent and a leather jacket came onstage and took the Cup. He grabbed the microphone and asked if anyone had seen Miro. Cho couldn't help it, he chuckled.

"Welcome to the club."

Quijano looked over from his desk.

"You say something?"

Cho hit pause and turned to Quijano.

"The kid wins the Academy Award of marijuana and doesn't even bother to show up and accept it."

"Maybe he was making a political statement. You know? Like Brando sending that Indian chick to make a speech."

"Native American."

"Whatever."

Cho considered it. Had Miro angered the Cannabis Cup people? Would not showing up be a reason for shooting him? He doubted it but it was something they should look into. He liked being thorough.

"You want to call *High Times* magazine and see what they say about it?"

Quijano laughed.

"I'm sure they'll love talking to me."

"Make the call."

Cho was trying to be Zen about the search for Miro but it wasn't working, and it wasn't helping his antacid do its job.

The detectives had dropped in and visited Miro's parents up the coast. They'd left their cards for him, but Miro hadn't called them back or tried to contact them at all. Not that Cho was surprised. What was the guy going to say? Still, you'd think that if the person who shot you was running around shooting other people, you'd be kind of curious about it. Wouldn't you?

Cho wondered if Miro knew the EMT woman or the guy who was murdered with her. And had they been a couple? Was it some kind of weird sex triangle?

It was like Miro had dropped off the planet. Maybe he'd gone underground or crossed the border to Mexico. Cho thought that if someone was trying to kill him, he might go there; that might be a reasonable excuse to go to the land of tacos and tequila. Of course, there was always the possibility that the wrong people had found Miro and now he was taking a dirt nap somewhere in the Mojave.

Cho needed a break in the case. He hoped it wouldn't be another body.

34

VINCENT SLID a green plastic bottle across the table toward Shamus. The bottle looked like something you'd get from a pharmacy, containing some prescription Valtrex, Vicodin, or Lipitor, only this label was clearly marked with a marijuana leaf and the words "Elephant Crush" in rainbow script. Below that it said "Cannabis Cup Winner." Shamus picked it up and looked at it.

"Is this the real shit? Where'd you get it?"

Vincent glared at him.

"You can buy this at the herbal cooperative in West Hollywood."

Vincent emphasized the "H" in herbal, just to be annoying.

Shamus wrestled with the child-proof top and popped it open. He took a sniff. The scent of fresh mangoes drifted into the air.

"Is it for real?"

"What do you think?"

Shamus didn't say anything. He clamped the lid back on the bottle and set it on the table. Vincent sighed and stroked his goatee. He looked thoughtful, in control, but really he wanted to strangle Shamus, choke the life out of him or beat him with a bat, whatever took the longest. Instead, he leaned forward, struggling to keep his voice under control.

"So here's the deal. First you're going to go to that herbal co-op and get this weed from them. *We're* the exclusive sellers, do you understand?"

Shamus nodded.

"Then you're going to find out where the little fucker is and finish the fucking job."

...

Shamus sat in the passenger seat and let Guillermo negotiate the nightmare traffic as they crept back toward West Hollywood from Santa Monica. He was clenching his fists, knuckles white and his nails biting into his palms. His anger pulsed inside him like hot magma. Yeah. He thought he'd killed that motherfucker. He'd put a bullet right into the guy's torso. That usually does the trick. Shamus knew that going for a head shot was a low percentage move. Why risk a miss? Maybe he could've fired another shot or two but that kind of noise just alerts the neighbors. They hear one shot and it could be anything, a car backfiring, an imaginary sound, a dog fart. Crack off a couple rounds and they know it's gunfire and they're peeking out their windows, witnessing the crime, IDing the car, and calling the LAPD.

Shamus told himself he hadn't done anything wrong. He'd done everything right. It was just bad luck that the guy lived to tell the tale.

What he didn't like was being talked down to by Vincent. *Fuck that shit.* He'd got into this line of work so he wouldn't have to deal with a boss and here he was dealing with a boss. Shamus was supposed to be the right-hand man, the go-to guy. Now he was getting scolded like a little bitch.

It really wasn't the way you were supposed to treat employees. It wasn't professional and Shamus thought of himself as a professional. He resisted the urge to pop a cap in Vincent's head. He wanted to. Fuck, yeah. But if he did that he'd have problems finding other people who'd be willing to do business with him. Going psycho might be the way things worked in Mexico, where you could execute someone who bugged you and put his decapitated head in a gym bag, but that was a throwback to the old cowboy days when the cannabis trade was illegal; now, with the semilegal nature of medical marijuana, it was impractical. Nowadays you needed to develop trust. You had to cultivate connections and build a personal network.

The interior of the West Hollywood herbal cooperative was exactly how Shamus had imagined: crappy leftover couches and chairs that looked like refugees from some old-folk's-home salvage sale, some kind of lame art on the wall that looked like dolphins swimming around a dwarf nebula in space, and a large glass counter holding baked goods like banana bread and some kind of whole-grain muffins made with hash oil and oat bran, presumably so the geriatric hippies could get high and still fight constipation. There was also an assortment of homemade candies chock-full of THC. A laser-printed "daily specials" sign was taped to the counter and offered a variety of Sativas, Indicas, and hashish. Highlighted as "highly recommended" was the Cannabis Cup–winning Elephant Crush.

Shamus kept one eye on the security guard as he went up to the counter. An attractive brunette was busy weighing eighths of bud on a scale, then popping them into prescription bottles. She looked up when she saw Shamus.

"Can I help you?"

Shamus spoke quietly yet clearly, keeping a polite, conversational tone to his voice.

"I have a gun. I'm not here to rob you but if you trigger the alarm or alert the guard, I will kill you and then I'll kill him."

The woman blinked. Shamus could tell that she was rattled; he didn't want that. He wanted her to stay calm.

"What do you want?"

"I want all your Elephant Crush and I want to know where you got it."

Shamus watched the woman's eyes dart back and forth, from the security guard then back to him.

"Tell me and you won't have any trouble."

He watched her swallow.

"A friend sold it to me."

"Miro Basinas?"

She hesitated for a moment, then nodded.

"Where can I find your friend?"

"I don't know. Honest. I don't know where he lives."

"He just showed up with the stuff in his car?"

She nodded again. Shamus saw her eyes dart back and forth again, a sign she wasn't being exactly honest. Shamus reached for his gun.

"You want me to shoot the guard?"

She shook her head.

"Actually, he rode a bike."

Shamus tilted his head back, looking down his nose at her. He wanted to appear imperious, intimidating.

"A bike?"

"A bicycle."

"In LA?"

She shrugged.

"I know. I know it's weird."

Shamus squinted his eyes, trying to give her the classic Clint Eastwood glare.

"I don't believe you."

He could see her hands trembling.

"It's true. I swear. He was dressed like one of those Mormon guys. Like a missionary."

...

Guillermo cracked the window and exhaled. This totally fucking sucked. Not that it was so bad to be sampling a little of the Elephant Crush that Vincent had given him—it was easily the best weed he'd ever had the privilege of blazin'—but it truly sucked that he was stuck in the car. That had been Damon's job. Damon was the fucking chauffeur. But now he was here, his ass asleep and the THC riding the swelling tide of his nervous system turning the pinprick tingle of bad circulation in his legs into a kind of needle-jab irritation. *Since when am I Shamus's bitch?*

Guillermo didn't want to end up like Damon. He wasn't going to be the butt of the joke, the whipping boy, the guy everyone made fun of. And he wasn't going to sit around waiting to drive Shamus to and fro like some kind of fucking chump. Besides, this was his chance to prove himself. If you want to be a star you have to step onto the stage. That's what they always said on that singing show he watched on TV.

That's what Damon had never understood. Guillermo needed to show Shamus that he wasn't like that fat freak. He wasn't frontin' or half-steppin' or any of that bogus bullshit, he was OG through and through, as OG as a white boy from Encino could get.

Guillermo got out of the car and popped the trunk. He pulled Shamus's AK-47 out from under a couple of blankets, snapped back the bolt, and calmly walked towards the co-op.

It was his time to shine.

...

Miro blinked. He read the e-mail from Guus again. The Dutchman was flying, in the air at this exact moment, on his way to save the day. And he was bringing a surprise. Miro sat in the swivel chair in the overly air-conditioned Kinko's business center and wondered what that cryptic message meant. Was he bringing some kind of professional hitman? A cleaner? Or did he have some kind of Interpol agent on his side?

Miro checked the ETA and realized that the plane would be landing that night.

"Fuck."

Daniel looked up from a weekly magazine—one of those free newsprint papers that are piled up in restaurants and CD stores—where he'd been scanning the ads in the back.

"What does 'full release' mean?"

"It means what you think it means."

"Really?"

Miro logged off the computer and stood.

"C'mon. I need to get my car."

...

Daniel and Miro pedaled up to the grotty little house on a cul-de-sac in Echo Park, locked their bikes next to a tree, and headed to the door. Miro's old Mercedes sat in the driveway. Daniel could hear some kind of strange music—Arabic sounding or Indian, mixed with one of the show tunes he remembered from a high school production of *The Fantasticks*—drifting out of the house along with a wall of burbling conversation. He turned to Miro.

"You sure this is okay?"

Miro gave him a reassuring smile and nodded toward the Benz.

"Relax. We're invited. Besides, that's my car."

...

Rupert opened the door and doubled over laughing like he'd taken a punch to the solar plexus. Miro patted him on the head.

"Don't wet yourself."

"Miro. What the fuck?"

Stacey stuck her head around the corner to see what all the hooting was about. When she saw Miro and Daniel standing there in their white short-sleeved shirts and ties her jaw dropped.

"What the fuck?"

Daniel fidgeted. Miro returned Stacey's stare.

"What?"

"You look like you joined a cult."

Miro looked Rupert in the eye and kept his expression blank, almost dour.

"A near-death experience will do that."
Rupert stopped laughing.
"You're scaring me, man."
Miro smiled.
"I need my car."
Stacey pointed at Daniel.
"He looks like a real one."
"He is."

...

It was, in many ways, a typical hipster party in a typical hipster home. A late-afternoon barbecue that might last until four in the morning depending on the vibe of the party, the strength of the drugs, and the endurance of the guests. The decor was classic alt-rock; a collection of random thrift-store furniture, framed movie posters from French New Wave films like *Masculine/Feminine,* a couple of guitar amps, a bookcase filled with old pulp-fiction paperbacks and new DVDs, a hand-woven Mexican basket filled with maracas and tambourines, a Vibraslap on top of the TV. Slightly grungy but boasting a kind of comforting retro-domesticity.

A dozen hipsters grazed in the dining room, crowding around a table loaded with bowls of guacamole, salsa, chips, carrot sticks, and *croquetas* from Porto's Cuban bakery in Glendale. The chatter was typical of these kinds of parties. Discussing the formation or dissipation of local rock bands like they were the weather, one low pressure system moving in, looking for a drummer, another band collapsing under the cold front of a nationwide tour. The latest indie films were parsed, cult novels discussed, and underground art shows reviewed. It was a cultured group.

Miro knew almost everyone there. Hadn't they been to a party at his house once? Hadn't he gone to their shows and provided high-grade cannabis to them? These had once been his people, the tribe he belonged to. But since the shooting he hadn't heard from any of them and now that he was back, dressed like some kind of freak, he realized that perhaps he'd never really fit in. *The tribe has spoken.*

A vinyl record spun on the turntable. Daniel stopped and stared at it. "That's a record?"

Rupert did a double take, shooting a curious look at Miro.

Miro shrugged. "Kids."

Daniel whispered to Miro.

"I've never seen a record before. Not in real life anyway."

The record was some kind of jazz, but not the bebop kind or the soothing elevator kind; this was experimental hooting, tooting, and clanging with a Bollywood beat. It was Rupert showing off his eclectic tastes. Miro would've put on some reggae, or maybe some Brazilian music, something soothing and lively and positive, but it wasn't his party.

Rupert plopped down on the couch. Miro sat down in an overstuffed chair across from him, his messenger bag swinging out and hitting the neck of a Rickenbacker twelve-string causing it to chime out a dissonant chord as it banged into the Gretsch Duo Jet on the stand next to it. Rupert looked dismayed.

"Those are collectible."

"Sorry."

Daniel sat on the couch next to Rupert as Stacey drifted off.

There were a few people huddled around the coffee table, passing around a large plastic bag filled with smoke. Daniel realized it was marijuana. He'd always assumed that you smoked it in a pipe or rolled it up in paper like a cigarette. Like in the movies. But there they were, carefully grinding up the leaves and putting it in some kind of machine and then sucking the smoke out of a big balloon. The bag came his way and he shook his head. He noticed that Miro wasn't smoking, either. In fact, Miro didn't do much of anything: he didn't drink alcohol or eat red meat. He claimed it was because his wound needed time to heal properly and Daniel had teased him, saying he was becoming a Mormon.

Miro turned to him.

"Relax. Go get something to eat."

"Maybe I'll drink a beer."

He'd gotten used to having a beer with Lenny at the end of his shift on the taco truck. He liked the taste of it; it complimented the flavors of a burrito and it made him feel happy. He didn't know why his church was anti-beer. It was, like Miro said about marijuana, made from ingredients God put on the planet. Why wouldn't God want people to drink beer and be happy?

He excused himself and walked into the kitchen.

The party was crowded but people moved out of the way when he approached, as if he were contagious, a leper in his missionary outfit.

Daniel reached into the ice chest and pulled out a beer, one from Mexico. As he was looking for the bottle opener, he heard a husky voice behind him.

"That one needs a little squirt of lime."
Daniel turned toward the voice.

...

Miro sat on the couch and watched Daniel. He had a brief
flash where he felt like he was watching a show on the Nature channel. He saw the prey, the innocent little Mormon
in his goofy white shirt and tie, standing in Rupert's kitchen
drinking a beer like a baby ibex at the watering hole. Circling
Daniel was the predator. It wasn't a lion or a cheetah, it was
a wild cat named Aimée LeClerq, a real star, a multimillionaire singer who made her career trading on a kinky sexpot
image to match her infamously husky voice. She was famous
for sexualizing everything she touched. She'd even written a
best-selling illustrated instructional pop-up book about fella-
tio called *Blow by Blow*. She'd starred in several films and even
posed topless on the cover of *Vanity Fair*. But her career had
gone into a slow fade after she hit forty. Now, fast approaching fifty, she devoted most of her energy to promoting animal rights and a vegan lifestyle.

Miro tapped Rupert on the shoulder.

"What's she doing here?"

Rupert grinned.

"She's starting a label and they're thinking about sign-
ing us."

"That's great."

Rupert shrugged and acted like he was stifling a yawn,
as if getting a recording contract was just some necessary evil
that true artists had to subject themselves to in order to get
their music to the people.

"If she lets us do the record our way."

Rupert stood and trudged off to the kitchen, and Miro turned his attention back to the scene unfolding in front of him. He would be the first to admit that human sexuality—the complex psychology of men and women mixed with the hormonal instincts more common in animal behavior—baffled him. A plant blooms and pollen drifts in the air, or bees, butterflies, and bats carry it from flower to flower; there's no ritual or etiquette to it, no sense of ownership or guilt. It just happens on the breeze. Like that fling he'd had in Amsterdam, a sexual encounter that floated into his life on the wind and then drifted away. There had been something different about that one, though. It's rare for two people to bring out the flora in each other.

Aimée, wearing a silk T-shirt that showed her nipples protruding through the sheer, clingy fabric, sidled up to Daniel. It was interesting to watch, Miro had to admit, as she reeled him in, laughing, touching his arm, working her sex magic, bewitching the teen. Miro wished he'd had an animal behaviorist with him, someone who could decode the finer points of the dance, point out the subtle mating cues. But then maybe he didn't need an expert because from across the room Miro could see an erection stretching the fabric of the young Mormon's church-mandated trousers.

35

"OH MAGOO, you've done it again."

Cho had to admit that Quijano did a pretty great imitation of Jim Backus. Cho laughed and shook his head as Quijano reached for the computer mouse.

"I've got to see this again. This shit is classic."

Quijano dragged the tab back on the computer screen, clicked PLAY, and they watched the scene unfold for a third time. It was hall of fame material, some of the best surveillance camera footage Cho had ever seen. He reminded himself to save a copy to show at the precinct Christmas party.

The camera was placed almost perfectly, looking down from a high angle as a Latino man stood at the counter talking to the female proprietor. A security guard loafed by the door, his legs crossed, looking at some freshly scooped snot from his nose, glistening on the tip of his pinky.

All in all, a pretty normal exchange was taking place; business as usual at the herbal co-op. That is until Mr. Magoo entered the scene carrying an AK-47.

Cho hit PAUSE. In the frozen frame he could see the Latino customer turning toward Mr. Magoo with the AK, a slight look of recognition flashing across his face. Cho couldn't see the proprietor's face from this angle, he could only guess what she was thinking as she reached down and triggered the silent alarm.

"C'mon, man," Quijano complained.

"Sorry. I just thought I'd do a little police work while you're enjoying the show."

Quijano snorted.

"Right."

Cho clicked it forward a few frames.

On the surveillance tape they watched the security guard finally noticing that someone has just walked into the store with a giant automatic assault rifle in his hands. The guard started to raise his hands in surrender but then, tragically, changed his mind.

"First instinct was the best."

"Usually is."

Cho clicked and the pictures slowed down.

It was Darwin's theory of evolution in action, unfolding on the surveillance tape, captured as it happened, digitized for posterity. The security guard says something as he starts to pull his Taser. Mr. Magoo spins, swinging the AK with him, but before he can get off a shot the Taser darts hit him in the chest and he starts to jiggle and shit himself as his knees buckle and he hits the floor. That's when the Latino at the counter pulls a handgun and shoots the guard in the heart.

Then, from Cho's perspective, it got interesting. The Latino started yelling at Mr. Magoo, waving his arms around, pointing to the surveillance camera. Mr. Magoo yanks the darts out of his chest and then swings the assault rifle up, giv-

ing the camera an excellent view of his face, and pulls the trigger, spraying a burst of bullets at the camera.

At that point the image goes black.

Quijano doubled over laughing.

"Oh my God, that's the funniest thing I've ever seen."

Cho thought about the murdered guard and decided it
wasn't that funny, not really. He shook his head at Quijano.

"You're a sick fuck, you know that."

Cho had a queasy feeling in his stomach that was un-
related to the In-N-Out Double-Double animal style he'd
demolished for lunch. Preliminary ballistics had tied the handgun that the Latino male had used to dispatch the security
guard with the same one that killed the EMT, the painter in
the river, and wounded Miro. This was the shooter. Now he
just needed to put a name to the face.

...

Ted sat in his car and waited. He wasn't sure what, exactly,
he planned to do, but he was sure that, somehow, Fran's death
had something to do with the skateboarder. Or maybe not.
Maybe he was wrong. It was a hunch and he didn't have any
other ideas. The police hadn't been helpful. They didn't know
anything about any backpack—Ted hadn't found it in Fran's
apartment or her locker—and they weren't interested in the
stolen painting from her living room wall. They were pretty
sure it was an open-and-shut case of breaking and entering
gone haywire. So instead of pursuing leads, the Glendale
Police Department was squabbling over jurisdiction with the
LAPD, trying to keep the case with them even though ballistics had proven Fran's murder was connected to several others

in Los Angeles. And when they weren't bickering with each other about that, the sworn officers of California law enforcement were spending their energies coming up with jokes, punch lines, and double entendres involving a firewoman with a strap-on and a hapless burglar. At least they'd figured that much out: crime scene investigators had found evidence that the front-door lock had been jimmied.

Ted knew that if it'd been him, Fran would've tried to get to the bottom of it. They might not have been the best of friends but they were partners.

Ted spotted the skateboarder a block or two away. The kid was wearing a sling that was rigged to be a shoulder immobilizer, meaning he must've cracked the shoulder joint or his collarbone when he wiped out, but he was still riding his board.

He didn't mean to tackle the kid. But the little fucker didn't stop when Ted asked him to. He'd just kept rolling, flashing his middle finger from his good hand as he rumbled past. So Ted ran after him and knocked him to the ground. It wouldn't be good for that shoulder joint, Ted knew. The kid knew it, too, because he writhed on the ground in pain.

"Motherfucker."

"Take it easy. You're only going to make it worse by moving around."

"Fuck you. I'm going to sue you."

"I asked you to stop."

The kid stopped moving when Ted showed him the gun. He had to do it discreetly; he didn't want anyone driving by to notice it.

"Don't kill me, man. I'm not holding."

Ted hadn't thought about killing anyone. The gun was just a prop, a visual aid to keep the kid from screaming, but now that the subject had been broached, Ted figured he should use it to his advantage.

"Holding?"

"Yeah. I don't got nothing."

Ted nodded.

"That's too bad."

"If I had anything, dude, I'd fucking give it to you."

"What was in your backpack the other day?"

Ted saw a flicker of recognition flash on the kid's face.

"Who are you?"

"Just answer the question. What was it? Coke?"

The kid shook his head. "Weed."

"Who were you taking it to?"

The kid shook his head.

"Dude. Do yourself a fucking favor and drop it."

Ted reached out a hand and gently poked the kid right where the acromion connects with the clavicle. The kid screamed in pain and scooted back.

"Who?" Ted asked again.

"He'll fucking kill you. Then he'll kill me."

Ted reached out again, positioning his finger, ready to tap the spot on the collarbone. The kid couldn't help himself, he blurted out a name.

"Shamus. Shamus Noriega."

...

Looking for trouble is a lot like shopping. You go from place to place, location to location, looking for that special something. Sometimes nothing looks right, other times they just don't have anything in your size. But when you find the perfect fit, when you can just erupt in an explosion of blood and fists and full-on balls-to-the-wall mayhem, well, for Shamus it was better than any drink or drug he'd ever taken. It was better than sex. And sometimes he felt that he enjoyed the shopping for trouble as much as the havoc itself.

But as the day wore on and they still hadn't come across any Mormon missionaries, he was starting to get grumpy.

Shamus turned to Guillermo.

"How come you see these Mormon kids every fucking day and then when you want to find one, they're nowhere?"

Guillermo turned the car off San Fernando Road onto Eagle Rock Boulevard.

"It's like with cops. They're never around when you need one."

Shamus made a face.

"What do you need a cop for?"

Guillermo shrugged.

"It's something my mom says."

"Why does your mom need a fucking cop?"

"It's just an expression. You wanna stop at Tommy's or something?"

Shamus scowled.

"Keep driving."

Now was not the time to stop for lunch.

...

Cho held a printout of the security camera footage from the herbal cooperative. It was a perfectly clear picture of a neatly dressed Latino holding a .45. Cho didn't know who the guy was—Quijano kept calling him the "weed whacker"—but he was going to find out.

Cho slid the picture across his desk and sighed. It was drugs. Of course. It's always drugs. *Always.* It was so predictable. Drugs were the irksome gas bag at the party, sucking the air out of the room, boring the shit out of law enforcement—a waste of time and energy, a stone fucking brain-drain. Cho wished the government would get off its ass and legalize drugs. At least *decriminalize* them. If the crumbs couldn't make any money dealing them, well, organized crime as we know it, the entire criminal underground, would find themselves struggling to make ends meet. Counterfeiting, prostitution, extortion, and trafficking in human beings only paid so much. Drugs were the moneymaker. Take that away and suddenly being a criminal isn't such an attractive lifestyle. No bling, no Hummers, no more bottles of Cristal and stable of foxy hos. The gangbangers were right, it *was* all about the Benjamins. Take that away, and you suddenly have a more civil society.

Cho leaned back in his desk chair and wished he could investigate a crime that wasn't connected with drugs, like a good old-fashioned gem heist or a payroll robbery, but that was a fantasy stuck in his brain from reading too many old detective novels, that wasn't reality. The truth was all drugs, all the time. Three hundred and sixty-five days a year. Twenty-four seven. Even a bank job was connected to drugs 99.999 percent of the time. It took all the fun out of being a detective. Not that every case was connected with drugs; there would always be an assortment of parasites, leeches, and bloodsucking freaks feeding off society, but legalizing the shit would go a long way toward emptying out the prisons and letting law enforcement concentrate on real crimes.

Detective Cho had been a logic machine since he was a little kid. It was just the way his brain worked. He had a knack for linking A to B to C, for following a thread from one end to the other. It wasn't like he was a genius, he just understood that things happen for a reason: every action is connected to something. It's the law of karma. *There is always a motive.* Sometimes the motive was stupid, like the time the guy chopped up his neighbor and tried to flush his body down the toilet because he'd borrowed a hedge trimmer and neglected to return it. The Roto-Rooter guy who had come to clean out the backed-up toilet discovered an intact jawbone blocking the pipe. Of course they discovered a meth lab in the murderer's house. How could they not?

Sometimes the motive was complex. This particular mess looked complicated but Cho was certain that underneath it, at the core, it was something very simple. Something like award-winning marijuana.

Cho's cold was gone but it had been replaced by a burning indigestion that put a vice grip on his stomach. He knew what his wife would say: that his career caused lifestyle choices that led him to be stressed out, undernourished from fast food and alcohol, and susceptible to illness. She wanted him to study Tai Chi or yoga and learn to relax; he wanted to learn karate and put his fucking head through a concrete block.

...

Shamus saw them first. A pair of missionaries pedaling down York Boulevard in Highland Park.

Shamus turned to Guillermo.

"Hit 'em."

"What?"

"Run 'em down."

Guillermo looked at Shamus.

"It'll kill them."

Shamus shrugged.

"Try to be gentle."

Guillermo checked his rearview, saw that no one was behind them, and angled the SUV so that he cut the missionaries off and forced them to crash into the curb.

The Mormons swerved in a futile attempt to avoid getting mashed but they only succeeded in colliding with each other and went tumbling onto the sidewalk.

Guillermo pulled over and Shamus jumped out of the SUV. A casual observer might've thought he was stopping to offer a helping hand or to give his insurance information to the unfortunate young men sprawled on the pavement. Maybe he was even going to give them a ride to the emergency room.

But that's no fun.

One of the Mormons was young and looked like a twelve-year-old reject from Junior ROTC. He had reddish hair buzzed military style and lay on the ground holding his wrist, which was bent at a strange angle, the bone broken and forming a lump where his wristwatch should be.

The other Mormon was older, his face flecked with acne, his hair glistening with Brylcreem. He glared at Shamus.

"What the hell, man?"

Shamus walked over and kicked him a couple times in the ribs. The Mormon holding his broken wrist shouted.

"Hey!"

Shamus turned to him. "My friend has gun. Now shut your mouth and get in the fucking car."

...

Miro watched as the party continued. Somehow, Daniel and the famous singer had gotten cozy, sitting in the corner talking about various interpretations of the Old Testament versus the New Testament and the Book of Mormon. Next to Miro, pretty girls with dark bangs and designer eyewear perched on the edge of the sofa as they drank wine and talked about music and restaurants and real estate with shaggy boys wearing cardigans over T-shirts logo'ed with names of obscure bands. Everyone wore cool shoes.

No one danced. They were all too self-consciously cool for anything that looked remotely passionate. Instead, they mingled and flirted, ate mini samosas and pot stickers from Fresh and Easy, dug into slabs of mediocre brie from Trader Joe's, dipped chips into salsa, uncorked wine, stepped outside to smoke cigarettes—even though smoking pot was perfectly acceptable inside the house—and basically postured the night away.

Miro looked at his watch. Guus's flight would be arriving in about an hour.

Miro walked up to Daniel and Aimée.

"I've got to go to the airport."

Daniel seemed torn. He looked at Aimée, staring at the outline of her left nipple peeking through her shirt, then looked at Miro. But before he could say anything, Aimée turned to Miro.

"I'll take care of him."

She said it in a way that made Daniel gulp. Miro nodded. "Okay, then. I'll be in touch."

...

Cho drove alone. It wasn't that he didn't trust his partner—in fact, he thought that if Quijano would stop posturing and pretending he was some tough-guy cop he'd seen on television, he'd make a fine detective—but the man he was going to see wasn't the type who suffered fools.

Cho found a space on the street and pulled into it. He killed the engine and sat there for a moment, letting everything go quiet, allowing his brain to spin. That's how it worked for him. Some detectives need clear motives and hard evidence. They need to have all the ducks in a row—a murder weapon, fingerprints, eyewitnesses, and confessions—before they figure a case out. But that wasn't the way Cho was wired; given enough information, his brain would turn into a logic machine, start parsing and processing like a kind of intuitive computer, connecting the dots, seeing through the bullshit, unraveling the lies, waiting for that one moment of clarity when everything lined up and he saw the truth.

Cho got out of his car and walked halfway down the block, past a botanica and a store that sold piñatas. Brightly colored figures of Batman, Sponge Bob, and the Powerpuff Girls dangled and danced from the awning and he had to fight the impulse to bust one open just to watch the candy fall out.

When he got to Chilango's Body Shop, he stepped over a puddle of motor oil and walked past a dozen or so cars scattered around the lot like heaps of crumpled laundry. He went to the office door and opened it slowly, acting casual. His coming here was surprise enough, he didn't want to get shot.

The office was what you'd expect. Piles of invoices and paperwork dumped on a metal desk, boxes of specialty paint stacked against a wall. An air conditioner thrummed in the window and an older Latino man chatted in rapid-fire Spanish on his cell phone. When the Latino saw Cho standing in his doorway, he snapped the phone shut without saying goodbye. His eyes narrowed and he glared at Cho.

"Detective."

Cho didn't expect a smile or a handshake, so he didn't offer one.

"Got a minute?"

The Latino nodded and sat up. He adjusted his guayabera, revealing faded neck tattoos under the collar.

"Your car need a custom paint job?"

"Something like that."

Cho stepped into the room and closed the door behind him. There was a Siamese cat asleep on the only other chair in the office so Cho didn't bother sitting. He pulled out the picture of the gunman in the herbal cooperative and handed it to the old man.

"Know him?"

The old man burst out laughing.

"You think this is funny, *pendejo*? You're fucking with me?"

"Why do you say that?"

The old man stroked his bushy gray mustache and adjusted the Dodgers cap on his head. "You looking for him?"

Cho nodded.

The old man chuckled. He smiled up at Cho.

"Nothing would make me happier than to see this *pinche puñatero* go down."

"So he's not one of yours?"

"He's nobody's."

Cho was surprised. He'd assumed the perp was affiliated with one of the gangs in the area.

"Why not?"

The old man shrugged.

"*Mala leche.*"

"He got a name?"

The old man became suddenly serious. His eyes locked with Cho's and his voice turned hard.

"One thing. I tell you his name, you gotta bury the motherfucker. That's the kind of guy he is."

Cho spread his hands in a noncommittal gesture.

"I'll see what I can do."

...

"These handcuffs are gay."

Shamus looked at the two Mormon missionaries sitting next to each other on the little bed. The one with the broken arm—and it was really swelling now—had his damaged limb handcuffed to the bed frame, while the other one, the one who thought he was tough, had his hands cuffed in front of him.

"Gay?"

"They're furry."

The tough Mormon kid held up his cuffs and showed Shamus the leopard-print fur handcuffs.

"They're only gay if they turn you on."

Shamus saw the Mormon's face flush bright red. He stroked his goatee and considered his options. While it would be easier to get the young kid with the broken arm to talk, it would be much more humiliating for the kid who thought he was a hard guy.

"Would you be more comfortable if I stripped you naked?"

The boys shook their heads.

"We're fine."

The young one, the one with the broken arm, finally said something.

"You can let us go. We won't tell anyone about the accident."

Shamus nodded.

"That's very generous."

The older one glared at Shamus.

"Why are we here? You ran us over."

Shamus punched him, hard, in the face. The kid caromed backward, blood spurting out of his nose. The Mormon with the broken wrist began crying. Shamus rubbed his hand and spoke calmly.

"Let's talk."

...

"No fucking cucumber cups."

The caterer looked at Vincent. "People love cucumber cups."

Vincent shook his head.

"They're like mini quiches. They cheapen everything."

"What about skewers? Like a Thai thing with a dipping sauce?"

"I don't know. You gotta hold a skewer in one hand and then a glass of champagne in the other. How can I shake hands? What if I want to point something out? I either spill my drink or I blind somebody with the stick."

The caterer pushed her hair back behind her ear and shoved her glasses up on her nose.

"Why don't you tell me what your dream appetizers would be and we'll work from that."

"I like a nice vegan spring roll. Fresh veggies wrapped in tofu skin. Something like that."

She made a note on a legal pad and nodded.

"How about mini sliders? You know, tiny hamburgers?"

Vincent shook his head.

"This isn't fucking White Castle."

"What about caviar? Little blinis topped with sevruga?"

"I'd rather do sushi."

"Duck confit taquitos?"

"Too messy."

The caterer put down her pad and pencil.

"Okay. Tell me, what do you want to accomplish with this event?"

Vincent leaned back in his chair and adopted a philosophical pose, like a man who enjoys nothing more than pondering the important questions of the day.

"What I want is for people to talk about this night. I want them to tell their friends about this amazing evening at the Compassion Club. It all has to blow their mind. The wine, the food, the decor, and especially the amazing cannabis."

The caterer nodded.

"We could make some special brownies. Grilled tofu and vegetables. A sprout salad. You know, do a Woodstock inspired barbecue-type thing."

Vincent sighed. He was about to tell her to leave, that he wasn't a hippie and this wasn't the sixties, when he got an idea. He opened a desk drawer, reached in, and pulled out a green plastic vial.

"Go home. Smoke this. Then talk to me about the appetizers."

He waved the vial in front of her.

"This is the star of the show."

...

Shamus had to admit that the tough kid could take a beating. But everyone has their weak spot. Shamus had spotted the missionary's when he had complained about the fake-leopard-fur handcuffs, so when he threatened to go "Abu Ghraib" on them—stripping them and making them butt fuck each other—he knew the kid would talk.

As it turned out, the Mormons didn't know much. But they knew there was a guy who lived by himself in an LDS-rented apartment on San Fernando Road. He was some kind of outcast and was probably the guy they were looking for. They didn't have the exact address but they'd ridden by the building a few times.

Shamus decided to check it out. If Miro was there, hiding out with some Mormon loser, well, he'd just have to kill both of them. Shamus didn't think he'd kill these Mormon boys; they'd been blindfolded when he brought them to the grow house, they didn't know where they were, and he figured they were too scared to get a good look at him anyway. Or maybe he would kill them. He'd figure it out later.

Shamus turned to the Mormons.

"I'm gonna go see if you're telling me the truth. For your sake, you better be."

"He needs to go to the hospital."

"Yeah, we'll see about that later."

As Shamus opened the door to leave, he saw Blanca, the old Mexican housewife who took care of the grow house, standing in the hallway holding a pump-action twelve-gauge shotgun in one hand and a bucket and scrub brush in the other.

Blanca pointed the gun at the older Mormon boy.

"*Limpiar mi piso.*"

Shamus laughed. The Mormon looked at him, confused. "What'd she say?"

"Guess you're going to do some God work after all. She wants you to scrub the floors."

36

IRO DIDN'T understand Rupert's reluctance to hand over the keys. He'd lent him the Mercedes making it clear that once he felt better he'd want it back. But Rupert acted like it was his car now; he'd even put a bumper sticker on the back that said "Drum Machines Have No Soul." That really annoyed Miro. He hated bumper stickers in general, and on principal, and just didn't understand why anyone would defile a classic car with free advertising for a lost cause. *Besides, what was wrong with a drum machine?*

Miro drove west on the 105, heading towards LAX, trying to think of something to do with Guus. He couldn't take him back to the roach-infested apartment, could he? And what about the cannabis? Except for the little bit he'd gotten from Amin, it was gone. There were other problems, too. The police were looking for him. People had been murdered. These are the kind of things that can put a damper on a vacation.

...

Marianna felt her stomach lurch. She wasn't sure if it was the baby kicking or her nerves getting ready to blossom into a full-blown panic attack. Her mind was racing, spinning out various scenarios that involved Miro being married to a supermodel and having nine children, or Miro being gay and having a boyfriend who was a movie star, or Miro being some kind of Hollywood playboy who swapped beautiful young women in and out of his bed every night.

She had a vision of Miro coming to the airport with a Vegas showgirl on one arm and a porn star on the other. What did she really know about him? What if he was involved with one of the flight attendants on the plane? What if he didn't really like her, but he'd been stoned and in Amsterdam so why not have a fling?

Marianna popped a peppermint into her mouth and resisted the urge to puke all over the polished floor of the Customs area. Guus turned and gave her an encouraging smile and a pat on the shoulder.

"I'm sure he'll be happy to see you."

Marianna smiled back; was her anxiety so obvious? How could Guus be so confident? She wasn't sure that Miro would be happy to see her; there are no guarantees in life and even fewer in love, but she'd come this far, the here and now beckoned, so she grabbed the handle of her wheelie suitcase and tugged it toward the exit and whatever Los Angeles had in store for her.

...

You'd be surprised how many people smile at you when you're dressed up like a Mormon missionary. It was like wearing a fucking Boy Scout uniform. Little old ladies grinned and men in suits nodded assuredly; it was as if the Mission was some kind of apprenticeship program designed to spit out well-groomed and polite young junior vice presidents of regional sales.

Usually nobody paid any attention to him at the airport. He would blend into the blur of people coming and going. But put on a clean white shirt and clip on a tie and all of a sudden you're an upstanding citizen, everybody's friend. Miro thought it was funny how Rupert and his hipster friends had been just the opposite, acting like he had become leprotic, a carrier of some fatal disease that caused terminal uncoolness.

Flights arrived. Passengers deplaned. An unbroken stream of slightly disoriented travelers drifted out of Customs and rolled their bags toward the terminal exits and ground transportation beyond.

Miro saw Guus first, the lanky Dutchman distinctive in his black leather jacket, his thick eyeglasses scanning the crowd. Miro straightened his clip-on and raised his hand to wave. That's when he noticed a swirl of bright red curls—wrapped with a bright green scarf—bouncing on top of the head of the most beautiful woman he'd ever seen. He felt his heart skip a beat.

...

Once Aimée LeClerq learned that Daniel was a virgin she bundled him into her chauffeured limo and absconded with him to her Italianate mansion in the Hollywood Hills.

The ride in the car was excruciating. Daniel sat next to the sultry pop star, inhaling the exotic spice of her perfume and looking at her beautiful face, the ambient light from the street somehow softening the age lines around her eyes. Even though he sat rigid—straight up and down and buckled tightly into his seat—he was drawn to her as if she had a magnetic pull or some kind of sexual centrifugal force that aligned his molecules and gave them a tug. As much as he tried to resist— and let's be perfectly honest here, he didn't try that hard— he couldn't help it, she turned on his sap machine.

Aimée looked at him and smiled. She reached a hand over and stroked his head, playing with his sandy hair. Her fingers crackled with energy and it sent a shiver down his spine all the way to the base of his balls. He'd only felt something like this once before, and that was when his feet slipped off the pedals and he stunned his scrotum against the bike frame.

"Mmmm. You are fresh. How old are you?"

Daniel swallowed.

"Eighteen."

"And it's really your first time?"

"In a limo?"

She laughed and smiled sweetly at him, as if he was some kind of puppy in a pet store window.

"Cute."

He reached out toward her, tentative, as if she might suddenly turn on him and bite off his arm. His finger touched her shoulder, lightly, as if she might not be real, his hand moist and trembling. She shifted in her seat.

"It's okay. Everyone's nervous their first time."

"I don't even touch myself."

She looked at him.

"What?"

"We're not supposed to touch ourselves, you know. We're not supposed to waste any sap."

Aimée smiled.

"That's very Tantric."

Daniel blinked at her. She stroked his cheek.

"I'll explain later."

"Okay."

She ran the tip of her index finger over his lips.

"But you're a young man. What do you do if you can't touch yourself?"

Daniel felt himself blushing, a rush of heat to his face, but he couldn't help himself, he told her the truth. For some reason he thought Aimée LeClerq would understand.

"I have to tie myself to the bed so I don't do anything."

Aimée's eyes lit up.

"Do you like tying yourself up?"

Daniel gulped and nodded.

And that's when Aimée LeClerq, multimillionaire pop star and sex icon to a generation, reached out, took Daniel's trembling hand and slid it into her blouse so that it was cupping one of the world's most famous silicone-enhanced breasts.

Daniel gasped. It was exactly like what the bishop had said. He felt his sap rising urgently, like it was being squeezed out of a tube. He squirmed in his seat. Aimée smiled.

"Oh, you poor thing."

She reached over and popped the buckle on his seatbelt, then shifted on the limo seat, slid down on her back, lifted her ass, pulled her panties off, and wrapped her personal-trainer-toned thighs around his torso.

"Come on. Let's make you a man. Get it out and stick it in."

...

It didn't take Ted long to locate the little house in Atwater Village. He had a friend who worked in the Department of Water and Power billing department who was happy to violate federal law and give him the address of the building where Shamus Noriega paid the water bill.

Ted parked his car a couple of houses away and sat there. He rolled down the window and scanned the street. It didn't seem like the kind of neighborhood a drug dealer would live in. Cute bungalows nestled under the trees; a couple of old ladies walked their chihuahuas. It was the picture of suburbia.

Ted pulled the Glock out of his jacket pocket and looked at it. He knew from movies that you needed to take the safety off to fire the thing but he didn't know which button was the safety. He wasn't even sure it was loaded. He pushed a lever and the magazine dropped out. It certainly looked loaded, there were bullet-looking things in there. He slipped the magazine back in and put the gun in his pocket. Hopefully he wouldn't have to shoot anybody.

...

The freeway was relatively uncrowded at this time of day. Marianna looked at Miro as he drove. She was feeling disconnected from reality. A strange city, this man she hardly knew, and this other person growing and moving around inside her body. It had taken Marianna a moment to recognize Miro. There was something about the goofy haircut, the glasses, and the cheap tie and short-sleeved white shirt that she hadn't expected. He looked like a cartoon caricature of a science nerd. Why was he dressed like that? Is this how he normally looked?

Now that they were in the car and she could see him up close, she was sure it was him. There was no denying the spark she felt between them, the attraction that pulled her toward him like they were propelled by an emotional-particle accelerator.

Miro peeked in her direction as he drove. She smiled at him, as if to reassure him that she had no bad intentions, that she didn't want anything from him, that she had come in peace.

Guus sat in the backseat and looked out the window.

"This is the famous traffic?"

Miro glanced in the rearview mirror.

"We're in the carpool lane."

Miro reached over and took Marianna's hand, feeling her soft warm skin, and gave her a reassuring squeeze. Marianna smiled at him.

"I probably gave you a shock."

Miro smiled back.

"Maybe I needed one."

Guus rolled down his window, took a sniff of freeway air, then rolled it back up.

"Does Los Angeles always smell like Japanese food?"

Miro laughed.

"That's the car. It runs on vegetable oil."

The carpool lane separated from the freeway—allowing a high-speed transition from the 105 to the 110—becoming a kind of futuristic flying buttress, leaping out into space high above the ground, then plunging down toward the city like a bobsled track. At its apex, the point just before the plunge, the Los Angeles skyline stood out, jutting up, a cluster of skyscrapers.

Marianna gasped.

"That is Los Angeles?"

Miro let the sunshine of her accent fill him, soaking it in, not realizing how much he'd missed it. Then he told her the truth, sweeping his hand in front of the windshield, indicating the vista from the ocean to the distant mountains.

"It's all Los Angeles."

Marianna took it in.

"*Puta merda.*"

Miro smiled and began merging into the crush of downtown traffic, the Mercedes's exhaust leaving the faint scent of tempura in the air.

...

Three times Ted had to piss in a Starbucks tall-size cup, discreetly open the door, and pour his urine out onto the curb. He was new to stakeouts, he didn't think about how guzzling bottled water out of boredom and drinking a double soy latte could cause severe bladder discomfort as the afternoon turned to evening and the evening turned to night.

Even if you have a cup to piss in, it's still not the easiest thing to do when you're sitting in your car. The angle is all wrong, gravity worked against him, and splash-back ricocheted onto his pants and the floor and basically made the car smell like some vagrant was living there. The pile of wrappers from the energy bars he'd been gnawing on didn't help. The heat seemed to make the boredom of sitting there even more boring, like some kind of tedium magnifier, and a couple of times Ted found himself drifting off to sleep, his eyelids slowly rolling down like those heavy steel security doors that protect storefronts at night.

...

Ransacking an apartment is not as easy or as fun as you might think. You don't just rip up cushions and dump out drawers willy-nilly. There's a method to the madness. You're looking for something, you have to be thorough. An experienced ransacker will have cut every mattress and cushion, deupholstered the couch and chairs, and looked in the toilet, the freezer, and the undersides of every drawer and cabinet. Once you've looked, sure, you break the shit up and dump it on the floor, that's part of the process. But when an apartment is as filthy as this one, you need a HazMat suit to properly ransack.

Finally finished with the job, Shamus was tired, sweaty, and covered in dust. He'd left Guillermo at a bar next to the ransacked apartment, with orders to keep an eye on the place just in case Miro showed up. Shamus needed a shower and a change of clothes.

Even though it was dark, he saw the dude sitting in his car. The guy didn't even try to duck as the headlights swept over him and Shamus pulled into his driveway.

Shamus had a momentary flash of paranoia, like maybe someone had put out a hit on him or the cops had gotten a grand jury indictment, but he relaxed when he saw the guy get out of his car and walk right up to him like he was about to slap him with a subpoena or letter from a bill collector or some shit like that. If the guy was a pro, Shamus would already be dead. That's why Shamus was surprised when the guy pulled out a gun.

"Shamus Noriega?"

Shamus nodded.

"I need to talk to you about something."

"Okay."

The guy hesitated.

"Can we go inside?"

Shamus smiled. This guy was no pro, he was shaking in his boots. Shamus could see the guy's hand trembling as he held the gun and it occurred to Shamus that he might be so nervous he'd accidentally pull the trigger. He held up his hands reassuringly.

"It's cool. You've got the gun. You want to come in, come in."

"Right. Okay."

Shamus slowly took out his key and opened his door.

"This okay?"

Shamus watched the guy look around, checking over his shoulder and down the street, peeking into the dark house, unsure what to do next and really jumpy, like some kind of crackhead idiot.

"Yeah. Yeah, go on in. Go."

Shamus could've dropped the guy. He could've pulled his own gun and killed him. Dropped his ass on the front lawn in a heartbeat. But then he'd have to move and he'd just got the place looking nice.

The guy waved the gun around.

"Go. C'mon."

Shamus stepped into the house and waited until the guy with the gun crossed the threshold.

"You want to close the door?" he asked.

The guy gulped, Shamus actually heard his throat muscles flex and contract, and pushed the door shut with his foot. Then he said, "Turn on the light."

"Okay."

Shamus flipped on the light and turned slowly, moving to face the guy. But the guy with the gun wasn't even looking at him, he was staring at the painting of Jim Morrison and the hippies on the beach.

"That's Fran's painting."

Shamus didn't wait for the guy to look back at him, he threw his elbow, hard, into the guy's face.

The gun clattered to the floor and the guy followed, dropping like a sack of concrete, out cold.

Shamus picked up the guy's gun and then went into the kitchen to find some duct tape. This whole day was turning out to be a fucking pain in the ass.

...

Miro didn't need to use the key, the door was already open. He could see wood splinters jutting up from the frame where the dead bolt had been jimmied. He walked in, trying not to make a sound in case someone was still inside, and looked around. What little he and Daniel had was piled in the middle of the floor along with the mattress stuffing, the pillow guts, and some broken wood that might have been the dresser or part of the closet. Loose tufts of kapok were mixed with the shattered glass on the kitchen floor.

Miro turned and looked at Guus and Marianna. They were standing in the doorway, their jaws dropped in disbelief, as if they'd just realized that the new world they'd heard so much about—the sun always shining, the air scented by orange blossoms, the champagne flowing poolside—was really just a ransacked, roach-infested dump.

Guus cleared his throat.

"So this is . . . what? Where you live?"

"This was my hideout."

"Your hideout has been found out."

Marianna appeared confused.

"Why are you hiding?"

Guus cleared his throat again and turned to Marianna.

"Someone shot him and stole his plants and seeds."

Marianna looked at Miro, a spark of fear flashing in her eyes.

"*Serio?*"

Miro shrugged.

"I'm okay now."

"But you have to hide?"

"Until I find out who did it. And who did this."

"So this clothing you're wearing is a disguise?"

"Yes."

Marianna heaved a sigh of relief.

"Thank God. I was really worried that the father of my baby was in some kind of cult."

Miro was about to say something but stopped midsyllable. He looked at Guus, who nodded.

"That's why I brought her. So she could tell you in person."

Marianna shrugged.

"I didn't mean to say it like that."

He had never really considered being a father. It just hadn't occurred to him. Not once. Not when he was in bed with any of his previous girlfriends and not when he visited friends and saw their little tykes romping around the room, pulling books off shelves, banging on pots and pans, and generally busying themselves creating cute kiddy chaos. It never crossed his mind that he might, one day, be the proud progenitor of some kind of miniature person. He was surprised by the intensity of the emotion he felt. Maybe it was because of his feelings for her. Maybe it was the near-death experience of being shot. Perhaps it was the fact that some kind of gangbanger death squad was tracking him.

It was all too much, too fast for Miro. His brain switched off for a moment like a computer freezing up from too much input: the ransacking of his hideout, the information from Marianna, and the sudden jolting realization that whoever had done this might be watching and that they might be in real and immediate danger.

His brain rebooted.

"We've got to go. They might come back."

Guus nodded.

"Let's go to a hotel and figure things out."

37

SHAMUS WORKED up a nice rich lather in the shower. He let the hot water relax his shoulders as it washed the funk and filth off his body. He was starting to feel better. He'd have to move the idiot intruder who was bound and gagged on the living room floor to the grow house —he couldn't risk leaving him unsupervised—and stick him in the room with the two Mormons, but otherwise things were looking up; they were closing in on problem numero uno, the Miro guy. Now that they knew that Miro was bicycling around dressed like a goof, it was only a matter of time before they'd find him and he could finish the job. Shamus reminded himself to go to the range and get in some practice. Normally when he shot somebody they went down and stayed down.

Shamus had just squirted a dollop of shaving cream into his hand—he liked to shave his head in the shower—when he heard his cell phone ringing in the bedroom.

Shamus stood, dripping wet with the phone at his ear, listening to Guillermo tell him that Miro and two other people, a couple, were in the apartment.

Guillermo wanted to know what to do, he couldn't follow them if they left because he didn't have a car. Should he go kill them?

Shamus didn't want him to kill them, that was *his* job, and the fact that a couple was there complicated matters. The hit would become mass murder.

If Shamus hadn't been distracted by the bound and gagged idiot inchworming his way out the front door, he might've told Guillermo to run over and hold the trio at gunpoint until he got there but as it was he threw the phone on the bed, ran out of the house naked, grabbed the guy by the feet, and dragged him back inside. Shamus didn't know how the guy had managed to get the door open but he wasn't going to give him the chance to do it again. He put one knee on the guy's chest to hold him down and proceeded to beat the living shit out of him.

Shamus finally stopped when he heard his phone ringing again.

...

Megamillionaire pop-rock chanteuse Aimée LeClerq had studied Kinbaku-bi with Natto Murasaki, the high priestess of Japanese rope bondage, at the latter's sex dojo in Osaka. The techniques combined fashion and kinky sex, two of Aimée's passions, and with practice she'd become a *nawashi,* a rope master. Aimée had even gone to the expense of building an entire boudoir in her home just for the practice of *tsuri* or "rope suspension."

She was using an Ebi Shibari tie on Daniel, his body restrained by coils of soft cotton rope and a series of tricky knots pulling and confining his limbs into a shape that left him effectively hog-tied on the bed.

Aimée then coiled more of the soft rope around his waist like a boa constrictor, wrapping between his thighs and, somehow, delicately separating his scrotum from his erect penis with an exquisite series of knots that looked like butterflies.

Aimée had bound him carefully, as if she was invoking some kind of ritual, turning sex into a spiritual practice. The cool rope stroked his skin, caressing him in areas that no one, not even a doctor, had ever touched before. His skin erupted in goose pimples, his body quivering under her fingers as she teased and tickled until he couldn't take it. Daniel spontaneously ejaculated into the air.

A delighted laugh bubbled up out of Aimée as she reached for a box of tissues.

Daniel blushed, slightly ashamed that he couldn't control his rising sap.

"Sorry."

Aimée smiled at him.

"I hope there's more where that came from, 'cos I'm just getting started."

Aimée then dropped to her knees in front of him, gently placed her hand on his penis as he trembled. She looked up at him.

"Is it true that Mormons consider oral sex unnatural?"

Daniel hesitated.

"I, I think so."

"You're not sure?"

"Well, Alma 5:57 says 'Touch not their unclean things.'"

She smiled at him.

"Is your cock unclean?"

As she asked this she gently wrapped her fingers around his penis and began to softly stroke it. Daniel looked down, his eyes meeting hers. He noticed that her fingernails were manicured and painted a bright, glossy red.

"I took a shower this morning."

"So do you think it would be okay with God if I put it in my mouth?"

Daniel thought he was about to have another orgasm. He tried to relax.

"I, I, I don't see why God would mind. Honestly."

Aimée stuck out her tongue and slowly licked from the base of his cock to the tip, like she was trying to keep a popsicle from dripping. Daniel shuddered.

"Wow."

Aimée put the tip of his penis in her mouth and gave it a good, hard suck. She pulled it out with a loud pop.

"I want to sanctify the area with a little washing and anointing, so there's no doubt that what we're doing is in accordance with the teachings of your faith."

Daniel, who'd had to close his eyes with all the sensations, looked at her.

"What?"

Aimée smiled and let the tip of her tongue tickle the edge of his glans.

"Do you trust me?"

Daniel nodded.

"Absolutely."

Aimée carefully spread a healthy dollop of shaving cream on Daniel's scrotum and began to shave his balls.

Daniel squirmed, but not too much, he didn't want her to cut him. And it wasn't as if he wanted her to stop. Having spent the first seventeen years of his life being taught that it was wrong to touch his genitals, that they were there for excretions and, later when he was married, procreation, the fact that a gorgeous woman was now caressing, cleaning, and shaving that part of his body was blowing his mind. Who knew so many sensations could be generated from the nerve endings between his legs? How come no one ever told him that being bound and shaved could cause him to lose himself in pure bliss? Why hadn't the bishop told him that surrendering his body to someone he trusted felt better than anything in the world?

Aimée took a porcelain basin, one that she'd purchased from an antique dealer in Paris, and washed his balls, his cock, and the surrounding area with a warm wet rag. She patted him dry with a soft cotton towel.

She smiled at him.

"Now I can suck your cock and God won't think it's unclean."

...

Detective Cho sat in his car and tried to relax. It had been a long, hard day filled with running around looking for people who didn't want to be found and then explaining to his superiors why he hadn't found them. He could tell them that Los Angeles was a giant city and if you really didn't want someone to find you, well, you'd be hard to find. But that wasn't what the captain, the commissioner, or the mayor wanted to hear. They wanted him to find the shooter. His scheduled vacation would just have to wait.

Detective Cho didn't know what was worse. Between his wife's fury, the barely concealed derision he got from the captain, and the chief's loosely veiled threat to knock him back to the night shift if he didn't make an arrest, Cho was starting to feel a tightness in his chest that he'd never noticed before. He felt lumps in his body that weren't there a week ago and his memory seemed to be playing tricks on him. Like he was about to stroke out, seize up, or contract some aggressive form of cancer. The funny thing was, the idea of dropping dead, of keeling over, seemed okay, pleasant even. Like maybe what he really needed was a nice long dirt nap. Cho recognized that this feeling wasn't healthy, and realized that he should probably take up yoga like his wife, or maybe even Buddhist meditation or something that would reduce his stress. Maybe drinking buckets of beer with the occasional tequila for extra fortification wasn't the best stress reducer after all. He'd look into this healthy lifestyle thing, maybe use the department's nutrition counselor and learn how to eat better. His wife would like that, too. They would be all yoga-and-brown-rice relaxed together. Oddly enough, that sounded kind of good to him.

But he didn't have the time or energy to worry about lifestyle changes right now. He called his wife and promised her a romantic, stress-reducing trip to Oaxaca. Maybe he'd take a yoga class down there.

38

IRO HAD BEEN dreaming. In the dream he was pursued by a black town car, the windows tinted obsidian, dead and unseeing like shark eyes. Miro was trying to get away, making evasive maneuvers in a pocket-sized sedan like a cross between one of those tiny Fiats you see in Italian movies and a Smart car. For some reason he was in San Francisco and trying to find a place he knew, a place where they made pinot-noir flavored gelato. As if a tasty Italian ice cream could be his salvation.

He woke with a start, having heard a sound, the crash of breaking glass or the rip-shatter of splintering wood or maybe it was just his imagination. Miro wasn't sure if the noise was from his dream or from inside the hotel room but he wasn't about to take chances. He reached for his messenger bag at the end of the bed and pulled out the handgun that Amin had given him.

A shaft of bright morning sunlight cut through a gap between the curtains and illuminated swirls of dust drifting in the air. Miro carefully walked toward the drapes and peeked out the window. The parking lot looked normal enough. No armed men approaching with guns in their hands. No one planting a bomb underneath his car.

He wished he could say he was just being paranoid but the fact was, somebody *was* out to get him. He couldn't believe that the ransacking of the apartment was a coincidence: it must mean that his gambit had worked. But the realization that he hadn't quite thought through the consequences of his ploy made him feel less than smart. He'd unleashed forces that he wasn't equipped to deal with. Still, a part of him felt success. He'd gotten to them. They wanted him dead, so he must be a threat; they must be afraid of him on some level. He'd have to warn Daniel—he couldn't have him get caught in the crossfire—and he'd have to do something to keep Marianna and Guus safe.

He turned back into the room and, as his eyes adjusted to the darkness, saw Marianna sitting up in bed looking at him. He realized he was holding the gun and suddenly felt strangely self-conscious.

"I don't normally . . ."

He put the gun on the dresser next to the bolted-down television set.

"It isn't even mine."

Marianna pulled the sheets up over her breasts.

"I think I should go."

Miro didn't want her to leave but he didn't disagree.

"It's not usually like this."

"This is because of the Cannabis Cup?"

He nodded and sat next to her on the bed. "I'm sorry," he said, "this is not how I want it to be."

Miro smiled at her and took her hand.

"But I'm glad you're here."

Miro felt his heart beating, throbbing faster than usual, the thump-thump-thump pounding out a primitive four/four time.

"I was thinking about you. All the time I was in the hospital. I kept thinking about you."

"You could've come back and found me."

"Believe me, once I delivered the seeds to Guus, I was going to find you."

Marianna smiled and looked down at his hand.

"I think I will choose to believe you."

"But you don't?"

Marianna smiled up at him.

"I told you I choose to. So I do."

Miro smiled at her and their eyes locked. She put her hand on his cheek and stroked his face.

"Show me where you got shot."

Miro pulled off his T-shirt. When she saw the scar, she gasped.

"Were you afraid?"

"Of what?"

"Dying."

Miro considered the question as Marianna ran her fingers gently along the scar tissue on his torso. She traced the line of the incision the surgeon had cut.

"I don't know. I didn't really have time to think about it."

She felt his body shiver, saw goose bumps spread across his ribs. She leaned forward and delicately kissed the scar where the bullet had entered.

"We have a saying, *Quem tem cu tem medo*."

"What's that mean?"

"Anyone who has an asshole has fear."

"Everybody has fear?"

Marianna smiled.

"Everybody."

Her lips worked their way around to the other side of his chest, caressing the scar tissue that had grown over the exit wound.

Miro's skin was still tender, the nerves hypersensitive to temperature and touch. A soft moan escaped his lips.

As she kissed his chest, right above his heart, he realized that she was crying. He felt her tears, warm and wet, falling on his chest. He put his arms around her.

"Hey. It's okay."

He reached up and touched her hair.

"Everything is going to be all right."

"Just like Bob Marley says?"

He nodded.

"Just like Bob Marley says."

...

Ted's tongue probed along the edge of his teeth, putting pressure on the upper and lower incisors, testing to see which ones were loose, and felt the swollen gums and dangling nerve endings of the two that were missing. His face felt like a hunk of boiled beef. More precisely, it felt like beef that had been put in a pressure cooker; his skin was puffy and hot, juicy and tenderized by the beating. The back of his head was throbbing and he could barely breathe out of his nose, it was so clotted with dried blood.

He remembered seeing Fran's painting, then trying to

escape, then Shamus Noriega's wet testicles dangling over his face as he got the living shit beat out of him.

Ted blinked open an eye. It must be his left eye because his right eye wouldn't open; it was swollen shut. He saw two young men in white short-sleeved shirts and ties sitting on a bed, staring at him.

"He's alive."

Ted closed his eye and reassessed. He couldn't tell if any of his bones were broken but it didn't feel like it. His hands were bound behind his back with what felt like a half a roll of duct tape. His ankles were bound, too.

He opened his eye again. One of the boys leaned forward.

"Hey, mister? Mister can you hear me?"

Ted was too tired to talk but he could nod.

"He heard me. He heard."

"Shut up. You want them to come in again?"

"But he's alive."

"So shut up."

Ted wondered if he was alive. Maybe he was dead. Maybe he was in some heavenly waiting room and these were two angels looking after him as he made the transition into the afterlife.

One of his kidneys confirmed the fact that he was alive by sending a shooting pain through his body that managed to pop his other eye open.

Ted looked at the two young men and noticed that they were wearing leopard-fur handcuffs. He moved his split and swollen lips.

"What the fuck is going on?"

...

Vincent hated coming to the Eastside. The traffic was brutal, it took him an hour to go from Santa Monica to Highland Park, and when he got there, well, then he was *there*. He hadn't come all this way for fun, though; there are some conversations that you just can't have on the phone. The Feds didn't agree with the state regarding the legal status of medical marijuana and sometimes they raided dispensaries or growers, and put federal wiretaps on phones. Discussing a drug operation was one thing, becoming an accessory to murder, maybe that's a conversation that should be had in private. So here he was. On the Eastside.

It was a shit hole. Dilapidated and dirty, the streets were lined with small *tiendas* selling everything from plastic flowers to long-distance phone cards to Santeria knickknacks to soccer jerseys. The butchers, the bakers, and the taco makers were there in the shape of *carnicerias* and *panderias,* all kinds of motherfucking *rias*. There was trash on the street and the crisp, clean billboards and graphic Diamond Vision screens of the Westside were replaced by storefront signage handpainted in the retina-searing colors that probably looked better in Mexico.

Traffic was different, too. The gleaming Mercedes and BMWs that cruised San Vicente and Montana Avenue were replaced by dusty Kias and souped-up Honda Accords. And then there were the trucks: shiny taco trucks parked every block or two, clouds of grease smoke pumping out of their kitchen exhausts; old delivery trucks repurposed to become rolling grocery stores, with clusters of green plantains swinging from hooks; ratty diesel-spewing death traps filled with used tires; and wheezing pickup trucks piled high with domestic jetsam. It was like a traveling carnival of dirty used crap and greasy food. A parade of junk. The clean, sun-spanked streets of LA morphed into some kind of developing-world diorama the further east you drove.

Vincent had heard stories of carjackings and gang shootings, white guys being attacked on the street, robbed and beaten, just because they had the audacity to venture into the barrio. These were tales of the predominantly poor Latino population running amok that were made popular in Academy Award–winning films and network television shows. The fact that these movies and shows were written by wealthy Caucasians living plush and protected 90210 lives on the Westside—people who couldn't find the Eastside without a location scout—didn't dilute the power these images had on Vincent's imagination. So when he crossed Eagle Rock Boulevard heading east he drove slowly, hypervigilant, his palms sweaty, half expecting some desperate immigrant to leap in front of his car with the intent of being maimed so that they could sue him or blackmail him or something bad like that. After all, he was driving a brand-new Prius.

He wound his way up a hill, the road narrowed by junked cars on one side, until he reached his destination. He drove past the house, just to be on the safe side, and then came back down the hill and parked a couple doors down.

Bernardo answered the door, gave Vincent a nod, and pointed him toward the living room where Shamus sat watching *los Jaguares de Chiapas* versus *los Rayados de Monterrey* on TV.

Vincent stood and watched the action on the television for a moment—he just didn't understand soccer—and then looked at Shamus.

"Do we have enough for the party?"

Shamus picked up a paper bag.

"This is about a pound and a quarter. There's more curing but it won't be ready for a few days."

Vincent took the bag and opened it. He was hit by the mango scent of the freshly dried weed. He looked inside and saw a bundle of neatly trimmed buds glistening with trichomes.

"Beautiful."

Vincent took a bud out of the bag and snapped it in half. He put it up to his nose and inhaled.

"Have you tried it?"

Shamus grunted. "Not yet."

Vincent noticed a grinder and a glass bong on the coffee table.

"Well, you are now. Now you're gonna see what this is all about."

Vincent sat down, dropped the bud into the grinder, and began cranking it into small bits. Then he opened it and studied the leaves.

"Amazing. It's ours. Elephant Crush, the reigning champion cannabis of the world."

He reached for the bong on Shamus's coffee table and stopped.

"What's wrong with this bong?"

Shamus looked up.

"What?"

"There's some, like, crud in it."

Shamus laughed.

"Those are bong barnacles, man. A naturally occurring phenomenon."

"Naturally occurring from what?"

"Sometimes I like to put Jack 'n' Coke in the bong."

Vincent gave Shamus a horrified look. Shamus shrugged.
"It's good."
Vincent shook his head.
"Got any papers?"
It only took Vincent a minute to roll a nice tight joint and hand it to Shamus. He watched as Shamus lit it and took a long, deep inhale. The distinct smell of ripe mangoes immediately filled the room. Vincent hadn't smoked any Elephant Crush since the Cannabis Cup and now here it was, grown in his secret grow house, cured to perfection, rolled up and burning in a curl of saliva-sodden paper just a few feet away.

Shamus took another deep hit and exhaled, his body sinking into his chair like an invisible elephant had just sat on him.

"Fuck, man. That's seriously the shit."

Shamus glanced at Vincent and then handed him the joint. Vincent licked his lips reflexively as he put it to his mouth. He trapped the smoke in his mouth, letting it cool slightly, and then French inhaled it through his nostrils and into his lungs.

The smoke was light, not oily or heavy, with no taste of skunk or fuel. It tasted like mangoes but not like the mangoes you get at the grocery store in LA, the taste was like mangoes you'd get at some kind of outdoor market on a sunny day in the tropics.

By the time Vincent had exhaled his second hit, he realized he was baked. He smiled at Shamus.

"Dude. I'm planning the best party. A world premiere event. This is gonna blow their minds."

He handed the joint back to Shamus.

"What do you think?"

Shamus, his eyes glazed by the THC in his system, his voice deep and mellow, turned and grinned at Vincent.

"I'd kill a lot of motherfuckers for this shit."

Vincent smiled. He was feeling giddy, flush, on top of the world. It was, easily, the best cannabis he'd ever smoked and he had a grow house full of it. He'd be able to propagate the Elephant Crush and keep it rolling off his production line for years to come. Not only would it make him millions, it would give him a name, a brand identity in the cannabis world. That was priceless. That was what made it all worthwhile. Vincent had done what any good businessman or corporation would do: he had seen a valuable resource and he was exploiting it. So what if someone had to die? It happened all the time, from Anaconda Copper to the diamond mines of Angola. You just had to recognize the opportunity when it knocked.

Vincent saw Blanca and Bernardo enter the room carrying three plates of rice and beans. For a brief moment he thought they were bringing them to him, but then they walked down the hallway toward one of the bedrooms in back. Blanca had a shotgun on a strap slung crossways over her shoulder bandito-style.

Vincent looked at Shamus.

"What's going on?"

Shamus shrugged.

"We've got house guests."

"You know you're not supposed to have people over."

"It couldn't be helped."

Vincent stood up to see what was going on. Shamus didn't move; Adolfo Bautista had just scored for Chiapas.

Vincent walked down the hallway and peeked into the second bedroom. He saw Blanca pointing the shotgun at two Mormon missionaries handcuffed to the bed while a badly beaten white dude lay hog-tied with duct tape on the floor. Bernardo was placing the food on the bed so the Mormons could eat. He put a plate next to the white dude but it didn't look like he'd be eating anything anytime soon.

Vincent went back to the living room.

"Who are those people?"

Shamus didn't divert his eyes from the game.

"We've had some complications."

"You want to elaborate on that?"

Shamus shrugged.

"The less you know, the better."

Vincent didn't like hearing that. He didn't like his employees, his subordinates, telling him what he did or didn't need to know.

"Maybe you should tell me what the fuck is going on."

...

Miro had never had sex with a pregnant woman before. He wondered if there was something special he needed to do, some kind of technique to ensure safety. There was, he realized, a steep learning curve ahead.

Marianna shifted her body, reaching down to find his erection and grabbing it firmly, giving his cock a strong tug. She looked up at him, a bright smile exploding across her face. That's when he realized that she wasn't sad, she wasn't crying because he'd nearly died, she was crying because she was happy he was alive.

Marianna threw a leg across his body and sat up, straddling him. She took a firm hold of his cock and gently guided
it inside her, muttering something he didn't understand, some
words in Portuguese.

...

Daniel was snuggled into a cloud, a cozy nebula of supersoft
bedding. The fact that he was nestled under thousands of
dollars worth of hypoallergenic down-filled duvet and a tangle
of one-thousand-thread-count sheets of the finest Egyptian
cotton didn't mean anything to him. The bedding was nice,
like a fancy hotel in a movie or something, but he felt amazing because he was a changed man. There had been a shift
inside him. Aimée had done something to him, released some
kind of energy, and he could feel an inner light glowing,
emanating from his body. Was this the feeling of exaltation
they talked about in church? Exaltation was supposed to be
the greatest gift of God and it came through being united with
a member of the opposite sex in a celestial marriage. Daniel
remembered reading that in *Doctrine and Covenants*. Exaltation was "the kind of life God lives." Exalted beings were
supposed to live in great glory, be perfect, and possess all
knowledge and wisdom.

That kind of described Aimée. *Maybe we are already
sealed in a celestial marriage.*

He peeked over at her, watching her sleep, noticing for
the first time the lines on her face and the gray roots at the
base of her hair. He saw the sagging flesh below her jawbones
and the crinkled skin around her eyes. She was older than him,
obviously, but he didn't care. She was still beautiful. Besides,

while her face showed her age, her perfectly formed, physically fit and surprisingly strong and agile body seemed ageless. Her muscles were tight, her skin was smooth and firm, and her breasts felt exactly like world-famous breasts should feel—full and soft and magnificent; like the countless photos of her without her shirt on hadn't lied. She was perfect and she possessed wisdom. She really was an exalted being, just like they described in *Gospel Principles, Chapter 47.*

Daniel saw himself as her young apprentice, eager to learn the mysteries of sex and willing to devote himself to its study and practice, technique and application. His mission was coming into focus.

But he also had a job. He was apprenticing to be a master burrito roller and he needed to get up, get dressed, and get on his bike.

As he slipped out of bed, Aimée stirred.

"Where're you going?"

"I gotta work."

"No you don't. Come back to bed."

"I'll be back soon. I only work the lunch shift. I'll bring you a burrito."

"Let Manuel drive you."

"I've got to get my bike."

She sat up on her elbows, her hair falling back, her perfect breasts rocking gently on her torso. Daniel couldn't help himself, he felt a boner popping to life. He tugged his pants up over his bulging cotton briefs and tried to tuck in his shirt.

Aimée smiled at him.

"Use the limo. I insist."

...

"What do you mean you had him?" Vincent asked.

Shamus glared. He didn't like having this conversation.

"Guillermo saw him with a couple of other people. That's all."

"Why didn't he shoot him?"

It annoyed Shamus when people said stuff like that. It just showed they didn't understand that it was complicated. You try to shoot one guy and you end up shooting three people; that's just asking for trouble.

"He's not a shooter."

He watched Vincent's eyes widen in disbelief.

"Why didn't you shoot him?"

"I got interrupted."

Shamus watched as Vincent began pacing the living room. Behind Vincent, Blanca and Bernardo were peeking in from the kitchen.

"Then what's going on? Why are you sitting here on your ass while he's still out there?"

"Don't freak. Guillermo's staking out his apartment. He went there once, he'll be back."

Vincent plopped down, a cloud of dust rising off the couch. He sighed and began speaking to Shamus like he was a fucking five year old.

"You know how important this is, right? The Elephant Crush is worth millions. But not with Miro alive. We can't sell it if he's alive. Do you think people are going to say 'too bad they almost killed that guy to steal it but heck it's really good weed so I don't care'?"

Vincent was standing again, waving his hands in the air.

"I've already sent out the invitations for the opening. The caterer is catering. I've got twelve cases of fucking Prosecco in my office. Do you understand? People are coming and they're going to want this weed."

Vincent picked up the paper bag of buds and started waving it in Shamus's face.

"If he's alive we can't sell it. If he's dead, well, we're carrying on his legacy. We'll put his fucking picture on the label. But you've got to deal with this. You understand that, right?"

Shamus didn't react. He muttered, "Yeah."

Vincent lost his shit. He shouted.

"So why the collection of freaks and geeks in the bedroom?"

Shamus shrugged, it took every ounce of self-control not to jump up and put his knee so deep into Vincent's groin that his balls would pop out his throat. You can't yell at a man like that. He was done with this conversation. Maybe he was done with Vincent. Shamus folded his arms across his chest and tried to concentrate on the soccer game.

Vincent sighed, sat back down, and put his face in his hands.

"Just find him and put a bullet in his head. Please."

39

THE EL RIO MOTEL on Colorado Boulevard, while having some distinctly off-ramp-adjacent charm, didn't offer room service, so Miro and Marianna walked a couple of blocks down to Zankou Chicken while Guus went in the other direction to find a coffee shop with free Internet.

For Marianna, whose appetite had seemed to quadruple in the last week, the perfectly roasted chicken with mysterious Armenian spices and slathered with an ambrosial garlic sauce was the ideal food. Miro sat across from her in the plastic orange booth as she attacked her food. The nervousness she felt about seeing him again, about telling him she was pregnant, all of that had dissipated. He seemed genuinely interested in having some sort of relationship with her. This made her happy and if he didn't walk around with a gun, she might even fall in love with him. But the nervousness she'd had was replaced by a sense of dread. On the walk over he had explained his gambit to her and why he needed the gun, and it was obvious to her that he was in over his head.

Marianna watched as he picked at his food.

"You forgot to keep a control."

"What?"

"You ran an experiment without a control."

Miro considered that.

"Okay."

"So let's analyze the situation. Take a different perspective. Figure out what is behind this."

Miro nodded. "I'm not sure I follow."

"Think like a scientist. Logically. Why you were robbed is obvious."

"Right."

She continued. "And whoever stole your plants and seeds will want to grow them. Correct?"

He started to see where she was going with this.

"Or what's the point?"

"So, they either have a greenhouse or they built one. This is a starting point. You must know people who grow marijuana, and the people who supply them with equipment and soil, things like that."

Miro nodded. "Right. Of course."

"All you need to do is locate them and then call the authorities."

Miro looked at her.

"The police?"

Marianna smiled at him sweetly.

"They already shot you once. That is a fact. We should trust the data and not let them shoot you again."

She picked up a piece of chicken from his plate.

"Are you going to eat this?"

...

The house was rented to someone named Shamus Noriega, a crumb that had been arrested a couple of times for assault but nothing really serious. Criminal intelligence, the organized-crime guys, had a file on him but he was, as best anyone knew, unaffiliated with any known gang. He was, apparently, one of those under-the-radar operators that are hard to get a line on. Cho leaned against the hood of his unmarked police cruiser and watched as Quijano peeked in the windows of the little house in Atwater. The guy wasn't there, that much was obvious.

Quijano came back shaking his head.

"It doesn't look like a crumb lives there."

"What do you mean?"

"I don't know, there's like art on the walls and stuff. It's kind of a nice place."

Cho thought about it.

"There's no way there's two Shamus Noriegas."

Quijano nodded.

"You want to sit on it?"

"I want to eat lunch."

Cho pulled out his cell phone and made a call as he walked around to the passenger side of the car.

…

It was, Daniel realized, all part of God's plan. Unlike the Baptists, Protestants, Catholics, or other Christianity-spouting organizations, Mormons don't believe in original sin. They don't think it's fair that God would punish all mankind for eternity because of the actions of Adam and Eve. In fact, Mormons believe that mankind should be tested, that temp-

tation, experience, and separation from God is an important
way to learn about life. You gain knowledge from experience,
from enduring trials and undergoing tribulations. That knowledge becomes wisdom and, with wisdom, you understand the
difference between good and evil. That's why the religions that
valued purity and innocence—all those chaste nuns and celi-
bate priests—those faiths were for chumps. Even the Amish
kicked their teenagers out of the house and told them to watch
reality television, get a hand job, drink a Budweiser, and
smoke a couple packs of Marlboros before deciding whether
or not to rejoin their community. You need a taste of the
secular to know what's sacred, although sitting in the back of
Aimée's limo he thought the secular was winning.

But while this made sense to Daniel—it seemed reasonable enough—some of the other strictures, the prohibitions
against masturbation and oral sex, seemed to counter the other
teachings. Why wouldn't the church want someone to experience carnal bliss? Wasn't there wisdom to be found in being
bound, shaved, and sucked off? Where was the sin in that?
Why was it considered unclean? Who was it hurting?

Daniel found some reassurance in the fact that the burrito, the godhead of food, was also tightly bound. If Daniel
was honest, if he was having one of those heart to hearts with
the bishop, he'd have to say that being bound by Aimée was
the closest he'd come to a religious experience. Not all the
classes, sermons, or prayers in the world could compare. Instead of making him doubt the existence of God, he discovered that there was a moment, right after he came, when he
actually felt proof of the existence of a higher power.

Only God could make something so profound.

...

Miro and Marianna stood in the middle of the store admiring the various hydroponic gardening systems, computerized drip irrigation setups, and the wide variety of fertilizers—both chemical and organic—on offer. The shop, tucked away in a strip mall in Koreatown, was the biggest supplier of indoor-farming equipment in Los Angeles. Miro had always liked the store's vibe. With warm bamboo floors, Japanese koto music plinking and bending its ting-tong sound from speakers, banzai trees in slate-colored planters, and shelves of books about indoor gardening, it was a cross between a high-end gadget boutique and a garden-supply store.

Takashi Goldberg, a middle-aged Japanese man wearing jeans, bright red clogs, and a Hives T-shirt, came out of the back room with a computer printout. He was the city's leading expert in all matters of cannabis cultivation and had written several books on the subject.

Takashi looked at the printout.

"There're only two big operations I've sold to in the last month. One was a couple of college kids from Occidental."

"Probably not who I'm looking for."

Takashi hesitated before handing the paper to Miro.

"Look, Miro. I'm only doing this because we're friends and, as a friend, well, why don't you just call it a day? You don't want to mess with these guys."

Miro cocked an eyebrow.

"Gang?"

"Ganglike. I don't know. But you heard about what they did to Barbara?"

A chill ran down Miro's spine.

"What happened?"

BAKED

"They shot her place up. Killed the security guard. Stole all of your stuff."

"My stuff?"

Takashi nodded.

"They took your Cup-winning weed. Nothing else. Not even the cash box."

Miro stood there, trying to process this. It had been part of his plan to agitate the bad guys but he hadn't thought anyone would get killed.

"Fuck."

Takashi put his hand on Miro's shoulder.

"Don't do anything stupid."

Miro didn't know what to do so Marianna reached out and gently took the paper from Takashi.

"Don't worry. I won't let him do anything stupid."

...

Quijano handed a paper plate dripping with pork fat and chilies through the window to Cho. Quijano shook his head.

"What happened to your 'eat healthy' plan?" he asked.

"This *is* healthy."

Quijano went around and got in the passenger seat.

"Right."

"What did you get?"

"Nopalito burrito."

"You eat cactus?"

Quijano nodded.

"They taste like green beans."

267

Cho bit into the first taco, taking half of it into his mouth, tasting the explosion of salt and pork and chilies and limes, and was just about to stuff the rest of the taco in his mouth when Quijano elbowed him in the ribs.

"What?"

Quijano jerked his head in the direction of the truck. Cho turned his head and saw what looked like Elder Daniel Lamb, young Mormon missionary and shooting-victim bedside sitter, stepping out of a sleek black Lincoln Town Car, pulling on an apron, and entering the taco truck.

Cho swallowed.

"What the fuck?"

"The Mormon kid?"

"Gotta be."

"Know any taco jockeys that come to work in a limo?"

Cho looked at Quijano.

"Now *this* is interesting. Let's run the plates."

...

Guus sat across the booth from the couple: the man was in his midfifties, looked like a hip music producer, and kept a porkpie hat stuck over his bald spot at all times; his girlfriend was a woman who apparently collected low-cut vintage dresses that were suddenly back in fashion after fifty years. The couple were hashish traders and had a loose-knit network of growers, manufacturers, and dealers scattered across the globe from Malawi to Chang Mai to Islamabad. Guus's coffee shop did a lot of business with them.

They sat, each of them drinking chocolate milkshakes and eating cheeseburgers, in a hipster diner in Los Feliz, shouting to be heard over a soundtrack that blasted everything from old Roxy Music to new TV on the Radio.

The hashish trader slurped his milkshake and smiled at Guus.

"I imagine you're here for the grand opening."

Guus pushed his glasses up.

"I'm here to visit a friend."

The woman leaned forward, her cleavage yawning open like it was about to consume the pile of french fries.

"They've got your Cannabis Cup winner."

Guus coughed.

"What?"

The man chewed his cheeseburger and swallowed.

"The Compassion Center. They're opening a fancy new weed shop."

The woman reached into her purse and pulled out an expensive-looking invitation.

"We can't make it. You should go."

Guus took the invitation and flipped it around in his hands. Sure enough, it announced a special exclusive first taste of the Cannabis Cup–winning Elephant Crush. Guus was especially irked that they'd put a little trademark sign after the Elephant Crush name.

...

Daniel sat in the back of the limo and touched the seat where he'd lost his virginity. He couldn't stop thinking about it. He replayed his deflowering over and over in his mind, recalling the sensations, the smells, the tastes, and the vision of her pilates-tight body stretched out before him. These daydreams made him weak in the knees, gave his skin goose bumps, and generally distracted him from his burrito-rolling duties on the taco truck. Lenny had noticed that he was not himself—Daniel's hands had been moist all day, causing some of his burritos to lack their usual structural integrity—and had let him take off early, right after the lunch rush.

Aimée had arranged for her driver to pick Daniel up and bring him to her house after his shift. It was not the usual way taco-truck employees commuted to work.

The anticipation of an afternoon with her had knotted his stomach and created a sublime tension buzzing around inside his body. He had even gotten an erection while he made a burrito for her.

He felt the burrito, still warm, nestled in his lap. His penis started to grow again. He couldn't help it.

...

They had waited until the lunch hour was over, then watched the limo return for Daniel. A check of the vehicle registration just showed that the car was owned by a limousine company. It didn't surprise them but it did make them even more curious.

It's easy to follow a limousine. It's not like they can hide in traffic or are fast enough to lose an experienced tail. As they drove, Quijano looked over at Cho.

"Pretend I'm stupid. Remind me why we're following this misfit."

Cho thought about it. He also thought about rolling down his window because he was about to let some gas escape from his body and wasn't sure how it would smell.

"Last time we saw him, he was riding a bike, hanging out with Miro Basinas. Now he's rollin' in a limo. I'd say something's fishy here. But even if he just struck it rich, I bet he and Miro will meet up at some point."

"But shouldn't we find the shooter?"

"The shooter's looking for Miro. Maybe he'll do us a favor and make an appearance."

Quijano rolled down his window.

"Light a match, motherfucker."

Cho smiled. He didn't know why, but farts were funny. They always got a laugh. Cho thought it was strange how flatulence embarrassed people. It was a completely natural function of a healthy body. Why was it so taboo? He blamed the church. Christianity was built on the notion that people were made in God's image. But would God fart like a donkey? Did Jesus cut the cheese? And if they did, what would heavenly gas smell like? An ambrosial potpourri or the sulphuric stench of a volcano?

They followed the limo until it stopped in front of an iron gate. They drove past and slowed. Cho checked the rearview and watched as the gate opened and the limo drove in.

"Who do you think lives there?"

"Let's ask the magic Ouija board."

Quijano typed some information into the computer mounted in the car and got a quick response.

"Aimée LeClerq."

"The singer?"

Quijano nodded.

"That's what the county records show. She owns the house. I've no idea if she's actually inside."

Cho stroked his goatee. He was puzzled. This, as the robot from *Lost in Space* so wisely said, did not compute.

271

"What would a nice Mormon boy want with a woman like that?"

Quijano looked over at him.

"You really want me to answer that?"

Cho's cell phone rang. He answered and then immediately reached for a pencil and his notepad to write something down.

40

IRO AND MARIANNA stopped at Lenny's taco truck. Miro needed to tell Daniel about the apartment and warn him not to go back for a while. Mostly he wished the young missionary had a cell phone. Lenny smiled when he saw Miro. He reached his hand out the window of the truck and gave him a warm handshake.

"You look great."

"Thanks, Lenny."

Lenny leaned forward, putting his face in the window. He smiled when he saw Marianna.

"This your girlfriend?"

Miro nodded.

"Yeah. Marianna, meet Lenny."

Marianna smiled.

"Hi."

Lenny grinned.

"You hungry?"

Before Marianna could answer, Miro looked at Lenny.

"I'm looking for the kid."

Lenny spread his hands.

"It was slow today. He just left."

Miro looked down the street.

"Maybe I can catch him."

Lenny laughed.

"He's not on his bike. A limo came and picked him up."

Miro couldn't help it. He cocked his head like a quizzical beagle.

"*En serio?*"

Lenny laughed again, a big booming chortle.

"Totally, man."

"If you see him, have him call me. It's important."

Lenny nodded, then looked at Marianna.

"You sure you're not hungry?"

Marianna pointed to the menu painted on the side of the truck.

"Could I get a taco?"

...

"Can you help me?"

Ted was still on his back on the floor. He lifted his hands up, reaching toward the missionaries.

"Please."

The two Mormons just sat on the bed and stared at him.

"Come on. Use your free hand and undo the tape."

The older of the missionaries shook his head.

"No way."

"Untie me and then I'll help you get those cuffs off."

"How?"

"I'll think of something. We can undo the bed. Or I can run and get help."

BAKED

The older missionary started to lean forward, then hesitated. The younger one, the one with the broken arm, looked alarmed.

"Don't. We don't know this guy. He may be tied up here 'cos he's a killer or something."

Ted sighed and dropped his hands.

"I'm not a killer."

"How would we know?"

Ted couldn't help it, even though it hurt he rolled his eyes.

"Yeah, and you guys are terrorists."

"No, we're not."

They almost said it in unison.

"How would I know? You're locked in here, too. So we must all be bad guys."

The older missionary reached a leg out and gave Ted a sharp kick in the head.

"Shut up."

Ted winced and made a silent vow to get even with the little fucker if he ever got the chance. But he didn't snap at them; he was hoping reason and logic might prevail.

"Look. I don't know what's going on but I know that they killed a friend of mine and they're probably going to kill us. We need to find a way out of here."

The younger Mormon shook his head.

"If God wants us to escape, he'll provide a way."

Ted wanted to shout at them, tell them they were fucking idiots, that there was no God and even if there was it's not like God is fucking Houdini, but he remembered his grandmother's admonition that you catch more flies with sugar than vinegar.

275

He needed to stay calm and sweet-talk them into trusting him. He took a deep breath.

"Right. And maybe that's what's going on here. God wants you to untie me so I can untie you and we can flee."

Ted looked up at the two young men, trying for a sincere and earnest expression. There was no response from them, like they'd suddenly entered a catatonic state. They weren't looking at him; instead they'd turned their eyes up to the ceiling.

Ted waited for what seemed like an appropriate amount of time. Finally he whispered.

"What are you doing?"

The older of the missionaries looked down at him.

"Waiting for a sign."

...

When you ransack a place, you don't normally plan on coming back and hanging out; there was no place to sit except on a shredded mattress, and the place now had a cheese stink from the carton of milk Guillermo had poured on the floor. Not that anyone thought there was something hidden in the milk carton, but fucking things up and making a mess was just part of the fun.

Guillermo shoved some ripped-up pillows and blankets against the wall and sat down while Shamus took the mattress, finished cutting it in half and then piled the pieces on top of each other.

"This fucking sucks, dude."

Shamus didn't say anything. It would get dark soon, and then it would really suck. Guillermo reached into a paper bag of In-N-Out burgers and began eating.

"You want one?"

Shamus shook his head.

Guillermo chewed.

"You think he'll come back?"

Shamus glared at Guillermo.

"Don't be a dick."

Guillermo nearly choked on his burger.

"What did I do?"

"You let him get away."

"It's not my fault that dude came to your place. And besides, if you'd left me with a car, I could've followed them."

Guillermo was right, Vincent was right, everybody was fucking right except him. Shamus turned to Guillermo.

"Shut up."

...

Detectives Cho and Quijano sat in their pale-blue Crown Vic a few houses down from a drab, gray-and-white tract house in an area that was remarkable in its unremarkability. It was a neighborhood gone to seed. While every house looked the same, more or less—not wealthy, not even upper-middle-class, but solidly suburban with large trees and picket fences and pickup trucks in the driveways—there was the rusting evidence of former vitality: corroded swing sets sagged in overgrown backyards and abandoned basketball hoops festooned with tattered remnants of rotted netting leaned over cracked driveways.

It was fucking depressing.

Cho almost said it out loud but then he remembered Quijano lived in Sunland, a neighborhood kind of like this one; the only difference was that Quijano took care of his house and had a couple of Jet Skis in his driveway.

Quijano rolled down the window and launched a loogie into the street.

"Not what I was expecting."

Cho looked over at Quijano. He sometimes forgot that his partner was new: he'd only been a detective for a year and still needed to learn a thing or two.

"What did you think?"

"I don't know. Bars on the windows, Dobermans, something badass. I keep expecting granny to cool a pie on the windowsill."

"I guess we'll just have to wait until SWAT gets here with the search warrant."

Cho saw a message coming through on the computer system and leaned forward. As they read the message, neither Cho nor Quijano noticed an older diesel Mercedes-Benz drive slowly past, leaving a trail of exhaust that smelled faintly like tempura.

...

Miro noticed a few things as he went past the house. He saw that the back windows were covered by aluminum foil, not, presumably, to keep light out, but to keep light in. Neighbors would notice if you had grow lights blazing until three or four in the morning. He also caught a glimpse of a large pile of organic compost mounded in the backyard. Typical of weekend gardeners but also a must for indoor farming. He rolled down the window and sniffed the air. His nose had found the wild-growing Hawaiian Indica in the national park and he'd smelled villagers smoking their homegrown sativa in Thailand. He thought, just for a moment, that he caught a whiff of mango-scented marijuana but wondered if his mind was playing tricks on him.

Marianna looked at him.

"What do you think?"

"It's an operation. But I really can't be sure."

"So now what?"

Miro considered it.

"I should really take you back to the motel. It's too dangerous."

They drove in silence for a moment and then Marianna turned to him.

"You don't have to have anything to do with the baby if you don't want."

Miro looked at her, surprised.

"Why would you say that?"

"I don't want you to feel like you are obligated. I want you to want to be involved as much as you feel like being involved."

Miro nodded.

"That's good because I want to be involved as much as you want me to be involved."

Marianna smiled and hooked a wayward strand of hair behind her ear.

"*Bom.*"

Miro reached out and held her hand.

"Does that mean we're involved?"

She nodded.

"Yes. I think we're involved together."

She saw Miro shift in his seat, as if an idea had made him suddenly uncomfortable.

"I still think it's too dangerous."

Marianna held her hands up.

"If it's too dangerous for me, it's too dangerous for you. We are involved now, you know."

That made Miro smile.

...

Miro drove back down the hill and found a small espresso bar on York.

"I need a coffee. Want a tea or something?"

She smiled, but it was a tired smile, the jet lag was catching up with her.

"Go ahead. I'll wait here."

When he came back with his coffee, Miro saw that she'd fallen asleep, her head leaning against the window. Sugar Minott's "Good Thing Going" was playing softly on the iPod. Miro slid quietly into the car and watched Marianna. Her hair was sticking up and a couple of tendrils stuck out the window like some kind of exotic red octopus; her face was soft, relaxed and lovely, and her skin seemed to glow.

Miro felt his body flood with a strange feeling. He felt a warmth toward her and it gave him a feeling of well-being, almost euphoria. This, he realized, was what being an animal —a warm-blooded mammal—was all about. He realized he loved her and wanted to stay with her, be her mate and companion and try to build some kind of life together.

Of course coming to that conclusion, for a *cannasseur,* a grower of controlled substances, was problematic. Would a stoner make a good parent? Would they let a cannabis farmer coach the youth soccer team?

He sipped his coffee and wondered what his next move should be. He'd found a grow house, but was it the grow house of the guys who stole the Elephant Crush? He didn't want to rat on some innocent indoor farmer, that wouldn't be cool.

Miro realized he'd have to go back to the house and go up to the door. If the door was open and they were growing Elephant Crush he'd be able to smell it in a second.

41

TRAFFIC IN EUROPE is different than traffic in Los Angeles; despite the cobbled streets and lack of open space for parking, it's much easier to navigate around Amsterdam or Paris. You might find yourself on ancient, medieval roads, or driving down a narrow mews, but wherever you were, whether in Brussels or Hamburg or Nice, your fellow drivers were, for the most part, kind and intelligent, courteous and observant even if they were tearing down the road like madmen. They were the kind of drivers who took a philosophical view of the experience. Because weren't we all trapped in a machine made of steel and glass and rubber and plastic? The European drivers recognized that it was inhumane at best, that the automobile was an isolating presence in the world, an invention that had kept people apart, that denied people time to sit on a tram and read a book or strike up a conversation. Apparently, this philosophical understanding, this detachment from being dominated by machines, hadn't made it to Los Angeles.

Guus had the hashish traders drop him at a car-rental place and now found himself behind the wheel of a Chrysler Sebring convertible, driving slack-jawed through the clogged, infernal mayhem of gigantic smoking SUVs—their rearview mirrors shaking with every thump and wallop of their expensive stereos—rattle-trap trucks and cargo vans, while a circus of tiny hybrids and Mini Coopers skittered in-between. They would careen toward a red light as if it were the finish line of the Indy 500, only to lock up their brakes, skid to a stop, and idle there, spewing fumes, and then start the race again when the light turned green.

As he drove he felt his forehead broil slowly from white to pink to a sun-kissed crimson. Perhaps renting a convertible had been a mistake, but he was in California and top-down cruising underneath the palms seemed to him to be the thing to do.

He'd decided to avoid the freeways. They seemed too fast: bone-break crazy and out-of-control like a ride at Disneyland that he wasn't quite tall enough to go on. But he couldn't have foreseen the demolition derby that ensued on the city streets, the slow hot slog through Hollywood toward Santa Monica and the Compassion Center's corporate office, with the inflectionless drone of the GPS digital-voice guidance system showing him the way.

...

Vincent shook a Klonopin out of the prescription bottle and popped it in his mouth. He washed it down with some Fiji water. His assistant had argued with him that it was ridiculous to buy fresh water from the South Pacific, plastic containers that had been shipped halfway around the world by supertankers, trains, and trucks just so people like him could find it at their local grocery store and drive it home in their cars. His assistant had told him that between manufacturing the plastic and the transportation costs, each bottle of imported water had the same carbon footprint as a 747 jumbo jet flying across the country. Vincent found that a little far-fetched. Besides, the water was tasty and he would recycle the plastic. Really. What was the big deal? Compared to the shit he was dealing with, remaining carbon neutral was small potatoes. It's easy being green and keeping your carbon footprint small when everything in your life is going fine.

But things weren't going fine. He'd decided to go ahead with the party. He had to or he'd be the laughingstock of Santa Monica. But the fact that Miro was running around was really annoying. Why couldn't that motherfucker stay dead? Vincent propped his head on his fist, stared off into space, and tried to think of what he was going to do.

Nothing came to him. If Miro made a fuss, he was fucked. The Klonopin wasn't working; maybe he needed Ritalin, that might improve his concentration. He opened a drawer, shook a pill out of a bottle, crushed it with a paperweight, and snorted it off the desktop. The pharmaceutical powder burned his nose but he started to feel more focused.

If the shit hit the fan he could always say he had bought it from a reliable source, that he didn't know it had been stolen. There was a certain built-in deniability. Worse case, he could blame Shamus and let him deal with the consequences. Who would people believe? Him? Or that psycho?

Vincent pushed back from his desk, went to the center of his office, and assumed a Downward Dog pose. He thought it might help calm him but it didn't; he couldn't get into it, he was too agitated. Then he remembered it was calming to do an inversion so he tried a handstand against the wall. That ended up making him think that the Klonopin wasn't getting digested, it felt like it was sliding back down his throat, so he stood up in the middle of his office, waiting for the powerful antianxiety drug to kick in. He considered that he probably should've just smoked some weed, but then he'd be stoned and he didn't want to be stoned. Not with this shit going on.

He tried a Pigeon pose, easing into the hip stretch in the middle of the floor. That's when Guus entered the office.

"We need to talk."

Vincent's assistant was right behind him.

"I tried to stop him."

Vincent looked up.

"It's cool. Get us a couple of Fiji waters."

...

Cho watched as Quijano snapped the magazine into his Glock semiautomatic and *ka-chunked* the slide, sending a round into the chamber, before turning toward him with a frown.

"What's your problem?"

"You're not gonna need your gun."

"How do you know?"

Cho pointed to the SWAT Team dressed in helmets, flak jackets, and ballistic assault gear jumping out of a couple of black SUVs and moving quickly toward the suburban tract home.

"Let the guys in the turtle suits secure the site. Then we go in."

"I thought we'd take the lead on this."

Cho shook his head.

"You watch too much TV."

It really wasn't like the way they showed it on TV. The SWAT team didn't go up to the front door and knock. They didn't identify themselves or give the occupants thirty seconds to open the door. What they did was jump out of their SUVs before they even stopped, sprint up to the front door with a battering ram, knock the door down, and swarm inside with overwhelming force. It was shock and awe in the suburbs and it worked. Shots were rarely fired. Nobody got killed.

Cho and Quijano sat in the car until they saw the SWAT captain stand on the front porch and flash a thumbs-up. Then they got out of the car and walked into the house. Cho could tell Quijano was disappointed that he didn't get to kick in the door and wave his gun around. He gave him a friendly pat on the back.

"Maybe you should apply to join the turtle suits."

"Fuck that."

Cho looked around and, for a moment, felt his heart sink. It looked like he'd fucked up royally. The house was completely normal and there was nothing about the couple of middle-aged Latinos—a man and a woman sitting on the couch in handcuffs—to make Cho think that they were anything other than hardworking, tax paying, innocent victims of a police pooch-screw. But then he noticed the steel-framed front door, obviously reinforced to prevent someone like Quijano from trying to kick it in, but not reinforced enough to give a SWAT battering ram much trouble. The SWAT captain came up to him, a big grin on his face.

"What've you got?" Cho asked.

"You tell me. You want to look at the farm in the basement or the hostages in the bedroom?"

...

Vincent looked at the Dutch dude sitting in the chair across from him. *What is it with these Europeans?* They come to LA dressed for a hipster's funeral: black T-shirt, a gray sweater, a black leather jacket, black jeans, black boots, and a bright red face. If a lobster decided to dress like Lou Reed, he'd look just like this Dutch tourist. Vincent wondered why the Europeans didn't check the weather. It was ninety degrees Fahrenheit in LA; maybe they thought that was cold in metric. Who the fuck knew?

Or maybe he was red because he was obviously angry. He kept demanding to know things. Vincent didn't know what he was supposed to say to the guy. He wasn't going to confess to anything. As far as he was concerned, it had all spun out of control and was FUBAR. He thought about something his shrink had said. *If it's out of your control, it's out of your control.* So Vincent decided to tell the truth.

"Look, I understand you're upset. But you had the exclusive in Europe. This isn't Europe."

Vincent was pleased to see the Dutchman squirm.

"Might I ask how you came to be in possession of this plant?"

Vincent smiled.

"I can't give you the name of my source. But someone came to me with it."

"It was stolen."

Vincent nodded in a show of empathy.

"If I'd known . . . but then someone else would've bought it. So you see it's really worked out for the best."

"How has it worked out for the best?"

"The universe takes care of you."

He watched the Dutch guy take his glasses off and clean them. Vincent's assistant stuck her head in the door.

"Vincent? The caterer's here."

Vincent smiled.

"Send her in."

The caterer entered with a box in her hands.

"Fresh, handmade, mango-infused truffles."

Vincent took one and tasted it. The chocolate dissolved in his mouth spreading a rich, bittersweet flavor tinged with an edge of mango. It tasted decadent.

Vincent pointed to the Dutch guy.

"Try one. Delicious."

"You're not going to get away with it."

There was something about the way the Dutch guy said this, his cold matter-of-factness, that was as startling as if he had stood up and screamed. The caterer stared at Vincent. Vincent felt his hand trembling. He took a breath. Inhaling, exhaling. Calmifying. Letting the Klonopin do its job.

"He's from Europe. These are great by the way. Perfect."

The caterer nodded.

"Excellent. We're all set for tonight."

Vincent nodded and the caterer left. Vincent turned his full attention to the Dutch pain in the ass sitting across from him.

"Listen. I have the Elephant Crush. I'm going to grow it and sell it. You can either play along and take a piece of the pie or you can go fuck yourself."

The Dutch guy sat there for what seemed like ten minutes before he finally said something.

"I believe I understand your position."

And then he got up and left.

Vincent wondered, briefly, if he would have to have the Dutch asshole killed. He took out a Post-it and wrote: Dutch guy? He stuck the Post-it to his telephone to remind him the next time he talked to Shamus, although it occurred to him that Shamus wasn't turning out to be the best hitman in the world. He might need to look for a new one. Maybe put an ad on Craigslist. He took out another Post-it and wrote: Craigslist.

Then he popped another mango-infused truffle in his mouth. This party was going to rock.

...

Miro and Marianna had sat in the car around the corner and discussed the pros and cons of going up to the house and seeing if they were really growing Elephant Crush. Marianna didn't think it was the best idea—she was afraid whoever opened the door would just start shooting—but Miro didn't know what else to do. He didn't feel comfortable dropping the dime on the grow op unless he was sure they were his plants they were growing. They finally decided that if they went to the door as a couple, pretending that they were looking for a friend, they might not get shot. If they were going to be a couple—and Marianna knew they had lots of things to discuss before that became a reality—they would do this together.

"Think of it as a date."

As it turned out they didn't have to go to the door of the suspected grow house. When they turned onto the street they saw swarms of police cars, unmarked cars, police vans, and all kinds of activity around the grow house. A uniformed officer yawned as he waved them past.

42

ALIFORNIA LAW—legislative statute SB 420—allows medical marijuana patients to grow six mature and twelve immature plants for personal use and for sale to a licensed cannabis dispensary, co-op, or collective. The four to five hundred plants in various stages of maturity in the basement of the Glassell Park grow house were well beyond the legal limit. SWAT had called Narco and now five drug detectives were snooping around the place, taking photos and doing a rough inventory. Somebody was going down for this operation, that was for sure, but Cho didn't really care. He thought the prohibition on cannabis was overcooked: it was no longer a scientific or rational debate but a political one, a hangover from the cold war era, the Old World morality that said anything that wasn't white and male was bad. It was bullshit. Was a puff of marijuana any worse than a cigar and a scotch on the rocks?

Cho knew some young and hungry assistant district attorney was on his or her way right now, ready to blow this thing open and make a name for him- or herself. The chief and the commissioner would follow, in hot pursuit of a photo op. They loved to get their names in the paper, puff up their chests, and preen in front of a pile of weed. Cho didn't give a flying fuck about any of that. He was getting close to Shamus Noriega. He could feel it.

Cho wished he'd learned Spanish. He spoke a little Korean but his Spanish was limited to recognizing when someone called him a bad name. He sat at the kitchen table as Quijano *habla*ed with the two suspects. Cho leaned forward and slid the photo of Shamus taken by the herbal cooperative's surveillance camera toward the couple and gave them an encouraging glare.

Quijano asked them if they recognized the man. The two Mexicans shook their heads but Cho knew they were lying. He could see it in their hesitation, their blinks and gulps. It'd just be a matter of time now before one of them cracked and told him what he needed to know. He turned to Quijano and affected his bad-cop voice.

"Make sure they understand that they're completely, totally, irrevocably fucked."

He smacked the table with a meaty fist just to see them jump.

Quijano nodded and translated a version of what Cho had said to them. Cho didn't hear the word "*chinga*" so he figured Quijano was soft selling, taking the role of good cop. That was fine with Cho; he figured that the suspects, Bernardo and Blanca Guardado, could probably speak English well enough to get the gist of what he was saying.

"Tell them we're going to deport them. Send their asses back to El Salvador."

"They're Mexican."

"I don't care. They're not going to some plush California prison on the taxpayer dime. Fuck that. I'm gonna personally feed these motherfuckers to the *tiburones*. Tell them that."

Cho got up.

"I'm going to talk to the EMT."

He walked off, leaving Quijano to translate what he'd said, not that Quijano needed to. Cho could tell by the expressions on the couple's faces that they'd understood him loud and clear.

Cho stopped and looked into one of the bedrooms and found two SWAT officers pulling guns out of the closet and laying them on the bed. There was a brand-new Benelli M4 Super 90 combat shotgun—the kind the U.S. military uses in Afghanistan and Iraq—a couple of old-school gangbanger favorites like a MAC-10 and an AK-47, plus a full gun-show sized assortment of .38 caliber revolvers and .9 millimeter semi-automatic handguns.

Cho looked at the SWAT officers.

"Any forty-fives?"

"Not yet."

Cho nodded.

"Let me know if you find one."

Cho walked out into the living room where Ted, the EMT fireman, sat on the couch rubbing his wrists. The two Mormons had already been interviewed and were now being driven to the emergency room for bone setting and psychiatric counseling. Apparently, the SWAT team's dynamic entrance—bursting into the room screaming and pointing automatic rifles—had caused them to shit themselves. They wouldn't be able to identify a picture of their mothers right now.

Cho looked at the EMT.

"So, Ted. Mind telling me how you ended up here?"

Ted glared at Cho.

"Doing your job."

Cho nodded; it was almost imperceptible, like he was agreeing with himself. It was an unconscious acknowledgment that, for whatever reason, Ted was going to be a hostile witness.

"Thinking of applying to the LAPD?"

Ted looked down at his wrists. They were red, rubbed raw by the duct tape. Cho handed him the photo from the herbal cooperative.

"Recognize this guy?"

Ted nodded.

"Shamus Noriega."

Cho raised an eyebrow. He sat down next to Ted and pulled out his notebook.

"Mind starting at the beginning?"

...

Daniel was floating in the outdoor Jacuzzi, letting the hot, bubbly water ease away the strain and muscle tension in his body from being yanked in opposite directions and suspended in the air. But he didn't mind the aches and pains. He remembered reading about a monk who wore a *cilice*—generally a hair shirt but in his case a spiked metal belt worn around the upper thigh—to induce a "mortification of the flesh." The idea being that if you denied yourself the experience of sensual pleasures your spirit would find God. Saint Paul said it best in Epistle to the Romans 8:13: "For if you live according to the flesh you will die, but if by the Spirit you put to death the deeds of the body you will live."

But Daniel didn't think that was exactly true; maybe it was the truth for some people but for him he found just the opposite. Although, he had to admit, it would be difficult to explain to the bishop and other members of the Church of Jesus Christ of Latter Day Saints how his mission, which had started off so disastrously, had become a success: it was leading him to find God.

Daniel looked up as Aimée walked out of the house carrying a cup of herbal tea and headed through the manicured grove of bamboo and tropical ginger toward him. Daniel splashed his legs in the warm water.

"You coming in?"

Aimée smiled at him. She was excited about something.

"I have an idea."

Daniel watched her sit on the edge of the Jacuzzi, folding her perfectly toned legs under her as she assumed a lotus position.

"How would you like to come to Japan with me?"

Daniel smiled.

"When?"

She touched his cheek.

"Soon. Tomorrow or the next day."

Daniel nodded.

"Let me go get my stuff."

...

Shamus sat in the passenger seat of his SUV. It was starting to get dark but that just made it easier to watch the small screen flickering in the dashboard. Shamus had made Guillermo wait inside the crappy apartment while he kept an eye on the entrance. It might be a while before the Mormon punk or that asshole pot grower showed up and there was no fucking way Shamus was going to hunker down in the debris and stench of that shit hole any longer.

Shamus watched as Tony Montana planted his face into a massive pile of cocaine. It was his favorite scene in the movie. He could watch it on a loop and never get tired of it. He could relate to Tony Montana. They had a lot in common. Both were self-made men, both had raised themselves up from nothing, clawed their way to the top, become major players in their respective fields, and both had *huevos* as big as they come.

As Tony Montana slumped in his chair and his mansion was overrun by his enemies, Shamus saw a lone bicyclist ride into the apartment building parking lot, lock his bike against a post, and head toward the apartment.

Shamus turned back to the screen just in time to see Tony Montana pick up a giant fucking gun and start killing everybody in sight. Maybe that was the thing to do. Go rampaging. Do what the T-shirt said. *Kill 'em all and let God sort it out.* Good advice for troubled times.

When Shamus crept up the stairs and entered the apartment, Daniel was already hog-tied on the floor and Guillermo was standing over him. Guillermo could barely conceal the pride he felt in roughing up the unsuspecting young Mormon. He turned to Shamus and grinned.

"What took you so long?"

...

Detectives Cho and Quijano sat in on the interview and listened as Blanca Guardado, the recently arrested resident of a marijuana grow house, spilled her guts. Apparently her husband Bernardo was a slob and a grouch, a man who didn't give her any money, never took her out, refused to help around the house, drank too much beer, was addicted to watching soccer on television, had the horrible habit of being a bed farter, and was an infrequent and inattentive lover. All of these faults and transgressions Blanca detailed in an unrelenting and rapid-fire Spanish that sounded to Cho like a newscast from hell. They had offered Blanca immunity from prosecution for her testimony and so far all they knew was that Bernardo was a pig and she was happy that he was in jail. Now her family would understand when she got a divorce.

Cho had tried to make an immunity deal with Bernardo, but Bernardo knew that talking to the cops was a death sentence so he did what he was supposed to do and kept his mouth shut. Cho couldn't tell if it was fear of his employers or if he was just happy to be away from Blanca.

Blanca's nonstop, interminable list of Bernardo's domestic shortcomings exhausted Cho. He wanted testimony. He knew she knew something but it was buried under a mountain of resentment and petty grievances and he was starting to think she'd never get to it.

And then, out of the blue, as if she sensed the detectives were losing their patience with her, like they might revoke their offer of immunity and put her back in that house with Bernardo, Blanca started naming names.

...

Miro couldn't help himself. He parked near the market and got out of the car. Marianna looked at him.

"What are we doing?"

He smiled.

"I want you to taste something."

She laughed.

"Now?"

"Well, yeah."

Marianna climbed out of the car and followed him into the local market. He headed straight for the produce section. There, past pyramids of oranges and cantaloupes and ruby-red grapefruits, were several bins of plums and peaches and *pluots* grown somewhere in the southern hemisphere—New Zealand or Australia or Chile. Their prices reflected their travels.

Miro selected the two that seemed the ripest.

They ate them in the car. Marianna grinned and kissed him, letting the juice from the fruit run down her chin.

"What did you call these?"

"*Pluots.* It's a hybrid. Three quarters plum and one quarter apricot. This was my inspiration. Where it all started."

She smiled at him.

"It's better than any plum or apricot I've ever tasted."

Miro smiled back.

"It's greater than the sum of its parts."

Marianna sucked on the seed and reached out for him.

"Like a baby."

...

Shamus saw it first. A squad car was parked in front of the grow house with two uniforms standing next to it. Streamers

BAKED

of crime-scene tape festooned the open door as crime-scene–
evidence guys hauled the marijuana plants out of the house
and loaded them into a truck.

"Fuck."

Guillermo started to speed up. Shamus grabbed his arm.

"Slow down, man. Don't draw attention."

Guillermo shot a look in the rearview.

"We got to get the fuck out of here."

"Get the fuck out of here *calmly*. They don't know
it's us."

"They got Bernardo."

Shamus watched the cops. They were busy scurrying
around, dismantling everything.

"Vincent is gonna shit."

Guillermo looked at him.

"What'll we do with the kid?"

Shamus shrugged.

"Fuck if I know."

...

Miro heard a knock at the door and quickly pulled the gun
out from under the mattress. Marianna looked at him, unsure what to do. Miro nodded his head toward the bathroom,
trying telepathically to get her to hide. She understood and
tiptoed in, closing the door silently behind her.

Miro crept up to the front door.

"Who is it?"

He heard a familiar voice.

"Guus."

He opened the door and let Guus into the room. Guus

looked around as Miro closed the door behind him, threw the dead bolt, and set the chain.

"Where's Marianna?"

Miro spoke to the bathroom door.

"It's Guus."

Marianna stepped out of the bathroom. She took one look at Guus's sunburned head and gasped.

"You need some lotion."

She went back in and came out with a tube.

Miro looked at Guus.

"It's pretty bad."

Guus touched his head.

"It'll fade to a nice tan in a day or two."

Marianna laughed.

"Until you start peeling."

Marianna handed him the lotion and Guus sat in a chair and rubbed some on his skin.

"This feels good. Thank you."

Miro sat on the bed, tucking the gun back under the pillows—it seemed to make everyone, including him, uncomfortable. It was a reminder that they were in danger, that life is short, that he might have to use it and kill someone.

"I think we found where they were growing the Elephant Crush."

Guus leaned forward.

"Really?"

Miro nodded.

"But the police found it at the same time."

Guus frowned.

"That is unfortunate."

"Yeah, to put it mildly."

Marianna sat next to Miro and they instinctively held hands.

"But we're not one hundred percent sure that it was the right place."

"We're seventy-five percent sure."

"So that's the end of the Elephant Crush?"

Miro sighed. It depressed him to think that all his work was now for nothing.

"Looks like it."

Guus clapped his hands together.

"Well, then there's nothing to do but go to a party."

Guus handed the invitation for the Compassion Center grand opening to Miro.

"We must not sit around feeling sorry for ourselves."

Miro read the invitation and looked at Guus.

"Holy shit."

43

T HE PROSECCO was on ice, the caterers were bustling about setting up serving stations, the florist had delivered several large arrangements, Compassion Center staff were polishing the bongs and putting a variety of cannabis in glass display jars, and Vincent was doing the most important job: grinding up some of the precious Elephant Crush bud in preparation for vaporization. He thought about rolling a joint and smoking it right then and there but realized he wanted to wait and make sure everything was perfect before blazing. He'd light up after the party was swinging.

He saw Shamus in his peripheral vision, standing by the door to the office in the back of the store. Shamus didn't say anything, he just motioned for Vincent to follow him. Vincent carefully put the Elephant Crush buds back into their large glass jar and followed Shamus into the office.

The office was small, just enough room for a desk with a computer and some cabinets for storing inventory. Guillermo leaned against the wall, his arm slung over a stack of cardboard boxes filled with rolling papers and glass pipes, looking like the badass he thought he was. This didn't surprise Vincent, he was used to the ridiculous posturing of

Shamus's hirelings. What did surprise him was the young man tied up and gagged, lying on the floor.

"Who the fuck is that?"

Shamus started to answer but Vincent interrupted him.

"Wait. More important. What the fuck is he doing here? When you came in, did you notice anything different? Like maybe today's a special day? Like, I don't know, we're having a grand fucking opening? There's going to be a hundred people here in about an hour."

Shamus ignored Vincent's sarcasm.

"The grow house got raided."

Five simple words. Five words that made Vincent's heart stop for a beat or two. The single worst sentence Vincent had ever heard in his life.

Shamus ran a hand over his scalp and looked at the kid on the floor.

"I didn't know what else to do."

Vincent needed to sit down. He could feel his knees giving out. His heart rate soared and he began hyperventilating. He perched on the edge of the desk and tried to catch his breath.

"What happened?"

Shamus cleared his throat.

"We were staking out the guy's apartment, that's where we found him." He nudged the bound Mormon with his foot before continuing.

"And when we took him back to the grow house, the cops were there."

"But how?"

"How the fuck should I know? Maybe they just got lucky."

Guillermo tossed in his opinion.

"Maybe there's a rat."

Vincent ignored him.

"They take the plants?"

Shamus nodded.

"I couldn't get too close but it looked like they got everything."

Vincent couldn't help it. He erupted in a spasm of anger that made his body actually levitate for a second.

"Fuck!"

Vincent sat back on the desk and let his head hang. He literally felt like he couldn't go on, like his life force had, momentarily, left his body and taken the fire exit out of the building.

"So that's it. We're fucked."

The three men stood there, letting the weight of Vincent's words sink in, feeling a submersion in the reality of what it's like being totally fucked.

Guillermo shook his head. "Man. This sucks."

Guillermo's comment flipped a switch in Vincent. His energy returned, charged by a fresh surge of pure uncut rage.

"Miro. That motherfucker. He's the rat. I know it."

Shamus shook his head.

"He can't find his dick."

Vincent glared at Shamus.

"You can't find your dick. Your incompetence is unbelievable."

"What?"

"If you'd just done your job, none of this would've happened."

Shamus's face flushed red and he struggled to contain the sudden urge to beat Vincent senseless.

"You screwed the pooch. Fucked the dog. You couldn't shoot straight. Then you couldn't find him."

The picture was becoming clear to Vincent. He stood up to say something more, but tripped over the kid tied up on the floor.

"And why? Please tell me why on *Earth* do you keep kidnapping people? Do you have some kind of compulsive disorder? Are you a kidnapaholic? Do you need to go to some kind of program?"

Shamus didn't say anything. Vincent looked at Guillermo, then back to Shamus.

"What a fucking mess."

He was about to say more when there was a knock at the door. Vincent opened it a crack and saw the caterer standing there.

"We've got a pretty good crowd out there. Shall we start passing the hors d'oeuvres?"

…

"We're going to a party at a pot club?"

"It won't be much of a party after we arrive."

Quijano looked suddenly nervous.

"Do we need backup?"

Cho rolled his eyes and looked at Quijano.

"It's a simple arrest. Do you really want to get the Santa Monica PD involved? The paperwork alone is a nightmare, not to mention those guys are dicks."

Quijano nodded and looked out the window.

"If we're going all the way to the Westside, can we get some sushi? I mean, we got time and there's a good place on Sawtelle."

"You kidding? I can't afford sushi."

"This place is reasonable."

"Reasonable sushi?"

Quijano looked at him.

"I thought Koreans ate sushi."

Koreans do eat sushi. Sashimi, too. But Cho had two kids who would be going to college one of these days and a wife who wanted a real vacation, so he tried to spend less than five dollars on lunch. It was his version of a retirement plan. This explained his fondness for eating out of trucks.

"It's not that. Let's just go and get this guy first and then we can go out somewhere you want to go."

"Anywhere?"

"You pick."

Quijano rubbed his hands together.

"I'm taking you to a place that makes the best hand rolls in town."

...

Miro drove. He still couldn't believe Vincent was behind this but the more he thought about it, the more it made sense. Vincent was greedy. And greed was always a good motivator.

As he got off the freeway and began winding through the pristine streets of Santa Monica, Miro realized that he'd never really liked Vincent. Vincent just gave off a bad vibe. He was like a morning glory vine, nice to look at, seemingly pretty, but underneath the purple flowers were roots that spread over everything, a parasite feeding off of other plants, slowly choking the life out of them. He was a danger to the entire cannabis community.

It occurred to Miro that the simplest way out of the situation would be to kill Vincent, just put a bullet in him and be done with it. It was kind of like pruning. You snip off the bad growth and the plant becomes healthier. It was the first time that homicide made sense to him. Perhaps that's how the guy who shot him had thought.

Miro looked over at Marianna. She was smiling. She knew they were in danger; she knew his whole world had come crashing down like a giant burning zeppelin but she was still cheerful. He liked that about her.

He looked in the rearview and saw Guus. The Dutchman wasn't happy. He wasn't smiling. He was pensive, chewing on his thumbnail. Guus looked in the rearview and his eyes met Miro's.

"Do you think you can do it again?"

"What?"

"The strain. Could you replicate it?"

Miro shrugged his shoulders.

"No. But maybe I could make something better."

...

That was the problem with bosses. That was what pissed Shamus off more than anything else. They didn't think things through. They just bossed people around and then yelled like a spoiled teenage girl if things didn't work out the way they wanted. Sure things were fucked up. It happened. You didn't have to start acting like a punk-ass bitch.

It occurred to Shamus that he should open his own medical marijuana dispensary—maybe he'd call it Farmacia Noriega—and he could become the go-to place for fancy pot. Why should he let Vincent take all the glory? Wasn't it time he stopped working for other people?

...

Vincent's jaw hurt from keeping his smile stretched out on his face like a fucking southern belle in a beauty pageant, but that's what he had to do. The damage had been done and he had a party to host.

It was surprising how crowded the store got even with only forty or fifty people milling about, drinking bubbly, eating hors d'oeuvres, and passing around plastic balloons filled with Elephant Crush vapor.

His employees, wearing crisp polo shirts with a redesigned Compassion Center logo, ground and vaporized the cannabis, the caterer's crew scurried through the crowd, the constant pop of Prosecco corks punctuated the air, and the thud of a mix tape kept the conversation louder than it needed to be. Through it all, Vincent smiled. He shook hands, he hugged, and he air-kissed the botoxed and surgically-stretched cheeks of the Westside elite. He was trying to put a positive spin on the disaster. Maybe it wasn't such a fucking mess. If all the Elephant Crush he had went up in smoke, he could announce that the entire crop had been confiscated by the police and it was no longer available. The reigning champion, the Cannabis Cup–winner would be extinct in an hour or two. In other words, this party was an epic, once-in-a-lifetime event. His customers would never forget it; it would be a defining moment in their lives and they'd tell their grandchildren about the night they smoked the Elephant Crush. They were some of the luckiest people in the world. Vincent realized that he'd started this to make history but, instead, he was going to become a legend. This would make the Compassion Center even more famous than if he actually had the cannabis for sale. It was victory snatched from the jaws of defeat. It was genius.

Of course there were some niggling details left to work out. Some loose ends to tie up. Vincent was sure Miro suspected that he was behind the shooting. That could make for an uncomfortable moment if they ran into each other. But then, Miro had no proof. Unless Shamus suddenly started talking, it was all just speculation, hearsay, and bullshit that Vincent could deny. Vincent made a mental note to get someone to put an end to Shamus. That was a problem that needed solving, sooner rather than later.

44

THE SMELL OF mangoes hit him in the face as he walked in the door. It was unmistakably Elephant Crush. Miro knew it instantly, the way a parent recognizes his kid in a crowded playground. He turned toward Marianna and could see that she recognized it, too.

Guus was already moving through the crowd, looking for Vincent, ready to do, well, Miro wasn't sure what they were going to do. He'd never had an evil nemesis before. Was he going to punch Vincent in the nose? Stand on the table and denounce him? Miro was torn between taking out his gun and shooting Vincent—which carried some severe consequences like a long prison term—or wagging his finger at him, which seemed kind of lame.

He took Marianna's hand and pulled her through a clump of well-heeled stoners: women in clingy dresses and men in business suits who looked like agents from some Century City talent agency. A waiter offered him a glass of wine. Miro declined it with a shake of his head but when he felt Marianna stop and tug on his hand, he turned and saw her popping a spring roll into her mouth.

There was a group of people by the back counter passing a balloon filled with mist. They were very animated, waving their hands around and loudly proclaiming it the best
cannabis they'd ever smoked.

Behind them was Vincent. He was standing behind the
counter next to a Volcano vaporizer, schmoozing his guests
like a cheesy Vegas emcee.

There was a shout, then a noise like the sound of smashing glass. And then there was some bald Latino guy with a
gun, pointing it at Guus.

Miro was surprised that no one was screaming. The
crowd had stopped talking but they weren't reacting; they
were just watching. It was an LA thing.

...

Shamus was still seething. Pissed off with himself, with Vincent,
with the whole fucking mess. This job should be mellow. It
was basically a pick-up-and-delivery kind of life. Run the
occasional errand. He shouldn't feel stressed out all the time.
Shamus figured it was Vincent. There was something about
him that just made everything a little more intense, more
personal, than it needed to be.

Shamus looked at Guillermo.

"Fuck this shit. I'm done."

Guillermo looked down at the Mormon kid hog-tied
on the floor.

"What about this guy?"

Shamus looked at the kid.

"Fuck it. Let Vincent deal with him."

Shamus walked out of the office. Guillermo followed.

Shamus was impressed by the turnout. You'd think a guy like Vincent would be happy that he had so many customers and clients. It was like a fucking fan club. Shamus grabbed a glass of Prosecco and tossed it back, only to have the bubbles rebel and race back up his throat into his nose. He made a face. This shit was disgusting.

Shamus walked up behind Vincent just in time to see some sunburned motherfucker in a leather jacket grab the big glass jar with the last remaining buds of Elephant Crush. He was shouting at Vincent with a funny accent, calling him a thief.

Then the guy slammed the glass jar into the floor, sending shards flying. That was enough for Shamus. He wasn't in the mood to fuck around. He pulled out his gun.

"Get the fuck out of here. Right now."

But the guy didn't move. He just stared at Vincent. He looked at Shamus. He was polite—cool, considering the handgun pointed at his head.

"I'm talking to Vincent."

And that's when Shamus saw Miro standing in the crowd.

...

There are all kinds of rules and regulations you have to follow when you work in law enforcement. Especially when you work for the LAPD. You're supposed to do everything you can to avoid having to make the dreaded "shots fired" report. The easiest way to do this is to not fire any shots. But sometimes that's unavoidable.

Cho and Quijano flashed their badges at the Compassion Center doorman. Cho even smirked when the guy told them it was a private party, like that would keep them out.

It was a swell party. Lots of successful Caucasians smoking weed, acting like they were on a day trip to Amsterdam. Cho was surprised to see Miro. He'd never expected to see him again—unless he turned up dead in Griffith Park—but there he was, pushing his way through the crowd.

It was at this very moment that Cho had the realization that maybe his wife was right: he'd been on the job too long, he needed a change of pace. Maybe he needed to have a life where he'd be surprised more often. But Cho knew that wasn't the case. He didn't need to make a change. He was just good at his job. That's all. It was like he could see the connections before they were real; when it came to criminals and human psychology, it was like he wore a permanent pair of X-Ray Specs.

Then there was a shout, a crash, and he saw Shamus Noriega pointing his .45 at some sunburned guy in a leather jacket.

...

Daniel thought of Colossians 3:5. *Greed is a form of idolatry.* If Paul the Apostle had seen what was going on in the Compassion Center, he probably would've e-mailed a copy to the two kidnappers and their boss. Not that they would read it. He knew what their problem was: they were idolizing the cannabis plant because it could make them rich. They were exploiting God's gift, turning away from the spiritual and focused only on what the money from the sale of the plants could buy them. It wouldn't buy them happiness, that was for sure, not like the happiness to be found in a tightly wrapped burrito or having your body restrained by soft cotton ropes. All they were going to get was misery, bad karma, and a one-way ticket to hell.

Daniel shifted, the ropes were looser than the ones Aimée tied and the amateurish square knots gave him enough play to reach up and take the gag off his mouth. He could hear a party in progress just beyond the door. They wouldn't kill him if people saw him, unless they were a bunch of vampires or something weird and then, well, then nothing was going to save him.

Daniel managed to get the rope linking his hands and feet together untied and was able to stand. His wrists and ankles were still bound, but he could hop, and twist a door-knob, and that's exactly what he did.

...

The Compassion Center's doorman hadn't bothered to frisk Miro, hadn't checked to see if he had a gun or a knife or a cell phone or a baseball bat hidden in his jacket; all he did was look at the invitation that Guus presented and wave them in.

Miro hadn't actually been planning to pull out his gun, he had just brought it along because he figured that's what you do when you confront your nemesis—you bring all the firepower you had. This assumption was based more on watching too many TV shows and movies than anything else. But when he saw the bald guy pointing a gun at Guus he decided maybe he should show his gun, too. Miro would be the first to admit that he was terrified. His hands were sweaty and trembling, his stomach was in knots, and his bowels were urging to be emptied into his pants. But he had to do something. Would Floyd Zaiger let his friends get murdered?

Miro reached behind his back, whipped his handgun out, and promptly sent it skittering across the floor. He lunged to get it just as the bald guy turned and fired.

For the second time in his life, Miro felt a burning hot bullet tear through his body.

...

Cho heard the shot and reacted. He and Quijano both drew their guns. Cho shouted the required warning.

"Police. Drop your weapons."

But Shamus Noriega didn't drop his weapon; instead he turned and pointed it at the detectives. That's when Cho noticed another guy, the guy he recognized as Mr. Magoo, the AK-47-wielding numbskull from the herbal cooperative shooting, pointing a handgun at him.

There's that cliche you hear sometimes, about how when something bad happens, like when you're in a car accident or if you fall off a ladder while you're cleaning the gutters on your roof, time stands still. It was like that for Cho. Nobody was pulling the trigger, no bullets were flying through the air. Time was standing still.

While Cho considered the possibilities of pulling the trigger and bringing a quick cessation of life to Mr. Noriega, Quijano had Mr. Magoo in his sights. Unfortunately, the crumbs had taken a reciprocal approach. If Cho shot Shamus then Magoo would shoot Quijano, or vice versa. No matter who shot first, someone would take one for the team and that really wasn't the way it was supposed to go down according to the police manual. Compounding this was the fact that there were forty or fifty innocent bystanders packed in around them. That meant one stray bullet, one misplaced shot, might kill someone who, from the looks of them, was either a high-powered lawyer or had access to one. This, as the city attorney would say, was a colossal clusterfuck in the making. It was the first time Cho had ever found himself in what is commonly called a Mexican standoff. If he looked it up in Merriam-Webster, Cho would find an accurate and eloquent definition: "a situation in which no one emerges a clear winner."

Which summed it up pretty well.

Cho didn't know if Miro was dead or not, but he could hear someone urgently muttering something in what sounded like Portuguese.

Cho wondered what the odds were that he and Quijano would pull their triggers simultaneously.

...

Guus was beginning to get a bad impression of the United States. What was this obsession with guns? Why couldn't these people behave like normal businessmen? It was too uncivilized, too cowboy for him. And what about the people? Why weren't they running? Shouldn't they be screaming for help on the streets? But they weren't. They were watching—some still chewing appetizers, some sipping their wine—like it was a drama staged for their benefit.

Guus backed away from the line of fire and felt a young woman in some kind of vintage dress press up against him. It was not an unpleasant sensation. He wondered if Miro was alive.

...

Vincent's brain was churning, trying to figure out how to put a positive spin on this mess. The party would now be remembered as the scene of a shooting. People might be afraid to come into the store now. He'd have to offer specials, cut-rate deals, and other promotions just to keep the business alive. Or maybe not. Maybe this would make the story even better. He just couldn't tell anymore. It was too complicated.

He looked over and saw a woman hold her glass out to the caterer for a refill. The caterer had not, obviously, thought this through. She pulled a cold bottle of Prosecco from the ice and popped the cork. The loud pop of gas escaping a bottle of sparkling wine from Italy coincided with Daniel's desperate hop, skip, and jump as he came careening out of the office.

Then the shooting began.

Two
Bullets

45

ARIANNA LOOKED as if she was about to burst. Her belly was enormous and round, jutting out in front of her and above her pants like an impossibly cantilevered blob. Miro held her hand as they left the midwife center, the *verloskundigen praktijk,* and strolled down Kerkweg, crossed the river where the street turned into Aardamsweg, and continued toward the bus station. His left arm was still sore from where he'd been shot but the bone had healed—with the helpful installation of a metal plate and a few screws—and he was able to use it as long as he was careful. He carried a copy of *Hello!,* the British celebrity magazine. There was a picture of Aimée and Daniel in Tokyo on the cover with the headline "Cougar and her Cub" splashed across the picture in bright red.

Marianna smiled at him.

"So, a girl."

Miro smiled back.

"I hope she looks like you."

"What do you want to name her?"

Miro grinned.

"Sativa."

Marianna shook her head.

"You've been working too hard. Or smoking too much."

"Lots of girls are named after flowers."

"Then how about Daisy?"

Miro considered it.

"I like it."

He took the scarf from his neck and wrapped it around her collar, hoping to keep her warm in the blustery Amsterdam wind, and planted a kiss on her lips. She smiled.

"I'm starved. Let's get some lunch."

Miro shook his head.

"I'll take you out to dinner, but I have to go back to the lab. Guus and I are onto something amazing. In fact, I've never seen anything like it."

Marianna smiled.

"Can you tell me? Or is it top secret?"

Miro leaned close to her and spoke in a whisper.

"It's got variegated leaves."

"Variegated?"

"It's got stripes."

Marianna smiled.

"Cool."

"I think it'll be really good, too. I still need to work through another generation, see if I can stabilize it. But it'll definitely be ready for this year's Cup."

She kissed him.

"What are you calling this one?"

Miro smiled.

"Zebra Crush."

...

Cho sent all the paperwork to the district attorney, to the Police Oversight Commission, to everyone who was supposed to get something from him. His report was pretty clear; all the loose ends were tied up. Ballistics matched Shamus Noriega's gun to Miro's shooting, the painter in the river, the EMT in her apartment, and the security guard at the West Hollywood herbal cooperative. They also matched it to a couple of random killings stretching back over the last six years.

Cho wished that he hadn't been forced to kill Noriega but what could he do? Two shots from Cho's gun had put a stop to more than just Shamus Noriega's heart. It also put a stop to any prosecution against Vincent. With Shamus dead, there was no evidence to tie the owner of the Compassion Center to the grow house or the shootings, and Mr. Magoo had caught a .9 millimeter slug right between the eyes. Quijano, it turned out, was a hell of a shot.

It bothered Cho that Vincent had gotten away with it but he figured the law of karma would eventually even the score. That seemed to be the way things worked.

Cho had even considered making a case against Miro—after all, his Cannabis Cup–winning pot had started all this shit—but there wasn't enough evidence. There were hundreds of plants but nothing that they could tie to Miro. Besides, the dude had taken two bullets. That was enough punishment for anyone. Too many people had died. And for what?

Cho reminded himself to make a donation to NORML. The sooner marijuana was legal the better it would be for everyone.

The case was closed, his vacation was starting, and he even had plane tickets to Oaxaca. They were going to stay in some ex-convent that had been converted into a fancy hotel.

They were going to eat *mole,* drink mezcal, and try tacos with roasted grasshoppers and cheese.

Detective Cho had stopped at a luggage store and picked up a new suitcase. A duffle bag with wheels, really. And then, just to see the job through, to have some closure, he'd followed the evidence truck out to Altadena, to a large industrial incinerator. He'd watched as they'd shoveled all the impounded marijuana into the burner. It was a lot, maybe a hundred pounds, with what they figured was an estimated street value of about six million dollars give or take the market value of the world's best cannabis. Cho watched as the workmen flipped a switch, the gas ignited, and the pot began to burn.

As he walked back to his car he turned and saw smoke billowing out of the smokestack.

The incinerator acted like a gargantuan vaporizer and the smoke drifted west across the city. It was, as it turned out, the first day in Los Angeles in over eighty years when there were no reported homicides or traffic accidents.

The smoke continued to blow out over the Pacific, catching the trade winds and beginning a trip around the world.

Two days later, a Chinese dissident, a fifty-three-year-old democracy activist and writer of erotic short stories, was released from prison in Beijing. A day after that, a suicide bomber in the occupied territories of Palestine changed her mind and went on a date with her boyfriend. They sat in the shade of an almond tree, shared a pomegranate, and talked about the future.

acknowledgments

THIS BOOK WOULD not have been possible without the intelligent and insightful editing of Jamison Stoltz.

I would also like to thank Mary Evans for her expert guidance; David Liss, Julie Buxbaum, Reid MacDonald, Patricia Go, and Allison Conant for early reads and encouragement and Caroline Trefler for a superb copyedit.

I give maximum respect, affection, and gratitude to Morgan Entrekin, Eric Price, Deb Seager and the hardworking team at Grove/Atlantic in New York City and to Brian Lipson, Ross Fineman and Samata Narra in Hollywood.

Big ups to Shana Stern, Amin Waliany, and Adam Caleb Braid for their technical expertise and advice on all matters cannabis, and to Karate Mike for the law enforcement point of view and general inspiration.

I'd also like to give a shout out to all the underground botanists and gardeners around the world, especially the Strain Hunters and DNA Genetics; to the organizers of the Cannabis Cup and all the great coffeeshops in Amsterdam and to NORML and all anti-prohibition activists everywhere. Special thanks are reserved for Floyd Zaiger for inventing my favorite stone fruit and to Olivia and Jules Smith for being the best kind of smartasses.

When his supermodel wife is kidnapped by Thai Pirates, Turk Henry, the aging bass player for megaplatinum heavy metal rockers Metal Assassin, is forced into action. The harsh Thai jungle, corrupt government officials, and his own raging sex addiction are just the start of Turk's problems.

Read on for the first chapter of Mark Haskell Smith's novel *Salty* . . .

One

PHUKET

The Andaman Sea stretches out for 218,100 square miles along the southern peninsula of Thailand, extending south until it tickles the shores of Indonesia, flowing west where it mixes with the dark water of the Indian Ocean. It is one of the most beautiful expanses of salt water in the world, teeming with pristine coral reefs and home to thousands of exotic sea creatures. Not that he gave a fuck.

Turk Henry stood on the beach and looked out at the ocean. It was amazingly clear, so clear it wasn't even blue or green or any of the colors you usually associate with ocean. It was like glass. You could see right through it, right down to the bottom. Clumps of seaweed, rocks, and sand; the occasional shadow and flash of fish darting beneath the waves. It wasn't like the water he'd seen growing up near the Jersey Shore, that was for sure.

Turk craned his neck, peering through his massive sunglasses—the kind that make you look like you're recovering from eye surgery—and looked for the boy. Turk liked the boy. The boy brought beer. Hand him a couple baht and he'd go sprinting off to the end of the beach where his parents and grandparents sat around giant coolers filled with beer, soda, green coconuts, whatever you wanted. He'd come racing back and hand you a beer. Ice cold beer; the three greatest words in the English language.

His wife had told him they were eight degrees north of the equator. She liked facts. Eight degrees north of the equator, for the layman, translated into unbelievably fucking hot. A zillion degrees Fahrenheit and humid like the inside of a dishwashing machine. Turk had never felt anything like it. The only thing that had even come close was when he and the rest of the band were stuck in an elevator with ten or twelve groupies. A couple of the girls decided to get frisky, and suffice to say an orgy broke loose. With all the fucking and sucking, the groaning and heavy breathing, the elevator got hot and humid in a hurry. A couple of the girls even fainted. Passed out from the sex. When the elevator doors were finally opened by the fire department, there were six or seven naked groupies lying in a pile on the elevator floor. That's how you become a legend.

But it was even hotter here, and Turk wasn't dressed for it. He'd rolled up the legs on his black linen slacks, the kind with the drawstring that hang loose and baggy and made him look thin, and dunked his feet in the water. The sea wasn't cooling or refreshing, it was warm. Almost like a bath. His wife had told him that the average water temperature in the Andaman Sea is seventy-eight degrees Fahrenheit. That felt about right.

Turk unbuttoned his black silk shirt, letting his large pale gut leap out into the sunlight, his skin so white that it bounced the light up, casting reverse double-chin shadows across his face and making him look vaguely vampirish. Despite the hiking of the pants and the unveiling of the paunch, he wasn't any cooler; sweat rolled off his body like he was melting. Fuck, he *was* melting. Where was that boy?

He turned around and looked for his wife. It was her idea to come to Thailand. She had nagged, pleaded, and cajoled until he finally broke down and agreed to sit on a plane for twenty-three hours—he watched five movies—as they flew from Los Angeles to Osaka to Phuket. It was her fault he was here, burning and roasting and sweating like a pig in an oven. Normally she was easy to spot—she was the only one here who actually wore a top. The rest of them, the Europeans and Australians, all lay out in the sun with their tits hanging out. They'd read books or play cards, sometimes get up and jump in the water to cool off; a couple of women were even throwing a Frisbee around, all of them topless. Not that it bothered Turk. He liked tits.

Sheila had told him that it was a five-star resort, superluxe, first class all the way. It was nice, he had to admit. It was isolated, away from the run-down little tourist town, smack in the middle of some kind of jungle with a private cove. The main part of the hotel was a modernist structure on top of a hill. It didn't fit with the local architecture, looking more like a billionaire playboy's fortress of evil than a Thai temple, but then Turk wouldn't know Thai architecture if it fell on him and besides, he thought the concrete and glass building looked pretty cool. The main lobby was a big open room with a soaring atrium. This was connected to a restaurant, a swimming pool, a fitness center with a personal trainer on standby, and most important, a bar that overlooked the beach and the tranquil little cove. The resort's rooms were actually freestanding cabanas dotting the beach and hillside surrounding the main building. You didn't get a room, you got a little house with a thatched roof, amid coconut palms and beautiful flowering orchids and other plants that Turk had never seen before.

He had to agree, it was very nice and if you were going to vacation in a third world country there was no better way to go. But it wasn't like he had never been in a fancy hotel before. Metal Assassin only stayed at the best hotels. It was in their contract.

If Sheila had told him that it was wall-to-wall breasts—like a nudist colony where only the women were nude—she wouldn't've had to nag him so much. There is nothing more relaxing for the stressed-out heavy metal musician than to kick back, drink a few cold ones, and watch a parade of nature's greatest triumph on display. If only Sheila were here to join in. Turk would be the first to tell you, his wife had a great rack. She'd put these other women to shame.

Turk remembered that she was off on some safari or something. She'd wanted him to go with her; she'd wanted him to ride an elephant. But he couldn't think of anything less appealing than straddling the massive gray hump of some monstrous beast as it lurched through the forest belching and farting like a sick Harley-Davidson. That was Sheila, though. She was always off doing something. She liked go to yoga retreats in Mexico or bungee jumping with her friends in some dusty canyon in Ojai; she'd spend an afternoon in an authentic Navajo sweat lodge or attend something called an "inspirational tea." Sheila made fun of Turk for not having an "adventurous spirit." But Turk liked to take it easy. Didn't people always say "take it easy"? Wasn't that something you were supposed to do?

He didn't mind that Sheila had her adventures; it was fine with him. That was the great thing about their marriage— they tried hard not to be codependent; they respected each other's space. Turk and Sheila were a mutual support squad, helping each other cope, keeping each other on their respective wagons. It may not have been the most passionate coupling in the history of the world, but it was certainly the most stable. Turk was happy to see Sheila go on her fulfilling adventures. He just preferred to putter around the house, listen to music, practice his bass, and maybe watch a movie in their home theater. Sometimes he swam in the pool. It was a quiet life, but it made him happy. Going snorkeling or jumping out of an airplane just didn't interest him. He often thought Sheila should've married an extreme-sport athlete, or maybe that guy who owned the airline company who was always jumping out of a hot air balloon on a motorcycle. She needed someone who enjoyed taking risks. That wasn't Turk. He enjoyed playing it safe. So while Sheila rode through a jungle on the back of an elephant, Turk did the safe and sensible thing and sat on the beach drinking beer.

His feet sufficiently soaked, Turk walked back to his umbrella and slouched into a chaise, grabbed a towel, and mopped the sweat off his head. He heard a voice speaking English with a light German accent.

"Excuse me, sir, but aren't you in Metal Assassin? You play the bass guitar, is that right?"

Turk looked up and saw a wispy young woman wearing nothing but a bikini bottom, her blond hair stuck in pigtails, her blue eyes gleaming at him from behind some Persols, and her perky little breasts pointing at him, looking almost accusatory, like he'd just done something wrong.

"Yeah. That's me."

"I love your music."

She smiled at him; beamed really. Turk was used to women throwing themselves at him. He knew it wasn't because he was super good-looking; it was because he was a rock star. Not that he was ugly. He had a chunky body—as round and expansive as the sound he conjured out of four strings and a massive Marshall back line; the kind of body a real bass player should have. It wasn't that he was out of shape; he worked out, and his arms and legs looked young and powerful, his articulated muscles standing in sharp contrast to his protruding beer gut. He had a large and colorful dragon tattooed up his right leg and his left bicep was inked with the Metal Assassin logo, the words written in flaming Iron Cross Gothic.

His face was fleshy, but handsome, with mischievous blue eyes and large curly muttonchops on the sides. His head was topped by a full mane of long stringy rock star hair that he had to dye to hide the serious streaks of gray sprouting from the temples. All in all he looked the part. He just kept his shirt on.

Turk smiled back at the girl. He'd had his teeth straightened and whitened just this year, for his forty-fifth birthday, and they looked so clean and gleamy that they appeared fake.

"Thanks."

"Really. You guys are my favorite band. I have all your discs."

Most of them did. Turk studied her nipples; they stood out like bright pink bits of Play-Doh that had been pinched into shape. He looked up at her face.

"Which one's your favorite?"

She bit her lip, appearing slightly stumped. Then she giggled.

"I don't have a favorite. I like them all."

Turk smiled and nodded. Sweat flipped off his head, scattering like he was some kind of wet dog.

"Cool."

The young German, or perhaps she was Swiss, on vacation from Zurich or somewhere, bit her lower lip, summoning up the courage to ask the big question.

"So? Tell me. Is it true?"

"What?"

"You are no more? Steve is really going solo?"

Turk nodded sadly, putting on that grief-stricken faraway look that the fans seemed to expect on hearing the news that Metal Assassin had finally called it quits.

"Yeah. He wants to do his own thing."

And not share the royalties. Selfish fucker.

"So, what are you going to do?"

Turk saw the boy trudging through the sand and waved to him. He then turned and looked at her. Normally, before he was married, before the years of therapy where he learned to recognize when he was in a *catalytic environment* and stop himself from *fantasizing* and *ritualizing* his sexual compulsions, he would've invited her back to his room for a quick shower and a longer blow job. But he'd learned to break that cycle. His therapist had drawn all kinds of little charts mapping out how his sexual addiction worked. The charts always ended with *anxiety, despair, shame, guilt,* and *self-loathing.*

Mark Haskell Smith

It wasn't easy for him; he was a rock star, after all, his entire life spent in a *catalytic environment,* but Turk had learned to control his destructive urges. He'd been surprised at how good it felt to have some power over his desires. His therapist had suggested that the behaviors and compulsions came from his having low self-esteem, and indeed, controlling those behaviors made him feel good about himself. In other words, Turk had discovered that denying himself a good piece of ass actually made him feel like a worthwhile human being. Go figure.

On top of that he'd taken a vow to be true to his wife and he was going to do it, even though it'd been the longest year of his life.

"Are you starting a new band?"

The Swiss-German girl seemed genuinely concerned, so he gave her an honest answer.

"I don't know. For the time being I'm just going to drink a beer."

The boy arrived, grabbed the baht from Turk's outstretched hand, and then went sprinting off down the beach.

336

© Martin Rusch

Mark Haskell Smith is the author of three previous novels—*Moist*, *Delicious*, and *Salty*— and is an award-winning screenwriter. He lives in Los Angeles, close to the Rambo taco truck.